Acclaim for Tracey Hooker's

LOVE MADLY

Wonderful—a journey of self-awareness and self-love.

—Don T.

The story was one I could relate to: love, loss, self-doubt, guilt and finally being happy and comfortable with who you are. Learning from the past but living in the moment.

—Karen B.

With tears in my eyes and love in my heart, I finished your book. The story was captivating, the characters relatable, the emotions genuine. The narrative was colorful and compelling.

—Patti J.

It was funny, heartbreaking, life affirming. I loved the message from the book and feel like it's something I really need to take in.

—Pam P.

LOVE
MADLY

TRACEY HOOKER

To Winnie, the corgi, who helped me write.

This book is a work of fiction. Any references to
real places or real people are used fictitiously.

Cover layout and book design by Leann Stelzer
leannstelzer@comcast.net

ISBN 978-1-7369360-0-9

Printed in the United States of America

Wild Primrose Press

Being deeply loved by someone gives you strength,
while loving someone deeply gives you courage.
—Lao Tzu

LOVE MADLY

Those Bastards

I WAS EIGHT YEARS OLD AND THE WORST HAD ALREADY happened. So, I begged my mom to let me ride my bike to school.

"I'll be fine, Mama," I said. "Please can I?" I pleaded.

"*May* I," Lidi corrected me.

My eyes met hers. "I guess Jamie needs her independence," she muttered to an invisible presence.

With her hesitant yes, I was off through the Phoenix ranch homes.

When the 3:00 school bell rang, I raced to the bike stands. I threw my Barbie lunch box in my basket. I could lose that banged up lunch box, like kids do, and not care. I never liked Barbie and her pink clothes or any dimpled dolls, for that matter.

I couldn't wait to get home. I was starving for a peanut butter and jelly sandwich on white bread. One, two, three—I pushed hard on the pedals and I was on my way. The wind blew through my hair that my mom tried to keep neat with a barrette. I pedaled and screamed, "Yee Ha!" like a cowgirl racing a tornado. Just as I rounded block six, with six more to go, fifth-grade boys appeared out of the alley, revving up their bicycles by making motor sounds. The pack of coyotes pointed at me and cackled.

"Oh, oh." My stomach tightened. "Those bastards," I said

to myself. I may not be able to out-cycle them, but I knew some
alleys that would shorten my ride to safety. For a skinny girl, I
could pedal fast. Still, the predators were close behind. I tried to
dodge them by careening down the back ways until I came to the
front of my house: 4050 North 58ᵗʰ Street. *Safe*! I leaped off my
bicycle and let it drop on the dry grass. One of the boys grabbed
me as I ran toward the front door. Caught in the coyote's paws,
I fell to the ground. "You bastards!" I screamed and kicked and
screamed again, scratching for what felt like my life. I wouldn't
succumb without a fight.

"Let's pants her!" The rabid dog barked. This intimidation
was the rage of bullies where I lived. I feared it, but almost
accepted it as part of neighborhood life. As they tried to grab
my pants, I never stopped fighting, though it started to feel like
a lost cause.

"What do you think you're doing, you little shits?!" boomed
my mother as she ran out the front door. She stood over us in her
peach-colored suit and matching heels. She seemed out of place
for a brawl. Her ladylike look was misleading. She wasn't scared
of wild dogs or sleeping alone.

The boys ran in three directions before Lidi could recognize
their faces. I cried in humiliation and tried to catch my breath
as I pushed the grass clippings off my clothes. I waited for my
mother to grab me and hold me or run after those kids.

"You're all right," Lidi said as she finger-combed my messed-
up hair.

I tried to believe I was okay. I gulped air, and my chest
heaved. I spit out grass like knocked out teeth.

"Bastards!" I yelled one last time before Lidi grabbed my
shoulders. The attack and potential for even worse violation
enraged me.

"You'll be fine," Lidi said. "Why don't you go to your room
and calm down." For Lidi, I knew I needed to get up the next
morning and be a big girl. I needed to get back on the bike. I felt

I had to take great care of my mom, since I only had one parent left. But now, I went to my room, closed the door, and sobbed in my pillow. "Why was my daddy gone?" I needed him.

I knew my daddy would have held me close. He would have chased down the boys and grabbed them by their T-shirts and threatened them with harm. He wouldn't have been able to help himself.

Daddy

I WAS HIS PRINCESS. HE WAS MY PRINCE. I LOOKED UP TO all six feet, green eyes, blonde hair of him. I wasn't the perfect child—not even for my daddy; but still, to him, I could do no wrong.

He taught me to ride a bike. I remember him cheering me on: "You can do it Princess!" he yelled, as he ran wildly, holding on to the seat, and then giving me a final push. I wobbled and struggled to gain my balance as I peddled faster and faster, Daddy running next to me the whole way.

When I finished my first ride, we hugged each other, and jumped up and down, and laughed. "I did it. Just like you said, Daddy!" He wiped teardrops from his eyes. "You're my precious girl," he said. "Precious" was a big word to a five-year-old, but he used it often enough that I knew it meant he loved me.

He taught me how to dive off the diving board. "Be brave." I remember him saying as I marveled at his perfect smile. His muscular arms stretched out ready to catch me, if necessary. For a long time, I stood at the end of the board with my toes curled around it. He waited. "Fear is your friend," he chanted. At the time, I didn't know exactly what he meant, but somehow it was soothing, and before long I made my first dive.

At night, I would cuddle up on the couch with Daddy to

5

hear a bedtime story: one of those chilling Grimm's fairy tales. I watched as his long fingers turned the pages of the book. "You've nothing to be scared of, Princess," he reassured me in a voice that he seemed to reserve for me. "I'll always keep you safe."

"I know Daddy," I would reply. I knew because he told me that every time when I woke up crying from a bad dream and he would tuck me in bed again and rub my back.

I believed in him just like I believed that every fairy tale had a happy ending. But there was a dark side to my daddy that he kept from my brothers and me. He broke my heart. And I made sure he was the last man to do so for a long time.

Hating Communists

Over time, stories circulated in my family about my father's death. It was hard to tell what was the truth or filled-in fiction. Here's what I chose to believe: My dad had developed insomnia because of his fear of communists. In the early 1960s, during the time of the Cold War, hating communists was rampant and considered patriotic among his friends.

Maybe it was the times, maybe it was his upbringing or his inclination, but my dad had an intense love for his country, and a profound fear of losing his freedom and his family.

Dad's terror of the potential launch of Russian missiles from the island of Cuba overwhelmed him. Knowing that Cuba was only ninety miles away from the United States put him in turmoil. My mother didn't share his angst.

Dad kept a pistol under his pillow and thought at times he could "hear army tanks" powering down the streets. He wanted to store weapons, food and secure an underground shelter for the family. Lidi wouldn't cooperate. She didn't believe in the crisis and kept us children unaware of Dad's worries. Bringing canned food and blankets to school and having under-the-desk drills was fun for us kids.

The different perceptions about the situation caused a rift in an otherwise romantic marriage. My mom always said that Dad was a sexy dancer. They had met at a dinner party at a mutual friend's apartment when they were in their twenties. Mom loved tall, lean men so it was passion at first sight, and the lore is that they danced close late into the night. They were a privileged pair: He was the son of a successful automobile businessman, and she was "The General's" daughter. Though both were of a similar conservative persuasion, Lidi did not take politics or current events so seriously. Over time, Dad's "moods" would overcome him. Lidi, on the other hand, was persistently positive, but she had a biting sense of humor that sometimes wasn't so funny to the sensitive, including my dad.

Two days before Thanksgiving, Dad started to drink early in the morning. He was agitated. He had dark circles under his eyes. He wanted to get away. He asked to be driven to his doting mother's home on Camelback Mountain to watch television and drink uninterrupted. Lidi was happy to give Dad a lift so she could run errands in the only family car. She was focused on planning a holiday celebration, not my dad's unraveling.

My dad was unable to relieve his anxiety about the safety of his family. After several drinks, he grabbed Granny's keys and took her new Cadillac for a ride to look for the "army tanks."

He sped down an empty highway. Police said he most likely turned the steering wheel too far to the right to avoid a tortoise. Instead, he ran it over and then swerved into an embankment where he rolled his mother's car. It burst into flames. My daddy burned to death.

Being picked up early from school by neighbors somehow had led me to believe we were in for a wonderful surprise. As a six-year-old it was easy for me to misread the silence.

I remember the moment Mom sat us down in the living room. As she told us the horrible news, she let out a deep wail, while clinging to my baby brother, who cried inconsolably in her arms. I sat in silence, shaking, with tears streaming down my face. My older brother must have gone numb. He didn't cry. He said, "That's the way the cookie crumbles." I'll never forget that odd response.

Our seemingly ideal family was shattered. Lidi is still too pained to talk about the unanswered questions of my father's death. My dad left behind a baby who never knew him, two traumatized children who struggled in school, and a distraught wife who had never worked outside the home. I had lost what made me feel safe. Gone was my invincibility. Gone was my Prince.

Before long, Lidi moved us far away from our bad memories to the beach in Los Angeles. The coast was a relief from the desert heat and the loss of my dad. Lidi had seemingly moved on. She avoided any discussion of my dad's demise and denied any longing for his presence.

After a while, it was like I never had a father. I'd learned it wasn't becoming to prolong my grief. What was left was a sadness that would envelop me when I would least expect it.

While many memories faded, I couldn't forget the unsaid family mantra: "If you ignore bad things, they'll go away." And I tried to believe Lidi when she would remind us, "You'll be fine. You're having a happy childhood." And it was mostly true.

The Best Guy Friend

Years passed and soon, like most, I was an adolescent with mixed emotions. During that summer of our 16th year, Paul was the best guy friend a teenage girl could have. He listened to me, accepted my sullen moods, and would eat anything Lidi fed him. We shared a love of the beach and the humor in every day occurrences. I felt calm and safe with him.

We had known each other for a few years before this summer and had been in math classes together in junior high school. But feeling awkward and shy then, I didn't carry on much conversation with boys.

In high school, my social skills naturally improved. It may have helped that my body had morphed from gawky to curvaceous. And my braces were gone.

During breaks in the school day, I liked hanging out in the center of the campus called "the Quad." That was where Paul would be. He often asked me what I had for lunch, hoping I would share something with him, which I always did, even if it was just an apple. He was part of the athletic group but also fit in with the geeky intellects. Me too.

That summer, there was a large patchwork of beach towels behind the lifeguard station where I hung out with my girlfriends and, before long, with boys, including Paul. Eventually, he was "borrowing" and then sharing my towel when he neglected to bring his own. I figured it was on purpose, but that was fine with me. I enjoyed his wit.

*****

Paul Primrose Sutter, like his namesake the primrose flower, was showy but, at the same time, retiring. As a loyal son, he had to be the best at everything. Even with emotionally absent parents, he succeeded in high school as an A student, a varsity football player and the star catcher on the baseball team. He aspired to play college baseball and enter a professional career in sports. But "Pop" intervened. "You will continue the family business," Mr. Sutter would remind him through his teen years.

Paul's family business was unique, at least to me. I didn't know anyone else whose family produced rock and roll television shows. For Paul, their work was nothing very exciting or out of the ordinary. Still, he had a great love for the music of the 1960s and early '70s and always had an ear for something new and different in the rock and roll world.

Paul weathered the erosive dynamics of a self-absorbed dad and an oblivious mom. He retreated to a few friends where he didn't have to talk about it.

What made Paul seem "inadequate" to my mom, as she liked to jest with him, was his pause in conversation. He was the only person I knew who did think before he spoke. At the same time, eating everything on his plate endeared him to Lidi, who didn't tolerate picky eaters.

Lidi had something to say about most of my friends who were boys to keep them at a distance. I considered her perspective. I wanted to keep her happy.

She enjoyed being a teaser. And she was adept at rapid-fire comebacks. I'm grateful for her fierce love of her children, but whenever possible, I avoided drawing her attention to myself.

Paul played along with Lidi's teasing. She was never successful in unnerving him, and this endeared him to her. Eventually he would respond with a joke. He told funny stories that sounded like they came from an old-timer's bar.

Paul loved my mom's home cooking, maybe because his mom fed him frozen dinners a lot of the time. He ate Lidi's stuffed zucchini, juicy pot roasts, Jerusalem artichoke soup and anything else she put on his plate.

He ate dinner with us as much as three times a week during the summer. He joked with my brothers. And he flirted with me.

Lidi teased Paul every night he ate dinner with us. "Paul, you're inadequate," she would repeat. It was sadistic, but she couldn't help it.

Paul would just laugh. I dared not ask her to stop for fear I would be the target of her teasing.

Paul fit in. He looked like us in a blonde, fair-eyed kind of way. But our limbs were long and lean. Paul had big bones and a muscular physique. He had strong, large hands that filled up a catcher's mitt. He could hurt somebody if he wanted to, but that never happened, not even on the football field.

I often stared at his big blue eyes. I couldn't help it.

He didn't force his way into the center of attention at the dinner table nor spout expletives and loud burps like my brothers and I did. I wish I could remember the dumb jokes he told, but I didn't, thinking there were always more to come.

Daily, Paul witnessed my siblings and me laughing, yelling, and threatening to beat the shit out of each other before Lidi came home from work. He never joined in but felt part of it just by being there.

Paul's Family

In the 1960s, Paul's parents introduced armchair rock and roll to the world's television audiences. Paul's dad started as a producer for variety television shows, but quickly found his niche in the exploding rock world. His mom was his dad's secretary. It wasn't long before his dad recognized her homegrown talents and smarts.

"They made a good team: Mom was the brains behind the scenes and Dad the show," said Paul. Paul's dad thrived in Hollywood and called many celebrities his good friends. His mom tended to keep to herself. But because of them, we don't have to go any further than our matching recliners to rock out.

Away from the office, the Sutters lived a private life that was partly normal and partly affected by the pressures of show business. They spent their money, but not as much on the extravagant as on the tasteful traditional. They lived in spacious comfort where it was hard for Paul's lumbering body to accidentally break things.

Their house fit in their neighborhood like a blonde kid fit in our school: neither new nor noticeable. It was a large white house with black shutters and manicured bushes. Potted gardenias cut in the shape of small trees decorated either side of the front door. Sometimes Paul would bring a flower or two from the gardenias, so I could immerse my face in their fragrance.

The inside of the house was pleasant but messy, with a modern kitchen and rooms in all white décor, except for Mr. Sutter's office, which was furnished in black. Photos of Mr. Sutter and famous people hung crookedly on the walls of his office. He stopped straightening the frames. It was futile. The earthquakes kept coming. Paul had to have met many of the celebrities pictured on his dad's office wall, but I don't remember that he ever talked about them.

He spent little time in his house or at his Dad's job, unless coerced to do mindless work. He circulated among his friends and only came home for food and clothes.

His younger brooding sister Beth ate bologna sandwiches in her room. She listened to Black Sabbath on the stereo with the volume turned all the way up. She was wearing the same heavy metal T-shirt every time I saw her. She gave me the heebie-jeebies when she answered the door with a scowl and a curt, "What do you want?"

Paul's mom, a petite woman with platinum blonde hair, red lipstick and black eyeliner, looked like the housewife version of Marilyn Monroe. Mrs. Sutter thought her husband was amusing. But she needed space from his whirlwind energy and his need for attention. For relaxation, she ate at the local Denny's. She would pick a booth in the smoking section and order the bottomless iced tea and a piece of pie. She loved her Winstons.

Paul told me she read everything, including Shakespeare. "I got my curiosity from my mom," he said.

For Paul, his dad's home behavior seemed "off the wall." When his dad was wound up from a day of financial decisions and ass-kissing from the stars, he would come home craving a rare steak and Jim Beam. He would walk out to the backyard in his boxers and grubby undershirt to talk to a giant sycamore. He would sort out the current day and make plans for the next one.

More than once, Paul would describe how his dad would carry on a conversation with the tree. He said, "Can you imagine this balding fat guy with a bottle, laughing and talking with a tree and even trying to put his arms around the trunk?"

"If I'm there, it's, 'Paulie, come talk to me!'"   "I can't stand being around him when he's doing that," Paul told me many times.

I liked Mr. Sutter, because I liked his fun-loving attitude. I guess Paul's dad would tease him about my "boy's" name and refer to me as "Legs."   His dad had nicknames for people he liked. He encouraged Paul to hang out with me.

But the tree hugging would be a little too much. I'd want to get out of there like Paul did.

"Why would he talk to a tree? I don't get it. He's crazy," Paul said.

"Maybe the tree is a good listener. It's hard to find a good listener," I suggested, wanting to defend his likeable dad.

Something about the Sutters was sad. They didn't make time to hang out with each other. That was the downside of show biz families. Paul didn't complain about his unusual family life. In that way, he was a mystery among his friends. He kept his feelings to himself (except with me), as if it was shameful to have them. He was loyal to his family despite their unconventional behaviors, but he avoided their company.

But I remember a time when Paul asked me to come along with his gregarious Dad for a "visit to some friends at the beach." Wearing only swimsuits and T shirts, we strolled along the Malibu shoreline toward the beach homes where the glitterati lived. We walked up to a spacious house with large windows where a tall thin man with a full head of gray hair greeted us and expected our visit. He was John DeLorean the auto executive and creator of the DeLorean sports car, later featured in the movie Back to the Future. I had no idea who he was, other than famous. Mr. Sutter introduced Paul and me to the old guy's young, stunning-with-no-make-up wife, Cristina Ferrare, a supermodel. The couple invited us to enjoy their jacuzzi.

Unaware we were going to soak with celebrities, I thought, "Why not?" I was along for the ride but felt that I was somehow part of Mr. Sutter's show. As I expected, in the company of the rich and famous, Paul was nonchalant, but friendly. I was unsure how to act, so I followed his casual lead. What ensued was a lively chat between Mr. Sutter and Mr. DeLorean while Paul and I listened and smiled at each other. At one point, Paul rolled his eyes discretely. We waited until we could politely exit and get back to the beach.

All summer, if he wasn't already at my house, in the early evening when his parents weren't around, he would leave a short note, "I'm going to Jamie's." He drove to my house in his jalopy with the rear-view mirror in a permanent tilt, and most of the time didn't call to ask or tell me he was coming. He said he would drool over the thought of my Mom's pot roast when he pulled up to our beach bungalow. He appeared at the front door, pushing his head in, sniffing like a bear looking for the forest ranger's Juicy Fruit gum.

I knew he was escaping home life. That was okay with me. He liked to hang out in my room and check out my music posters. He touched everything he was curious about.

"You still listen to the Beatles, Jamie?" he said as he touched the four photos of John, Paul, Ringo and George taped to my closet door.

"Yeah I listen to the Beatles. Doesn't everybody? I love that song, 'What would you do if I sang out of tune,' I sang. 'Oh, I get high with a little help from my friends.'"

"Really, Jamie? You get high?" He turned around and looked at me, waiting for an honest answer.

"Yup, Paul, but I do it naturally. I fell back on my bed, then sat up and bounced on my butt. "Can we get the hell out of here now?"

"Don't you want to know my sins?" said Paul.

"Not really," I replied. I didn't want to hear about my friends' sins—or drug habits—and I didn't want a habit myself because I tried to stay in top shape as a competitive swimmer. Paul seemed a bit disappointed that I wasn't curious, even though he had nothing to tell about except some drinking after football games. I already knew about that.

The Beach

THE RUMBLE OF PAUL'S CAR THAT HE CALLED OLD BLUE woke me way too early many mornings during the summer of '73. His ailing car readied me for this season's ritual: he crawled into my bed and rubbed his calloused feet against my legs. I guess this could be considered affection, although I thought it an odd way for him to wake me up. It was not very romantic.

We mostly didn't date beyond hanging out at the beach. We seemed to hold fast to the preservation of a friendship over complicating romantic interests. And perhaps, way back in our subconscious, was the Catholic voice of our childhood telling us to "abstain from sin." Even with my good intentions, I could have done without that guilt-laden reminder.

Paul was enthusiastic about being one of the first people on the beach. Still, he tried to wake me up gently, knowing what a grump I was in the morning. "Jamie, you beach babe." he would whisper, "Wake up. It's time to go to the sea, sea, sea." Mostly, I was already awake but pretended not to be.

"You great white walrus. Get outta here!" I would whine. "How'd you get in?"

"The back door was open like it always is, sleepy head." We mostly forgot to lock up at night. We felt safe in our little beach house.

"My brothers didn't wake up?"

"They're out cold."

"Come on, Jamie," as he snuggled his large, muscular body up to mine and patted my head. He felt warm and comfortable. I wanted to fall back to sleep. My Mom was long gone for her daily swim and to her job as an office manager. I wished I could be as disciplined as Lidi, and she wished it too.

Paul and I would nod off together for about a half hour, with our noses almost touching, I smelled the toothpaste on his teeth and the manly soap on his chest. He ignored the light snores I directed at his face.

Unlike a lot of my girlfriends, I didn't want to grow up too soon. Sometimes I felt my father's sudden death had slowed my maturity. And, having experienced mortality, I was just a bit more cautious than the average teenager. Although I must admit I thought about it, I continued to be ruled by the mantra that sex carried grown-up responsibilities and possible consequences. I wasn't ready for that, and Paul didn't seem to be either. We were content to cuddle.

The real purpose of Paul's early morning visits was to get me to go to the beach with him before the afternoon wind churned up the ocean. "Jamie, the waves are breakin' perfect for bodysurfing," he would say to entice me. The water is clear—I bet we'll see our feet. Maybe we'll see some dolphins," he would say.

I loved watching the dolphins ride the morning waves, but I hated waking up early. I would tell Paul that I wanted two more hours of sleep. "Get out of my face!" I would growl, as I put the pillow over my head. He would take the pillow off to see if I was mad.

Earlier in the summer, I had tested myself with a thirty-five-day backpacking trip. This was a gift from my wealthy Uncle Larry. My uncle tried his best to fill a father role for me and my brothers. He thought I would use his money for something exotic and relaxing, like a trip to Hawaii. I chose the test of a rugged trek in the Wyoming Grand Tetons with a bunch of "fucked-up rich kids," as I called them. After that grueling hike—with a backpack that weighed half as much as I did and a daily 5:30 a.m. wake-up call—I was permanently averse to early morning wake-ups. I told Paul, "I don't want to catch the worm, and getting up before the sun does is fucked up." He would put the pillow back on my head to stop the tirade.

This conversation would happen almost daily. Then he would help himself to our Cocoa Puffs as he tried to convince me to "rise and shine." Paul was persuasive because he was patient and accepting. His upbeat attitude was a great motivator. He had good instincts, too. He would back off at a certain point, and he knew when a punch line would change my mood for the better.

The morning would continue with decisions about breakfast. I never wanted to eat much, and I knew we could walk the six blocks back to my house for lunch.

Once I saw him glancing at my body. I had changed from by bedtime boxers and T-shirt into my tropical print bikini. I loved that bikini so much I wore a hole in the butt by the end of the summer.

"What the F are you looking at?" I asked in an accusatory voice.

"*Absolutely nothing,* Jamie," he said with a smile and a giggle he could barely contain.

"Good," I laughed quietly and looked down at my feet. I laughed more when he was around. I needed his kindness in my life.

Every day that we could, we would walk a half a mile to State Beach, clad only in our swimsuits: no shoes, no hat, no Coppertone. We had that one beach towel that I used and shared with Paul. It just about fit our two bodies.

Paul didn't need much. He was content with his blue trunks and an occasional torn or stained shirt. Sometimes he didn't bother with the towel, he would just lie in the warm sand and push it over him.

I would challenge Paul to bodysurfing contests and taunt him about my being stronger in the water. Encouraged by my mom, I competed in swimming. It helped alleviate my moodiness, and I loved the camaraderie that came with being a part of a team. My long muscles and broad shoulders, inherited from my swimmer mom, gave me natural abilities. I was strong and had an efficient stroke, but not enough competitive gumption. I was a solid second place finisher. Maybe I could have been more than just "The Plugger," as I was called. But much of the time, I was distracted by the screaming fans and preoccupied with the kicks and arm strokes of girls in the lanes next to me. Then I would remember I was in a race.

Paul couldn't help smiling when I bragged about "winning the competition" when it came to riding the waves. He laughed and would be close to grabbing me in a hug.

As he emerged from the ocean, I found myself admiring his Adonis-like looks, his sun-bleached, slicked-back hair, and his glistening athletic body. I don't know if he knew how good he looked to a 16-year-old girl.

The beach was quiet in the mornings: only a few surfers sharing observations on the form of the waves, some squawking seagulls, and the whish of ocean reaching the sand. There were no screaming children and mothers or screaming girls being chased by flirting boys. The morning beach was ours. The ocean in front of Life Guard Station 11 was ours, too.

Our beach conversations were mostly about music and life philosophy. He loved the Grateful Dead. I remember once he asked me what I thought of the band. "I don't know, I guess death is a weird thing to be grateful for," was my snarky remark.

Not appreciating my humor, he continued that he wanted to take me to their concert. His dad had given him the tickets. "I just think you're the only beach babe who'd get it," he said with a smile.

"The Dead concerts go on and on and on and I have swimming early in the morning. Besides, what if I don't get it? Will you still be my friend?" I rolled to my belly on my towel, so I could look at Paul's face, which was now two inches from mine.

"I … I … I … am always your friend, Jamie, you know that."

I liked getting philosophical with Paul. "Life's too short," I would say. It would catch him off guard and he wouldn't know how to respond. "We need to enjoy life and appreciate the good times and the bizarre ones. Did you know that you have a soul that tells you how to live life? You may not even know that you have one because you're too busy with baseball and football, but I know you do. You have a good one. The truth is you have the most amazing soul I think I'll ever know," I told him one time.

"Jamie, you're getting weird on me," he replied. Paul wasn't quite prepared for my deep thoughts, but that didn't stop me. I figured he would get it later. I knew I shouldn't say anything, but I couldn't help myself.

"You'll understand better about your heart and what it's done for me. I'm glad you're my friend," I said. That was as close as I got to telling Paul how much I cared about him.

"You're welcome, Jamie. I'm not sure I'm as good as you say," he answered. We had this conversation while our cheeks rested on our crossed arms and we took turns scooping sand with our toes and depositing it on each other's behinds.

"Sometimes you think about your Dad, don't you?" Paul ventured.

With that question, I sat up, and Paul did too, and we stared at the clear waves of the morning ocean, careful not to look at each other.

"Yes," I said reluctantly.

"Sometimes I see a tear in the corner of your eye. I wish there's something I could do, Jamie."

"You can't do shit about this."

"I know, and that's cool."

"It just sucks. It happened when I was a little girl. I should be way over it. But sometimes I feel the pain so deeply and when I least expect it."

"I can't imagine fucking losing my dad, even though he can be a pain in the ass." I didn't acknowledge him.

He changed the subject: "You know, last year at lunch, I'd hear you laughin' your head off. It cracked me up," said Paul.

He would tell his friends, "This girl's a fox." (Things got back to me.)

Even though I had developed into a more attractive, seemingly happy, young woman, not far underneath was an uncertain, melancholy self. I combated my insecurities partly through my fashion statement. When I wasn't in a bikini, I wore my severely torn and patched up jeans, an oversized cowboy shirt, a black leather jacket that I found in my grandparents' basement, and I mostly went bare foot.

This way, I felt wild and rebellious. Lidi ignored my expression, but to shop owners, I looked like the kid who was going to steal something. I was also suspect among my female friends' parents. I was labeled "a bad influence." Little did they know that the so-called bad influences were under their own roofs.

Many of my conforming friends were the ones having sex, drinking to excess, and smoking copious amounts of pot. Luckily, Paul came into my life just when I was edging toward taking benign rebellion to the next level.

Even as a self-conscious teenager, I still felt Paul's attraction to me. I knew, because I would catch him staring a moment longer than a glance. Sometimes he stared at my lips. He seemed to want me for his very own.

That summer, he had my attention. We weren't physical, but we were intimate in that we shared feelings with each other that we didn't share with others. We had a trusting friendship, and it was natural for us to nurture each other's worthiness. It was a closeness that we both had craved for a long time in our short lives. But such profound intimacy would be fleeting, like teenage relationships could be, and mostly absent from our adult life.

A Grateful Dead Date

"Hey, Jamie, you're really going to like this," Paul said when I opened the door to a clean football stud. He was a mirage, dressed in tan corduroys and a button-down white shirt with clean sneakers. We were going on a date—the only real one we had in high school. And for the first—well maybe second time—he looked sexy, even with the middle button of his shirt absentmindedly undone.

"*You* look hot. I haven't seen you look so put together before." I had to say so, even though I could feel my face turn red. Paul just shrugged his shoulders.

He stared at me up and down. "Is that a new crop top? Cool color." He had to feel the material at my neckline. He always liked to feel things.

"We'll see ya later, Lidi," he said to my mother, who was standing close by with her hands at her hips. "I won't keep your daughter out too late, but don't wait up for us cause it's the Grateful Dead."

"Grateful who?" she said frowning, as if she didn't know that I was going out, even though I gave her ample notice.

"They'll play for a long time. Don't freak out and don't call the police," he said with a wide grin. Paul squeezed my hand and pulled me out the door.

"Bye Mom!" Lidi didn't approve of my top that tied in the

back and at my neck, so I couldn't wear a bra. But I knew Paul was safe. He wasn't going to make any moves on me.

"We gotta go, Jamie. We don't want to miss anything. We have bitchin' seats, right in the middle in a box near the stage. We'll have a clear view of the band. I brought us a picnic with some good stuff: oranges, pbj's, and some Grateful Dead doobies."

"I don't do that."

"That's okay, just kiddin'. I know you're in training," and he grabbed my biceps, which were enlarged and tight from miles of swimming practice.

I took my camera, since we were going to the Hollywood Bowl to see the Grateful Dead's famous Wall of Sound—a giant edifice of speakers. All night long, I tried to count them. It was a black throbbing pattern of rectangles and squares, and I never came up with a final number.

At random moments, while we hung out at the beach, Paul would break out into exuberant off-key choruses of Dead songs, like "Truckin …" I think it was a life-long behavior. After a while, I started to sing with him, even though I didn't know the words. At the concert, I got to hear what he was singing about; the band members' harmonizing outdid Paul's renditions, so the evening was worthwhile.

Since Paul brought the picnic, I brought some drinks and a blanket. L.A. nights could get cold. There was no other band, just the Grateful Dead. They started at 9:30 and played until 2:00 in the morning. We wiggled to the music most of the night. At a certain point, I crossed my arms and lay my head on the picnic table as the long, winding melodies lulled me to a semi-sleep. Paul could have kept going all night long.

"Is everything good, Jamie?" Paul asked as he put the blanket over me and his hand on my back.

"No prob, Paul. I'm having a great time, really. Can I have your sweatshirt?" I said.

The Amusement Park

After my junior year in high school in 1974, I spent a good part of my summer vacation in San Diego staying at my Uncle Larry's condominium in Mission Bay. It happened to be down the street from Paul's friend's house, where he was vacationing.

We were bored, especially being with the grown-ups. We had had enough of the beach, and we needed some excitement.

"Wouldn't it be a trip to go to P.B.'s Amusement Park?" Paul threw out. Neon lights and carnival music were a welcome change from hanging out near adults and listening to their old music. We were all in. So, Paul drove me and two of his buddies there for a carefree evening.

Paul and his friends were out to have a wholesome good time. I was excited to be in their company but tried not to show it. I felt like a tagalong with these naturally foxy guys. Their T-shirts and shorts showed off their muscular arms and legs from days of boogie boarding and body surfing. Their chest muscles bulged through their baggy shirts. Without any fuss, they were impressive Southern California specimens.

The amusement park had plenty to amuse. Fireworks shot over Mission Bay like the Fourth of July. Yellow, green and red blinking lights decorated a giant Ferris wheel. The swirling lights on the roller coaster and screaming sirens as the cars turned corners scared you into thinking that you were heading straight into the dark ocean waters. You could smell the oil greasing the rickety wheels. If it wasn't so much fun, the sound would be deafening. We spoke with hand signs and exaggerated mouthing of our words.

Music from the swinging shipwreck blared. Penny arcades popped and howled, and giant bells rang when the boys effortlessly hit the weight to the bell at the top. They showed off their flexed biceps after each success. The boys preferred to ogle some cute girls in bikini tops and bell bottoms rather than go on rides. Everything looked right on these beach bunnies: nice butts, perky breasts, large white smiles, and long, shiny hair parted down the middle and hanging down their backs. The girls traveled in a six-pack. One girl kept track of the rest of her friends like a mother goose and her goslings, spreading out, then she signaled them to come back together. Now and then, the boys stopped to flirt with them. I trailed behind.

"You don't mind, Jamie, do ya?" They would ask. I didn't care. None of them were my boyfriends, but Paul and I stayed close to each other. He was protective. Paul gave me a giant pink bunny that he won by shooting water into a plastic dolphin's mouth.

Everybody got hungry. Paul bought cotton candy that he shared with me. He pulled off pieces of the pink cloud and stuffed it in his mouth. He ate it like it was his dinner. He offered his cotton candy to the cute girls. They were more important than his chuckling friends.

It didn't bother me too much that he was flirting with those girls. We were 17 then, and the unspoken passion from the summer before had drifted away. A year made a difference. But we were still good friends.

We all scattered, attracted by different arcades. I wandered over to where you could throw pennies in small bowls and win a Siamese fighting fish.

Behind me, there was laughing, and a slang Spanish being spoken. I didn't like what I heard. I turned around toward Paul, who was standing by himself not so far from me. Close to him was a kid who had a barely grown in mustache and was no more than five feet tall. His hands were scarred with crosses. He had tattoos in large dark letters—"ODIO" on his left hand and "AMOR" on the right. He had only a stub for his right pinky.

I stopped breathing, I stopped thinking. I stared and grabbed a piece of my hair and put it across my nose and smelled my shampoo's fragrance. It was an odd but calming habit. There were fireworks overhead—Bam! Boom! Crack! Crack! Crack! —which startled me.

Paul didn't notice the trouble walking toward him.

"Hey Mister Chingado Güero, da me un qwaartur," the kid said. I remember the kid had combed-back hair that fell past his shoulders. When he smiled, you could see his two front teeth were covered with gold. Paul responded, "Huh?" He didn't speak Spanish, but I understood the kid's feigned, polite, yet insulting, request.

"Oh, this is not good." I cringed."

"Give me un qwarrturr, cabrón," the kid said, as he held out his hand and laughed.

"Oh, a quarter?" Paul said.

"Yesss!" hissed the kid.

His mouth was smiling, but not his eyes; they were like a jaguar's, focused and ready to pounce on their prey. The kid kept looking behind him at his group of compadres, who were laughing and jabbing their fists in the air as if they held knives in their hands. Paul looked around for his friends and didn't see them. He didn't see me signaling him to run.

I could see sweat on Paul's forehead as he realized he was in trouble and that he was alone. The kid rocked back and forth shifting his weight from the front foot to the back foot, staring into Paul's squinting eyes. Sweat dripped down Paul's sideburns on this breezy night. Even being a defenseman, he was not used to confrontation. Neither fight nor flight seemed like good choices. But he was a large muscular male. The other guy was so small it was no contest. So, Paul chose "fight" in his own way.

"No, sorry, man, I don't have a quarter." Paul raised his eyebrows as if saying "Isn't that good enough? Now scram!" The kid stayed and reached into his pocket. Paul's face crunched like he was ready to tackle the opponent. No one else but me noticed that the kid had pulled out a shiny four-inch switchblade. Paul didn't move. Nor did I.

I froze and watched thirty seconds turn into drawn-out terror. With expert speed, the kid thrust the knife at Paul's lower belly and pierced it three times. Paul grimaced, but did not quite register the magnitude of what had just happened. He stepped back in an agile football move. The kid's gangster friends laughed, holding their sides. The kid jumped toward Paul and plunged his knife three more times into Paul's lower belly. The small teenager had to stab this big white guy more than once because he had to kill him. That was a brutal gang initiation. Only his homies and I witnessed the horror.

I screamed Paul's name and he looked over at me. "Oh, God!" he yelled at the top of his lungs. He dropped his cotton candy and grabbed his belly where dark red started to run between his fingers. Then he crumpled to the ground.

Soon he lay in an enlarging pool of blood as his wounds drained him of life. Lights kept blinking and music kept blaring as screaming teenagers surrounded him.

The blood poured out of his body, but being young, his heart was strong: it kept pumping, but very fast. Time began to slow down as Paul became weak and helpless. The paramedics could have used assistance in picking up Paul's large, limp body, but Paul's two friends who huddled near him didn't react. I didn't either.

Paul stayed conscious and he held his arms to his chest to hold in the warmth that was leaving him. He licked his lips, getting thirstier, or maybe he noticed the sugary taste of cotton candy in his mouth.

The kid, assuming he had completed his job, darted in and out of the crowd pushing people aside and disappeared into the loud night. He could brag to his superiors and his friends who were witnesses that the white guy fell dead.

When Paul reached the emergency room, the EMTs tried to protect other patients from Paul's gruesome appearance. I later found out he had lost nearly half of his body's blood. It was smeared from his bare feet to his soaked hair, and his shirt and shorts were drenched.

It took a while for his parents to arrive. They had to travel two hours from Los Angeles. I couldn't see or touch him. I just sat alone, waiting and crying. My body shook as I gasped for air. He couldn't die. I put my face in my lap and let time pass. Someone put their hand on my back to comfort me, but I couldn't tell you who it was.

No one lives after that. Paul was lucky.

What could I have done to prevent it? I'm not sure anything.

But I kept playing in my mind how I could have stopped it. I sensed that kid was planning evil before he asked for a quarter. Instead of alerting Paul, I froze.

A few weeks later, I remember walking into his hospital room. As I walked through the door, he had a big smile on his face. He looked pale and half his football size.

"Shit!" I didn't mean for that to be my greeting. Though I guess he was healing well, I was shocked by what I saw.

He was still too weak to move much. I wanted to crawl into the hospital bed with him, but I kept my distance and hoped my jean miniskirt and crop top would offer some consolation.

"Ya want to see where I was stabbed, Jamie?" he said with a smile.

"Hell, no! But I'm glad you're okay," I said.

"That was a close one, Jamie."

"Too close. That was totally fucked up."

Somehow, that seemed to be enough about the trauma, so Paul moved the conversation to a more superfluous subject.

"Jamie, where did you learn all those bad words?" he asked with amusement in his voice.

"Why? You like them?"

"Only when *you* say them."

"I've had a foul mouth since I was very young. I started off with 'bastard,' which I got from my mom yelling at my dad. They loved each other madly but still could get into some verbal spats. Later, I discovered that the word 'shit' would shock boys. I liked the shock factor. But it doesn't seem to work with you."

"Not really," he concurred.

"Then I added 'fuck' to my repertoire when I was about 12. I've been told that only people who have limited vocabularies resort to the forbidden seven. I like my limited vocabulary. Speaking of that, did I ever tell you the time the comedian George Carlin picked up me and my best friend Gracie when we were hitchhiking on Sunset Blvd?"

"Oh yeah," he said. "You were dressed as identical nerds."

"Yeah, his monologue about swear words is hysterical but George was in a serious mood when he gave us a ride. We were the funny ones that day."

"I remember that. You girls seemed at home with your look, sporting horn-rimmed glasses, braids up like Pippi Longstocking and your retainers on your teeth. I couldn't believe you hitchhiked like that."

It was a good change of subject. Paul once again was helping *me* relax and feel comfortable.

La Virgen de Guadalupe

AFTER GRADUATION, PAUL AND I ENROLLED IN SEPARATE universities and, without conferring, both ended up in Arizona. I veered north to a small college in the mountains. He traveled south, to the University of Arizona in Tucson, for warmth and baseball. We didn't keep in touch to any great extent. At that time, long-distance calls cost too much, and I wasn't a disciplined letter writer. But missing our friendship made us meet one last time in our young lives.

After an unexpected call from Paul, my party-girl roommate Bridget and I decided we needed to venture south for a fiesta in the desert. By happy coincidence, my Tucson cousin, Isabel, matriculated at the same school, so of course she too had to come along. My cousin and I shared one-sixteenth Mexican blood from our great-grandmother. In our adult years, we toasted her with tequila shots during our Thanksgiving reunions in the Saguaro desert.

We drove four long hours to Tucson. When we reached our destination, we burst out of the car whooping "Ay yai yai yai yai!" as we circled in place with our shawls spread like the wings of an eagle.

The warmth of the late fall night wrapped around me like a Mexican serape. This time of year, you could usually see your breath when taking an evening walk in the desert. The party organizers took advantage of the unseasonable warmth and decided on an outdoor fiesta honoring Our Lady of Guadalupe.

The fiesta parking lot was situated a half-mile away from the event to help keep the dust off the tamales and rellenos. But we still could hear mariachis harmonizing as they strummed their giant guitaras en juntos. We sang along. The trumpets punctuated the singers' verses. My cousin and I jumped to music familiar from our childhoods. Isabel and I were proud of our heritage. "Hurry up!" we yelled, "Vamos a la fiesta!"

With only one phone call between us, Paul and I agreed on a meeting spot. I hoped we would find each other. It was a hazard to wait in the parking lot with drivers drunk on tequila.

Paul and I hadn't seen each other since before high school graduation. And since we parted, I had fleeting angst about not having his calmness in my life. We were going our separate ways without much forethought; even so, it seemed to be a natural progression. Besides, there was a whole world of men out there, and I intended to date a few of them.

Paul found me in the crowd. He was dressed in a clean white shirt and grey corduroys. He looked subdued for a Mexican fiesta. For the second time since I had known him, he wore something without holes or stains that fit and showed off his assets. He wanted to make a good impression. He must miss me, I thought. I know I missed him. But I had begun my future, and that included a hockey player boyfriend and unsettling emotional outbursts between the two of us. I wasn't going to bring the boyfriend up unless I had to.

"Hey, Jamie." He stared and hesitated when we finally met.

"Fuckin' A, do I have to do the work?" I said. He smiled and put his arms around me. I felt the power in his muscles. The hug moved past a shy high school one and lasted longer than past good-bye ones.

I smelled his aftershave. No strong musk, just something that felt like he wanted to show he was thinking about me. We kept hugging as my cousin and roommate looked on. I finally introduced them and said we would meet them at the party.

With nowhere else to go, Paul and I started to walk back to his car to catch up in a quiet way. Paul grabbed my hand. It was that catcher's hand, powerful and calloused. He was going to hold my hand most of the night. I let him.

We hung out on the top of his jalopy's hood, snuggled close. Paul's car was parked some way from the rest of the parking lot to avoid any mishaps with zealous partiers.

It was very dark in the desert. You could hardly see the giant saguaros watching over the grande fiesta. The sky had its own party. It seemed like every five minutes shooting stars flew across one horizon to the other.

The night's performance made Paul and I "ooh" and "ahh" as we squeezed each other's hands. This was our chance to catch up, but we didn't say anything for a long time. Still, I felt in the company of more of a self-assured, independent young man rather than my teenage beach buddy. Maybe I had grown up some too.

We didn't even look at each other. We just felt each other's warmth. I shared my shawl with him. He didn't complain, but he had been shivering as the night grew colder.

Finally, I blurted out, "Paul, how noisy do you think the universe is? From here, it is silent. If heaven is so much fun, how can it be so quiet? What's next for you, Paul?" Having so many inane questions thrown out, coupled with a "future" query, made him squirm.

He sighed, "Oh, Jamie."

"I know. Who wants to talk about it? I hate the future shit. But I've plans to have a career and be an independent woman. I don't want to depend on any controlling fucked-up man. No offense."

"None taken," he said, "because I'm not that man."

"Why don't we go dance," Paul suggested. We were all talked out. We quickly walked to the party, hand in hand.

It was a perfect night to honor Our Lady. Strings of translucent lights illuminated the perimeter of the party. La Virgen de Guadalupe is beyond an icon. She is a protector and good fortune. Her likeness hung over an altar decorated with rose petals. She was dressed for the party in her sapphire blue robe with gold stars. Brightly colored crepe paper flowers adorned the bars where the hibiscus tea and margaritas were served. The band members were dressed in starched white shirts and bolo ties. Their black pants were decorated with silver buttons all down the legs.

The smell of green chili with garlic permeated the air. We gorged on the authentic food and appreciated the change from dorm chow. Paul and I laughed late into the night. He held me tight when we danced. I felt secure in his arms. It was nothing energetic, just holding and swaying from side to side. It felt like a long goodbye.

Joe

I MET JOE NEARLY A DECADE AFTER PAUL BECAME A DISTANT memory and I had made a few bad choices in boyfriends. I felt safe with Joe, and he made sure that I stayed out of harm's way. Just before we met, I had fled a volatile relationship with a seemingly "charming" guy who turned out to be physically abusive. I then ruled out the charmers.

When I met Joe, I knew I had found my husband. We came from opposite sides of the country and landed in Denver, Colorado, to go to graduate school.

It was easy for me to fall in love with Joe. He wanted to take care of me. And even though I claimed fierce independence, a large part of me wanted to be taken care of.

When I first met him on a dance floor in a downtown Denver bar, I noticed the height difference. According to him, he was the "perfect height" at five feet five inches. He was "just like all the movie actors," he would tell me, like "Tom Cruise with a Jewish flair." Not that his being three inches shorter than I was important, but my legs occasionally loved sexy high heels, which stood him a half a foot out of my view. That was fine by Joe. He was proud of tall me.

Joe had a tender side. He would write me little love notes, saying things like, "I just want to take care of you, Little Flower." We cried at the same movies—those uplifting inspirational ones.

When we made love, I felt sexy and desirable. He brought me flowers, and he would pick my favorites—stock and hyacinths, which have a sweet fragrance.

It was my vulnerability and spontaneity, I think, that attracted him to me. Practicalities made me fall for Joe. I could rely on him to do what he said he would do. Unlike me, he was punctual and organized. He got things done and anticipated my basic needs.

I thought we were a good pair. More than once, we ended up buying the same card for each other. When we took walks, even our breathing seemed coordinated. Often, we would sniff aloud right at the same time.

We had the same political convictions. We went on camping trips. We both loved Mexican food, especially bean burritos smothered in pork green chili.

I loved Joe's broad smile. At a party, he was the most confident man in the room and adept at circulating among strangers. Women liked him for his listening skills: he didn't reveal his own opinion but smiled and nodded his head up and down.

He was reassuring and encouraging and was an integral part in my early success in my career.

I knew he would never be distracted by more important things and stop paying attention to me. I knew our future kids and family would be his number one priority.

I appreciated that he came from sturdy, doting parents and an intact family. To me, having grown up mostly with a single parent, that was a precious commodity.

I overlooked what I considered the small things when Joe and I were dating. Joe could be moody. He could be impatient with "stupid people." And sometimes his comments stung. I chalked up his East Coast sarcasm as mostly amusing. He was always congenial in public, but not so much behind the wheel, where his cynicism spewed like a Manhattan taxi driver.

Getting Married

Joe was strong for his size. He would pick me up off the couch and place me in his bed with ease. He was fearless, except for facing the unfamiliar and his qualms about marriage, which I didn't take seriously. Joe rarely worried, I thought. I only saw him fret over the fluctuating value of his retirement investments.

After dating for two years and moving in together, it made sense to get married and start a family. I thought Joe agreed. Looking back, I realize he was reluctant. But I paid no attention to his hesitancy. A week before we married, Joe dug a deep hole at his work at a waste water treatment plant, which he called the "turd mill." "You don't have to dig the hole, Joe. And it doesn't have to be so deep or so wide," said his staff. But he was frantic.

"Stop, Joe! It's done!" they yelled.

"I can't stop. I'm getting married," said Joe.

I believe that digging a deep dark hole was the way Joe expressed his anxieties about the uncertainties of marriage.

Joe kept digging because he wanted to see where the hole would lead and because he didn't want to think. He was 38, and marriage was the only contractual agreement where he felt out of control.

Digging didn't fix anything. And it inflamed his shoulder. During the wedding ceremony, he held his arm at a right angle to protect himself from stabbing pain. During the reception, he used a guest's pink silk shawl as a sling and avoided walking and dancing.

I didn't blame Joe. When it came to the wedding day, I was anxious and uncertain too. I had numbed myself with beta blockers that lulled me away from the ceremony and into a pleasant vertical nap just before we exchanged vows. The ceremony was a little boring. Our rent-a-reverend talked too long about the "special" moments, using that adjective when he didn't know what else to say about two people he hardly knew.

Neither the gentiles nor the Jews appreciated that the ceremony was a mixed religion gig for their benefit. Poor Joe was annoyed until the ceremony started. Then he plastered on the broad smile and held my hands. In the video, you can see him shaking them to wake me up.

Having a country western band may have been an abomination for the East Coast relatives, but the cowboys played Hava Nagila and everybody danced, except Joe. The men and boys hoisted my new husband and me in our chairs. I thought my drunken friends might forget what they were doing and let us fall. Our doubts and fears gave way to oblivion from continuous drinking; my ever-inebriated Uncle Larry paid for the alcohol. Uncle Larry tried to give me an out two hours before the wedding. Joe still resents him, even though Uncle Larry is long gone, dead from liver disease.

Joe carried me over the threshold of the wrong room. There was trash everywhere and the sheets and blankets were strewn across the carpet. Empty champagne bottles littered the floor, and a pile of used condoms lay on the nightstand. Was this room telling us something? "Fuck! This can't be our room," Joe said. So, he dropped me because he couldn't hold me any longer with his bum shoulder. That put me in a bad mood for what was left of the night. Digging the deep dark hole had screwed our nuptials and screwed our screwing.

To this bride, Joe quickly became an enigma. Just minutes before the ceremony and photo shoots of us looking like the happy loving couple, Joe was mad. But in retrospect, he was scared and had only anger to show it. Still, during those less-than-blissful moments, I was wondering if I could get along with this man "until death do us part." It occurred to me as I conjured my best wedding smile that I grew up with mostly just a mom, and I never saw her get along with a man for very long, let alone a grumpy one.

The Honeymoon

AT THE BEGINNING, OUR MARRIAGE WAS GREAT, UNTIL OUR honeymoon. The honeymoon was a generous gift from my mom's sister, Aunt Marina. Always looking out for her family's "best interests," she informed me, "For your wedding present, I'm sending you love birds to Hawaii." I couldn't say no to that. But I neglected to consult my fiancé. It was a done deal before Joe could express any misgivings. It is hard for a honeymoon to go wrong when the venue is a small lush island and your hotel room overlooks the ocean. And anyway, who would expect a honeymoon to be a flop?

Just a warning: If your husband is fair-skinned and parts of his body haven't had a suntan since he was twelve years old, beware when he decides he wants to sit in the sun. Not long after sipping a Mai Tai on the sunny hotel room balcony, Joe's body broke out in bright red bumps that soon itched and eventually oozed and bled. He then refused to venture into tropical paradise. I knew our honeymoon was "aloha" of the goodbye kind.

We tried to have fun. But I learned something new about Joe. He dreaded going where he hadn't been before, which was anywhere on the island. For the first three days, he stayed inside and ordered room service for all three meals each day. He didn't change his boxers, let alone put on a swimsuit or shorts. I assumed a big city guy was up for anything. But the idea of "exploring" caused him to recoil in Woody Allen anxiety. I hadn't met this Joe before.

As I walked the shore alone while Joe watched from the room with his beer and boxers, I thought, maybe we should have memorized those *10 Do's and Don'ts of Relationship Etiquette* that I saw in a Dear Abby article. This situation didn't break the deal, but it came close.

Maybe honeymoons aren't for men. The bride ought to take the maid of honor and leave the groom home with his best man to set up the man cave. Your new spouse can forget scenery. Forget about making love surrounded by ocean breezes; forget waves lulling the happy couple to a peaceful sleep.

Assuming the maid of honor is your best friend, you know she won't get a sun rash. At least she would warn you ahead of time. You and your maid of honor could pine away about the absent men, then pack it up for a fun week.

It seemed like it was more than sun poisoning that kept Joe in the hotel room. "I don't need to go out, Little Flower, I can look at the beach sights on the hotel Channel 6. They've gotta slide show of island scenery and stuff to do," he said.

"Wonderful, Joe. Would any of those activities be something you'd want to do?" I asked in my most patient voice.

"Oh no, I'm happy here at the hotel. But it's a gorgeous island. You go and have a good time, Little Flower. I don't think he was oblivious to my desires, just overwhelmed.

"We might as well've been in our basement with that giant television you just bought." My good humor was waning. I was a newlywed with promise. I had loved my fiancé, but liking my husband might be a challenge. "What's wrong, Sweetie?" I asked him. I'd never seen this wimpy side of Joe.

"I'm recovering from a traumatic experience," Joe said. I almost laughed, looking at him curled up in the fetal position on the bed with the channel changer in his hand.

"What trauma? Is there something I should have known about before the wedding?" I said. My stomach churned and my heart beat like it was coming out of my chest. I was in my black bikini with a black sarong wrapped around my hips. My ever-virile man didn't even notice my provocative attire.

I was cold. He had turned the air conditioning on full blast. The windows and sliding glass doors were shut and locked, the curtains pulled together.

"Don't you want to take in the tropical sounds of the island and the salty smell of the ocean?" I ventured.

"No, that's okay. I'm more comfortable this way," he replied.

He went on, "Anyway, you wanted me to *ask for marriage*. Why would I *ask for marriage*?" he seemed to wonder aloud. His face was white, and his hands shook, still curled up, he picked up a bottle of water from the nightstand. I watched his Adam's apple move up and down as he gulped the water. His right cheek twitched to punctuate his distress. Was he kidding? No, not at all. I realized he had never proposed to me. I had simply moved forward with wedding plans after we started living together.

Still, I felt like I was in a Saturday Night Live skit. It was too silly to be true and it would be a hilarious story for a monthly gathering of my women friends if I could get over the rejection.

"Asking for marriage is like asking for a promotion without a raise," Joe advised.

"I'm glad you think marrying me was a promotion for your life, but isn't it a little late for this discussion?" So I tried to cheer him up about the horrible predicament he was in. I said, "I don't know, Joe. Neither of us was that excited about marriage. Maybe that's why we picked each other. After my dad died, my mom's interaction with men was all downhill. I grew up believing men were trouble, a disappointment, and not anything to take seriously. Present company excluded."

"You tell me this attitude about men now?" said Joe.

"Yeah, I was commiserating." I should have stopped talking. "Being in my thirties, I wanted to get on with my life and I'd had enough of the 'living in sin shtick.' I knew I wanted a family. I think you wanted one, too. Don't you? We'll make cool progeny. That's my hope. It'll be like backpacking—leave the world a better place than when you got there."

"I hate to backpack, Jamie."

"You have buyer's remorse, Joe. Your purchase was worthwhile," I reassured him. "We have great credentials for a happy marriage: We have good sex, masters' degrees and money. You cry at the same movies I do, and you've a wicked sense of humor. I laugh at your fucking jokes. Besides, how many shiksas do you know who speak Yiddish? Give me the channel changer so I can turn off this mashuguna TV. I'm finished with this tour of the island. How about we go to the beach tomorrow?" I said.

"I'll worry about that tomorrow," said Joe as he turned away.

"You don't have to worry, Joe." I let the conversation stop there. Joe was already asleep; thanks to the pain killers he took for his shoulder. I turned off the light and opened the curtains and sliding glass door to the balcony. Tomorrow would be a better day.

I stepped outside, rubbed the moist air on my body, and took a deep breath while I stretched my arms over my head in a moonlight salutation. The moon lit the ocean swells like a giant disco ball. I wanted to remember the beauty of this moment. But it would have been so much better with my spouse.

I heard the waves crash on the shore and the rhythmic swoosh each time the ocean came further up on the sand. A couple walked down the beach holding hands. It was a romantic evening, even if my husband's day ended a while ago. I wrapped myself in a blanket and basked in the island sensations. This was familiar and comforting, but if I thought it through, I would have anticipated a better place for my man. I was only thinking of myself. This honeymoon was a West Coast girl's chance to get an island paradise fix.

I came in from the balcony. I missed Joe despite his hesitance. I left the sliding glass door open and shut off the air conditioning. Then I untied my black sarong and let it fall beside the bed. Joe didn't see this sexy move. I crawled ever so gently beside him. My fingers lightly rubbed his back. I would go easy on him tomorrow. He was in physical pain and traumatized. I didn't take seriously the part about "asking for marriage." I pretended that this was a situation comedy, only there was no laugh track.

Joe didn't move, and I couldn't hear him breathe from where I was. His arms folded across his chest. For a moment, I fantasized that Joe dying in his sleep would be an easy way out of this "unwanted marriage." But he was alive and comfortable.

I tossed and turned in the bed, careful not to bother Joe. "Stop ruminating," I told myself. From my side of the bed I saw that the wind had stopped. The sea was like glass, except for the ruffle of tiny waves against the sand. I could see the dark shapes of palms in the moonlight and another couple holding hands by the edge of the water. I wish Joe could share this beauty with me. Would he ever?

The next morning, I cheerfully said, "Time to wake up." I was determined to be happy and ready for a fun day with Joe. The room was filled with light. Joe made himself a cup of coffee with the Fiji water and Starbucks coffee left for honeymooners.

"Let's go to the beach," Joe said. I was still a bit wounded from the conversation last night, but I smiled.

"I'd love that."

"Let's eat breakfast first," he said. For him, nothing bad had happened.

The buffet offered a spread that honeymooners who had made love half the night would crave. I ordered a veggie omelet, a fruit bowl, whole-wheat toast, two slices of bacon and two glasses of orange juice. Joe had bran flakes and a grapefruit.

"Joe, there are some luscious bagels and cream cheese and beautiful salmon and fresh mahi mahi. Get some and I'll take a bite." He declined but tried a piece of mango from my plate and then spit it out in his napkin.

"It's not ripe. There's nothing here I can eat. I gotta watch my cholesterol—everybody has to in my family." He had to watch his cholesterol? Since when? This was a side of Joe I hadn't experienced. For a moment, I was lost in my thoughts imagining our offspring spitting out food in a nightly ritual.

"And you know I'm not a big fish eater," he said. I took a deep breath.

It took us only 20 minutes to drive to a beach on the other side of the island. The water was turquoise blue. Schools of brightly-colored fish swam around us and through our legs. Joe was in the water for only a little bit when the fish brushing against him began to freak him out.

Later that day, we went snorkeling. I saw small sharks and a large eel. Joe stayed in the boat and kidded with the captain as they smoked cigars. I came up from my exploration of the underwater wilderness, and the guys threw their cigars into the water. They floated by me like two giant turds.

Orchids

AFTER YOUR STORE-BOUGHT ORCHID BLOOMS, YOU LOSE the excitement and are left with a plant with shiny green leaves. These plants can live anywhere, but have little prospect of repeat color, unless you give them the right care in the right place. Without the exquisite flowers, it's just a plain frustrating plant. People often toss them. Some people do that with marriage. I tried not to.

Joe was East-Coast novelty to me, with a sharp sense of humor and stable genes for reproduction. I was fun to him, spur-of-the-moment, with nice boobs and a firm ass. After over twenty years of marriage, we stopped bringing out the best in each other; there was not much blooming in our lives, even though both of us still had many virtues to contribute to the union. Early in the relationship, except for the honeymoon fiasco, lust and family hid any need to think about intimacy.

Not long after we married, we had two boys. Raising them was fun with Joe. When they were babies, Joe was the one who changed most of the poopy diapers, bathed the squirming bodies, and read favorite books over and over again. When the babies cried at night, he insisted on being the one to hold them until they stopped. When the kids were preschoolers, sitting around the dinner table was our favorite time. The most important question of the day was "Did you see any animals?" Mostly Joe saw the "exotic" ones. Because his work was situated away from the city, Joe spotted eagles, hawks, snakes, coyotes, and lots of prairie dogs.

Soccer and baseball dominated our lives as the kids grew older. We camped and fished in the summer, snowboarded and skied in the winter. Family vacations were split between East and West Coast beaches. Joe was an involved dad and loving toward his boys. We had many good times and few glitches as a family. The boys were smart—book wise. They did fine in school. As teenagers, they pulled pranks, lit firecrackers with their friends, sneaked alcohol and pot. We became aware of these activities through their encounters with the law. Getting them into college was a relief.

As time went on and the boys no longer were at home, Joe became crankier. Partly, I think he was getting to hate his job at the turd mill and was burned out from the commute. He perpetually under-slept, with a 4:30 alarm for work.

During the first hour after Joe got home, he would put his mean on or forget to take it off. He was full of nagging criticism and numerous "fuck" bombs that I tried to dodge. But this was not easy for a wife who struggled with maintaining her personal space and abhorred blatant or even subtle criticism. "There's too much food in the refrigerator," meant too much money was spent. "There are dirty dishes in the sink," meant "What were you doing all day?" Honestly, I never was meant for home making.

I swear it was the caffeine that turned Joe into Mr. Hyde after he indulged in multiple cups of coffee. In that Hyde state, he brought his male coworkers to tears. Everybody "was stupid" after Joe dosed himself on those tiny energy drinks in the afternoon. Sometimes I would say, "Have you had some coffee, Joey?"

"Why do you care? I'm fine," he'd say.

"How 'bout we take the dog for a walk to use up some of

that energy?"

"Fine, let's go now," he'd demand. He hated waiting. "You're taking too long, as usual. Today Jamie!" he would start pacing.

"I'm not that fast like you New Yorkers. What's up with you?"

"Quit with the questions," he'd say.

"Then why the hurry?" I'd ask.

"Jamie, there is no why? It just is. You walk like an invalid," he often said.

"Sorry." Ugh! Why'd I say I was sorry? I didn't mean it. "Is everything all right?" I'd ask.

Growing up small, Joe may have been a target for bullies, but his mouth was unbeatable. His cutting words could penetrate the tender part of even a big brute's heart. No one could keep up because no one could get to his sensitivities. If this weren't real life, he would be funny, maybe he would even be my favorite tweaked cartoon character. Luckily, our boys never took him seriously.

As he grew older, Joe couldn't tolerate interrupted sleep. One night I woke him up because I needed to talk. My daytime fears entered my night dreams. Joe didn't want to participate in my anxieties. He had his own, the main one being his 4:30 a.m. wake-up time. There were many moments in the middle of the night when I wanted to talk. I'll show you how one of the last conversations went:

"Joe, please wake up."

"Why?"

"I can't sleep. I need to talk to you about the children." I said.

"And so, I gotta be awake because you're awake? Don't bother me. I have to get up in six hours," he said.

That was a good point. I guess I didn't need to talk to him. I rolled over and dealt with it myself.

Disgusted

COLORADO SUMMERS BRING RAGWEED AND BERMUDA GRASS
and who knows what other allergens. You don't have to go
outside. It blows through the screens and hitches rides on dog
fur and human hair. One day last summer, I sneezed a ferocious
five times. It was so forceful that it startled Joe out of his nap on
the family room couch. He remembered his afternoon dream—
crazy sex with his wife. But my multiple screaming orgasms were
uncharacteristic after so many years. Joe had started out as a
pleasing lover. But as time went on, he wanted kinds of sex that
I found distasteful and he sulked if I refused to participate.

I bolted through the screen door from the garden to clean
up my nose, which drained clear fluid like a leaky faucet. It was
too late. It dropped to the slate floor right in front of Joe. I
looked up at him waiting for his reaction.

"Couldn't you use your sleeve at least? That's disgusting,"
said Joe.

"It's been a really bad year for allergies, Joe, one of the worst.
My eyes itch. It feels like someone is running a tiny feather
across the end of my nose and eyes. Every long sleeve of mine
has been used as emergency tissue," I said. I contorted my face to
fend off the sneeze at the top of my nose and crossed my legs, so
I wouldn't pee in my pants. Before a second round of screaming
sneezes, I raced to the bathroom.

"I have no control over this. All I can do is stuff a wadded tissue up my nostrils," I said when I came out of the bathroom.

"You have control more than you think," said Joe." "Figure it out," and he walked away.

Later that day he told me, "You are a fucking embarrassment!" when he caught me with a runny nose in the supermarket. He turned his back and walked away again. He didn't offer to find me tissues, and I didn't think to open a box, even though they were there to my right in aisle five.

"When are you going to learn?" Joe said as we met in the checkout line and things were under control, much to Joe's relief.

"Learn what?" I said.

"To be prepared."

By the time our children left for college, Joe had grown incapable of being nice. Me too. His callousness colored all his goodness. My defenses colored mine. Each bit of sarcasm eroded my good nature.

During last winter, I parked our brown sedan too close to an SUV. The snow was two feet deep, with higher drifts lining the edge of the streets. Of course, we don't have snow tires. We never thought them necessary for our front-wheel drive car.

Joe wanted the car for an errand. "What the fuck were you thinking?" He yelled across the street as he began digging the snow away from the front wheels.

"What do you mean?" I said.

"This guy can't get out. You're parked too close. Why did you park here? No one can get out of this snow."

"Hey, Joe, be careful, your grandpa died shoveling snow. By the way, what's the value of your life insurance these days?" I yelled back.

He ignored me. "What the fuck?" He continued. "I can't believe you parked here. What the fuck were you thinking?"

"That kind of talk makes me want to walk away."

"I don't care. I just can't believe you're so stupid," he said.

"Well, thanks for digging me out,"

"Yeah, yeah," he said.

My Morning

EVERY MORNING I OPEN MY EYES, NOT WANTING TO WAKE UP. Slumber is a time to escape to an extraordinary life of connection and contentment. My dreams are full of yeses, caresses, "I'd love tos," and "I love yous."

Conflict can be stimulating, but nothing feels good about clashes. I have grown tired of them. My everyday life with Joe is full of disagreement. Joe thrives on being disagreeable—while it sucks away my good nature. Perhaps life with me is so dull that arguments and insults are better than quiet—for him.

When I lie in my warm bed, gearing up for another day, I try to fight off the nagging fears and big questions like "Am I wasting my life away?" The fears feel like spiders crawling all over my body. They almost overwhelm me until I counter them with my mantra of gratitude—not for the spiders, but for a warm bed, clothes and food.

What am I most grateful for? The well-being of our children. There's a delicate balance in a mom's psyche between *wondering* if your grown offspring are all right and *assuming* they are just fine. "You always worry," my kids say over the phone. "It's hard not to," I think, but I don't reply. I'm grateful that Joe fathered such good people—that's his strength, I must admit. I'm not feeling grateful about much else.

I finally get up, my joints a bit stiff. I feel better when I start moving. One by one the spiders disappear. I look in the bathroom mirror, hoping something has changed for the better overnight. I walk downstairs to feed Indigo, my happy corgi, and eat a bowl of shredded wheat with bran. We crunch together. Then I climb back upstairs to get dressed. Joe is long-gone to work, leaving before it is light. He is a hard worker—I'll admit that, too. He rarely calls in sick. The house is lonely without him in the morning, but it is lonely with him too.

I have eight tasks on my To Do list, but I don't want to do any of them: One is to write something, anything, even a thank you note. Two is to practice yoga. Three is to prepare for the fitness class I teach at the senior center. Four is to get refills for my antidepressants. Five is to dust the blinds. Six is to scrub the kitchen floor. Seven is to clean the toilet. Eight is to brush out the fireplace. And I wish upon a star.

Botanic Gardens ... June

By our last anniversary, which we both forgot, Joe and I settled into "blame and defend" communication. In my early years, I never thought I would be unhappily married and dependent upon a man. Over time, the chronic negativity, with only sporadic joy, can bring you down until you are ready to legally change his name to "Asshole." Do you want to run? My time was coming.

"Give me a man who tells me I'm beautiful. I could get used to it. There is nothing wrong with a flow of positive words and good deeds. That would be instant love," I confided to my long-time neighbor and friend Sophie as we explored Denver Botanic Gardens on a sunny June day. I could talk to Sophie about family difficulties. She understood because she had had two husbands and a rebellious teenage daughter.

Sophie and I had been friends since our children were babies. I would walk my newborn around the block, and she would call from her front porch to see if I wanted to have a glass of wine. One evening, I finally said yes. I couldn't resist the neighborly gesture. The walks relieved me from postpartum blues, but one time, the wine and company sounded like a better way to do that. Sophie reminds me that I was hard to get to know. She had tried many times to invite me over. She said I was "aloof." I think I was preoccupied.

Sophie knows almost everyone on her block, and calls many of them friends. People dance and eat homemade pasta at her parties. She has a delightfully eclectic group of friends. She is sincerely interested in other people's stories. Sophie probes for the truth and advises even when not asked. I usually appreciate that about her.

The Denver Botanic Gardens was a perfect place for Sophie and me to catch up, be outside and get a little exercise. June is a flashy month for flowers. Strolling through the Gardens was also an escape from my wifely duties and the guilt of not being employed. "The part-time jobs aren't making a difference in the college tuitions for our boys, Sophie."

"Why don't you get a real job? It would make you independent and more powerful, and Joe wouldn't be so stressed. You could stop complaining about your husband and do something," said Sophie.

"I think I'm unemployable," I said.

"Only in your mind," she said.

I reminded Sophie that I had been out of the full-time workforce for a while. I decided I needed to be around when my kids were in their teen years. But somewhere, I also lost my mojo when it came to meeting the demands of the full-time workplace. My skin was so thin I could see through it. The worst was the grueling employee evaluations. Not that I was a bad employee. Far from it. But I never was good about taking criticism.

I liked my part-time job where I had to think fast and be accurate, but it only lasted six months out of the year.

"Scoring kids' proficiency tests can be entertaining," I told Sophie. "You should see what the kids say when they get aggravated, like: 'I don't remember a fucking thing,' or 'My teacher didn't teach me any of this shit.' One kid was even more graphic. He drew a picture with a demand to 'suck my dick.' There's a statement."

"I fantasize writing 'fuck this' on a work evaluation," I said.

"You can't do that in the real world," Sophie said, just in case I forgot what being employed was like.

"I know," I laughed.

Sophie and I passed a basket of cascading purple and orange petunias. I looked down at my outfit. "I'm that, Sophie," I said as I pointed to the bright basket. I'm not a khaki skirt, starched blouse, black jacket and pumps woman."

"You'll have to get used to it again, Jamie."

After our visit, I said goodbye to Sophie and thanked her for letting me vent. I could count on Sophie to be honest with me, though gentle. I wasn't any closer to a job, but I could face emails with a more relaxed mind. When it cooled down in the early evening, I went upstairs to read a few.

Leftie

FROM MY OFFICE WHERE I WRITE STORIES, SILLY POEMS, AND a few resumes, I can see down into the backyard. I was grateful for this view that allowed me to enjoy the afternoons when my boys used to play rough and tumble outside.

Their play wasn't as fierce as when my brothers and I were kids. We would start gentle, then one would throw a ball in someone's face. Then my younger brother would pull my hair. He would freeze and stare at me, anticipating what might come next. I would scream so that the neighbors could hear. Everyone would stop moving, and our world would be silenced except for the rustling of the sycamore leaves.

I remember that day during the late afternoon of June 28. I could hear aspen leaves flutter outside my office window, and that was it. The boys were in college. I was existing. There were no new emails. My desk chair swiveled and bent back so I could view the ceiling. My pulse was resting, but it increased as I realized I was doing nothing—a hot, dull, I-couldn't-even-tell-you-the-color-of-the-ceiling, nothing.

When had I last been this bored? When I was a teen and my Mom dragged me with her to visit her friends who had marital problems. Old people's marriage problems were mind-numbing.

My eyes began to droop while I tried to make figures out of the orange peel texture of the wall. I wasn't hungry, and I wasn't thirsty. I wasn't thankful. I tried to muster guilt for the sin of sloth. That thought passed.

It must be ennui. But "ennui" was the same as bored, only in a sexier language. At that moment, nothing pleased me or made me unhappy. I felt empty, like a giant black hole in my space.

Now, my breathing increased, and my hands began to tingle.

"I know ..." I had an idea. I made lips with my left hand and thumb and it started to talk to me.

"What's wrong?" Leftie said.

"I need passion," I said.

"How can I help? Leftie asked.

"Let me kiss you." I noticed that Leftie's lips were dry from gardening without gloves, which repulsed me.

"I'm going to kiss you anyway," I said.

At first it was a sweet peck, but Leftie said, "More." It was a long-ago kiss ... deep ... satisfying. Joe ran up the stairs in bare socks trying to sneak up on me. He loved to get a reaction.

"What Joe?" I asked in my most bored voice after I lifted my tongue away from my hand.

"What are you doing with your hand there?" he asked with his giant "gotcha" smile.

"Having an affair."

"Is that all you can get?"

"For now," I said. His smile left.

Joe retreated—not getting in the last word like he usually did. My pulse increased again, this time from the guilt of fantasizing about an affair.

June 28

SUDDENLY, I WAS GETTING ACTION. MY COMPUTER SCREEN started to move as a few surprising notes appeared in my in box. The first was sent from my best girlfriend Gracie J. The J initial didn't stand for anything. Gracie and I met when we were in the seventh grade when we realized that we laughed at the same absurdities about school and growing up. I liked her instantly.

Aside from her ever-enthusiastic folks, I was the biggest fan of her musical and dramatic talents. We shared an odd sense of humor that only we appreciated. We thought that was our best attribute.

Gracie J. invited me to her bas mitzvah. I was the only shiksa. She sang the Torah like an ancient Hebrew princess. After her ceremony, I danced slow and close with a cute Jewish boy. He had frizzy brown hair, a nice smile and was most attentive. It was then that I decided I was going to have a nice Jewish husband.

So, this June 28, Gracie J wrote me, "Hey Jamie, how are you? You missed the last high school reunion. The girls were gorgeous. But some of the real skinny ones have passed their scarf and barf stage and now are chubby. Most of the boys are bald, spreading, and think they're funny. Your old buddy Paul was asking about you. I gave him and a few other people your email. Remember Sally Hutch? She always liked you. Anyway, expect a few messages. Knowing you like I do, I figured you'd be okay with that." Let's talk soon. Love and kisses, Gracie J."

Then the second email appeared. "Hi Jamie, it's me, Sally Hutch." I remember Sal as Paul's friend and his summer roommate during college years. She was a classic Irish beauty with shiny auburn hair and an infectious, hearty laugh that was all the funnier because it came out of such a tiny girl. She wore Adidas tennis shoes every day of her life, including to the prom with her shamrock green formal.

"I hope you're doing well, Jamie. You should have been at the reunion. I would love to see your skinny tush sometime. Is it still skinny? Mine is. Paul Sutter was there. He's trying to find you and I guess I found you for him. Can I give him your email? By the way, he's not getting along with his wife. But pretend I didn't tell you that."

That was a mouthful. But that was Sal. She asked the pointed questions and maneuvered relationships. I thought for a split second and then responded. "Hi Sal, Great to hear from you. Sure, give Paul my email," I wrote. "I'll keep the wife conflict to myself. I mean, so what's new with anyone who has been married for over 20 years?" Maybe I should have kept that thought to myself. This should be fun.

After all the back and forth emails with Gracie J. and Sally, Paul sent me a note. I hesitated to open it. What was I getting myself into?   Obviously nothing, I told myself. It was just a simple reconnection with a long-ago buddy. I was overreacting.

The note was a letdown. It was nothing chatty like the girls' notes. "Hi Jamie, it's Paul, can I call you?" he wrote. I was uncomfortable; one could maintain distance with email. But I was excited, too. I wondered if I would recognize his voice. I had things to say to this middle-aged man, or to the young man I knew. But I wasn't prepared for an immediate conversation with someone I had not spoken to in some thirty-five years. I didn't want to lose this opportunity, so I wrote back an innocuous, "Hi Paul, sure, give me a call."

I didn't expect him to call me anytime soon. But I hoped. I tapped my fingers on my desk and shook my foot under the desk. I wanted time to race, but it stood its ground. I hummed "Rock Around the Clock."

My dog Indigo was asleep with her tongue hanging out, and the birds were flying from branch to branch in the aspens. I looked back at the computer screen. Then I got up from the desk chair to go downstairs for some ice water. I almost tripped over Indi as she slowly put one paw in front of the other, yawned, and performed a downward-facing-dog stretch.

As I walked back upstairs to my office, in my mind, I spit out questions. After all these years, why was he looking for me now? Did he like his work? Who did he marry? Did he have kids? Where did he live? I thought he seemed troubled at the 20-year reunion when I only watched and didn't talk to him. Was he still kind and a good listener? Memories of Paul's comforting effect on me as a teen had lingered. His caring and understanding were crucial to me at that time.

What if he asks me personal questions? I shuddered with the thought of telling my story. I could change the subject fast. People liked to talk about themselves, but Paul, not so much. I really wanted to know how he recovered from that gang attack. My memories were still vivid.

Paul must have read my email and waited five minutes, long enough to hesitate and determine whether it was a good idea. Then my phone rang. Indigo startled from her second nap with the loud ring. My right hand shook as I reached for our avocado green princess phone—there would be no shitty cell phone reception for this conversation.

"Hey, Jamie."

That was all he had to say. His voice sounded the same as it

was as a teenager. I waited for him to say, "Let's go to the beach."
I trusted this voice. It calmed me. This was good, and this was
trouble.

Margins

THERE WERE MANY TIMES I WANTED TO BE BACK IN TOUCH with my friend Paul. A cancer diagnosis was one of those times.

I watched the nurse practitioner extract what looked like a small flying saucer connected to a blood vessel on the inside of my left ankle. Ten days later, the nurse called me to say that they had to send the specimen to the Mayo Clinic, which identified a rare sarcoma. "You're kidding," I said, as if any health professional would joke when they called to say, "It's cancer. Oh … kidding!"

People start behaving a little different when they get a cancer diagnosis. "You took so long to get me the results, I thought you were going to tell me you lost my records," I said.

"No, Ma'am," said the nurse.

"This must be serious."

"Well, it is malignant," she said.

"So, what do I need to do?"

"Well, it can be life threatening and you need to deal with it immediately."

"I thought I got the thing taken out."

"There was more at the margins."

"What margins?"

"I can't say. You'll need to speak to your doctor."

"Well, then, please get her on the phone now. I'm ready to speak."

"I can't do that."

"There's nothing comforting about your phone call is there?"

"No, Ma'am. But I'm sorry."

"Thanks." And I hung up, made dinner, went for a run and slept without interruption.

A couple of weeks later, after "the margins were clear," I was left with a two-inch oval divot in my ankle; I told curious friends and acquaintances that a shark bit me. People liked that explanation.

Nothing was funny about cancer, but I couldn't take it too seriously. A part of me was too delusional to deal with something that was a lot out of my control. Joe worried for a while. He even cried in relief after the operation. Then he lost interest in "the whole dramatic event," as he called it.

The surgeon had shaved a thin piece of skin from my upper thigh to cover the wound. At the re-check, I said, "Doctor, there's been a miracle." I pushed my pants down on one side to reveal my pencil drawing. I had taped the Virgin of Guadalupe on my thigh where the skin had been shaved off. The doctor stared and smiled politely. My husband cringed. I laughed by myself.

Even though I was cured, the diagnosis made me want to reconnect with people who understood me. I wrote Paul a letter and sent it to a work address that I found on the Internet. The letter was returned, stamped "wrong address."

Maybe Paul had some reason beyond curiosity for wanting to connect with me. I'm not sure who he thought I was at this point. And I wasn't sure who he was, but I was intrigued.

"You missed the last reunion," Paul started.

"Yeah, but the one before I was there," I said.

"You didn't talk to me."

"You were with that bimbo."

"I know. She was just a date. She wasn't my type. How are you, Jamie?"

Good that he changed the subject … "I'm great!" I lied.

"That's good to hear. Me, too."

"I'm glad. It's so nice to hear your voice. I have a million questions," I said.

"You always did, and I'll answer them. Can we continue this conversation again? I'm at work and I have an appointment I need to get to."

"Sure, that'd be great."   I had hoped for a longer chat but maybe he was testing my receptibility.

Our conversation made me forget the hot day and the long, sweltering nights that kept me tossing and turning. At night, our brick house becomes an oven. By midnight, I tear off my nightie and wipe myself down with a wet washcloth. When the moisture evaporated, I would start tossing again. I imagine Paul didn't feel that midnight heat. His house must have air conditioning. And he, no doubt, lives close to the ocean.

Just his voice brought back good memories. I realized how dissatisfied I was with my life. I'm not sure if it's just that I had chosen to be dissatisfied. I'm embarrassed because, at my age, I've read enough books and had enough therapy to find peace with myself. Shouldn't I be cheerful every morning? I should say to myself, "Good morning, you. It's a beautiful one at that. You're looking good in that body, and I love your hairstyle with that pony tail on top of your head." My attitude needs a tuneup, and I'm not sure if neglect or my make and model are affecting it.

This phone call caused me to further reflect about my life. Why had I let problems go on so long? Why couldn't I fix what was broken? Was it all my doing? Already, Paul felt like a solution to my marital disenfranchisement. I had been unhappy for so long, but I wasn't sure if the blame was fifty-fifty or whether my spouse or I was the 80 percent contributor. I never really knew how to be a good partner. What would I do to this nice guy?

Poor Paul. I hadn't even had a substantive conversation yet. God help my anxious soul and his trusting one.

"Jamie, don't be so hard on yourself," I thought. I felt good about my career choices, even if it rubbed Joe raw, what with national travel and peer admiration in the former one or the current one that paid just above minimum wage for seasonal work. With my current job as an evaluator of standardized tests, I had more time to raise my boys, who were exploring their independence. I was exploring my creativity. Isn't that okay? Don't answer that.

I was starting to write rap songs. That's bizarre, I know. But when you drive your kids here and there and that's the music that placates them, well, then you start to think "I can write that," don't you? Well, I did. I wrote one for my younger son Justin's fifteenth birthday titled, *Don't Bounce Him All Around*, and subjected his friends to a singalong. They loved it. It's just gritty poetry. I don't know why more moms aren't writing rap.

Morning Glories … August

Light blue morning glories almost don't look real because of their iridescence. This stunning flower doesn't last long, but the vine is relentless, winding in and out of all the cracks in a fence. It has a mind of its own and won't give up, even if you lop it off at the head. When it starts to overwhelm, that's when a flower becomes a weed. If I didn't stop bothering Paul with emails, I feared I would become a weed in his mind.

After that first brief phone conversation, we wrote emails back and forth to get to know each other again. It was emotionally safe. They were short and carefully worded, delightful messages, like: Hey Jamie, do you still have that great smile? It used to catch me off guard. It made you shine even through mad and sad. I hope you are smiling now.

Then they stopped, and I wondered where Paul went. He didn't say. He must have gotten tired of this email game. I didn't. One day I wrote, "Where the heck are you? I hope you're walking on the beach enjoying the summer nights, because I haven't heard from you in a while."

"Hi, Jamie," he replied immediately. "I'm in Scotland, checking out the greenest golf courses in the world. I'll send you pictures of my favorite ones. I took a breather on the emails because I didn't want you to think I was being forward. But I'm glad you wrote. I'd love to visit you sometime and see Lidi. She was like a mom to me."

It's hard to tell a person's true thoughts in an email. The more emails I got, the more I wanted to know the adult Paul. I wrote him, "I forgot about your obsession with golf. Thanks for all the photos of spectacular golf courses around the world. Honestly, I can't get excited about golf courses. I know I'm a killjoy. But a liberal gets that way in the dry environment of this state. Do you still like me? I'll send you a few pics of the mountains."

"Nothing has changed about you, Jamie. I forgot you're a mountain girl. I remember that long, wild trip you took in Wyoming when we were kids. I was so impressed that a girl could handle 35 days with the bears, bald eagles and no showers. I'm not offended. On the contrary, Jamie, I always appreciated that you spoke your mind."

"You should definitely visit us," I wrote. "I would love for you to see my side of the world, and Lidi would get a kick out of teasing the adult Paul. We could take a car ride to Red Rocks for some nostalgia. Didn't you start your roadie job there?"

What was I doing in inviting him here? He wrote back, "I'd love to see you guys, but I don't know if you will want to see me." I wasn't sure about the hesitation, but I was curious.

The Mile High ... September

I DIDN'T KNOW HOW I WOULD REACT TO PAUL'S VISIT. WOULD we recognize each other? In high school, we were athletes. That was part of our attraction. Falling in like in high school made sense. You maneuvered from instinct and intuition you didn't know you had. There were few layers to peel away. You had young, toned bodies. There were no fake boobs, no Botox, no work demands, no guilt, no children—just fun and infatuation.

We stifled our passion for each other in high school. At the same time, we protected our friendship. It was a sacred emotional space that somehow survived over the years. This enduring affection was unknown to our spouses and kept from our conscious selves. It would have stayed tucked away, except for Paul's phone call. Now it was unlocked, and our curiosity heightened.

Waiting at the airport arrival area, I wondered why he was taking so long. There was only a crowded one-way escalator from the train. He found a suitable alternative and rode an elevator up one floor. I held my sign overhead that indicated I was waiting for, "Old Boyfriend." This sure singled me out from the crowd. I didn't see him until he waved and yelled, "Jamie, Old Boyfriend is over here!" I had looked past him for a lean blonde baseball catcher even though I had seen a recent photo of him on the Internet. "Holy shit!" tumbled out of my mouth. Approaching me was a very large man with giant blue eyes, the ones I remembered from long ago. He had deep worry lines between his eyebrows, and his shirt was wet under his arms. After reality set in, I recognized Paul right away, only it looked like he was enclosed in one of those flabby suits that actors wear to play the part of a morbidly obese character. Paul was easily twice the size of the young one I knew at the beach. This was the reason for his hesitation to visit.

This giant bear ambled over to me and laid his inflated hand on my shoulder. "Hi Jamie," he said with a half smile. "I like your sign."

"Hi, Paul, Welcome to the Mile High. You're looking … good." I said.

"Don't bullshit me, Jamie," he said.

I could work with this, I thought. I still felt that tingle of excitement. I did worry about what I should and shouldn't say. But we needed to be ourselves. I wondered if the affection I felt from long ago would revive with this big reality.

We gave each other an obligatory hug. I couldn't get my arms around him. (This extra luggage has to go, I thought).

(I want to grab your) "*bottom*," he said. I wasn't sure I heard right the first part of his sentence.

"What?" I said.

"Are you parked on the *bottom* floor, I hope?" he said.

Then we kissed, a short one. (His lips are soft. I am feeling this. I dare not be too) "*forward*," I said.

"What did you say Jamie?"

"*Forward*, I am parked near the front," I said.

The altitude already affected Paul. He was out of breath walking the short distance to the baggage claim. I was relieved, in a way, that this friendship just couldn't go into the physical realm.

When we waited for his luggage, I said, "Paul, can we get this tension over with?"

"I'm not feeling tense, Jamie … well, maybe a little," said Paul as he wiped the sweat off his brow with his handkerchief.

"How 'bout we go to that two-star motel five miles down the road and explore each other's bodies." His body shook in amusement as he let out a short giggle. The suggestion was part jest and part curiosity to see what he would say.

"Jamie, I've got plenty to explore, baby. Check out this relationship fat." His hands held his belly.

"I see it Paul, front and center," I said.

"I appreciate the thought, really, but I don't do motels on the first date … if you can call this a date," said Paul.

He was the gentleman, mostly, and I sounded like the untamed she-wolf. My immodest comment spewed out of my synthetic-hormoned body. I was married with children. Why would I tease him like that? Was I teasing? I really didn't know how I felt about obesity and love. I was hoping the obese part would be short term. Nevertheless, my question left a residual smile on Paul's face for the time during his stay with us.

I chatted on about nothing, trying to relax him—or was it me—as we walked through the hustle and bustle of the Denver airport and parking lot. He patted my shoulder as if to say, "Take it easy."

When we reached the car, we stopped to face each other and felt compelled to hug again. Our hugs were different. His was a gentlemanly one, maybe tentative, that seemed to express a fear of rejection. Mine was one of gratitude to be with my dear old friend who had given me solace long ago. We held each other for a long time. My head was on his chest. I could hear his heart beat, even through layers of insulation. I had to think about what this new Paul meant to me.

I watched as Paul tried to fit the seat belt around his waist. I wouldn't drive away until I heard the click of the over-extended belt. (When was the last time he wore one?) He watched me watch him. Sweat dripped from his red cheeks. He winced or maybe smiled.

"I love this woman," he mumbled.

"What did you say?"

"I'm loving this, Jamie."

As we drove away from the airport, I said, "We're going to have a good time. But I need to say one thing. I have finally found you. Or you found me, really. Now I don't want to lose you."

"I get it Jamie. And I'm taking care of it. This is a huge burden for me, as you noticed. Just flying here reminded me of the embarrassment of being a big person traveling on a plane. I'm the kind of passenger that travelers dread. At least I have the means to go first class. Even so, I know people wonder if I can squeeze into the tiny first-class restroom. I don't try. I hold it. When the plane landed in Denver, I was the last one out. Can you imagine remaining calm with a bladder ready to burst? I waited behind to avoid bumping into people. Finally out, I found the private family toilets. If I can help it at all, I avoid public restrooms.

"I can only imagine the humiliation you must've felt," I said.

"I stepped into the empty elevator to descend to the airport train. I was going to squeeze my way down the escalator but there was too much of a crowd for me to maneuver. When I entered the train, people stepped back to give me room. I lifted my arm to hold on to one of those handles hanging from the ceiling. Sweat was dripping from my armpits and soaking the sides of my shirt. I caught the eye-rolling and grimaces, and my stomach gurgled loud just to make things worse.

"I wondered what your face would look like when you saw me."

I felt my heart pound harder than usual from being a mile high. I knew enough to take deep breaths and drink from my water bottle, as conspicuous as it was when I gulped down half of a 32-ounce bottle that I bought in one of your airport stores. Was it worth it, Jamie?"

"Well, I hope you answered 'Yes.'"

"Well, I wasn't sure. All I could think was that we are an odd couple with your slender figure and my stocky overdone physique that resembles my Canadian fishermen ancestors. As I got off the train, I saw the sign for the elevator and had to push my sweaty way through the giant school of fish heading the opposite direction. When I reached the top and saw this long blonde holding a large white sign that said, 'Old Boyfriend' in big black letters, I knew everything was going to be all right."

"It would be wrong for me to say I know how you feel. But everything is going to be all right," I said under the influence of new-relationship enthusiasm. "Okay, let's get this weekend started."   A few miles outside the airport, I pointed to Mount Evans and Pikes Peak and the rest of the majestic Rocky Mountains while I steered with my less competent left hand.

"My beach girl has grown into a tree hugger. I like it," he said.

"Let's get some lunch. I'll take you to my favorite park," I said. My anxious self started to creep in when I realized the professional stature of my passenger. Paul was a successful Hollywood producer. I left my career to raise my boys during their trying teen years. Paul had money and houses and shiny new cars. Joe's supervisor position in the wastewater plant and my seasonal job, coupled with two boys in college, added up to very little left over after we paid the bills. We drove our twelve-year-old automobiles and were grateful that we bought early in one of the most valued neighborhoods in Denver. Our house was our best investment.

I sank in my seat and sipped on water and then some more. The car was quiet.

"What's up, Jamie?"

"Nothing." I turned on the radio to a hip-hop station and beat my clammy fingers on the steering wheel.

"So, Jamie, it's good to see you," Paul said. "What have you been doing since we last emailed, which I think was yesterday? I'm ready for you to fill me in on the things you don't mention in notes."

"Shit! I got off at the wrong exit." I couldn't think. I pinched the tissue between my eyes. My face started to itch, and then my arms, and my breathing became shallow. I had to get control before, before—I don't know what. Paul let me be just like when we were young.

"I'm doing nothing, absolutely nothing," I said.

"I don't believe you, Jamie. I know you have all sorts of things up your sleeve and brilliant ideas in that amazing brain of yours," Paul said.

That's all I needed, a little recognition and validation.

Validation: that was part of the attraction that I couldn't explain to friends when they later wondered how I could be into a fat guy, while a fit, svelte husband sat in front of the television at home.

"Well, how about sandwiches in the park," I said after getting back on the freeway. I took a few long, deep breaths and settled down. "I'm taking you to the local sandwich shop where they pile them high with roast beef and cheese and smother the bread with mayo. But you can get a vegan sandwich with nothing on it," I said to Paul.

"I'll take the 'nothing' sandwich." Instead of the motel, we rested, completely clothed, under a giant elm tree at City Park. Not far from us was a noisy beer festival. People were dressed in brightly colored costumes decorated with feathers and sequins. It looked like everyone had ridden a bike to the fair. Paul and I would have been there twenty years ago. Now we were under the tree.

He ate very little of his lunch. When would I see the true eater? While we lay there, I asked, "What's relationship fat?"

"The kind you get when you're no longer in the market for babes," he said.

"Is that what all *this* is?" I pointed to his belly with my hand like it was a pistol.

"Not really. But I like the line. Can we change the subject for a little while, Jamie?"

"Sure." And we enjoyed each other's company in silence.

Then Paul piped up, "I know what you're thinking, Jamie."

"What?"

"That I'm an old man."

"If you're old, then I'm old, and I'm not old," I responded.

In the shade Paul intermittently closed his eyes to enjoy the cool breeze blowing through the trees. I kept my back in the sun to keep me warm.

"Actually, I was wondering why your hair is brown instead of blonde and why you have no gray hairs. Something like that," I said.

"That's my real color, no shit," he said. "And, I was wondering about your shiny blonde hair. You have no gray ones anywhere I can see."

"Amazing, isn't it? I just ask my hairdresser Cecilia, 'Will you please take all the dreary gray hairs away?' And an hour later, they're gone."

"You fooled me, Jamie."

I didn't mind fooling Paul for a moment. But I didn't like telling him fibs. Then I looked into his blue eyes; I always loved his empathetic blues, and I waved my hand across his torso "I'm taking care of it," he said with some impatience. I've already started to lose weight."

"Really? How easy is it to lose weight?" I stopped there with the interrogation.

He didn't respond. "Jamie, let's enjoy the moment," he seemed to say with his eyes. He grabbed my slender fingers and squeezed them and kissed the top of my hand. We closed our eyes to enjoy each other's company.

I thought, as we left City Park to get into my car, he was breathing like a buffalo, and he could barely keep up with me. I couldn't seem to give it up. But he deserved a break, since he was at 5,280 feet and he came from sea level.

I had said what I needed to say and, although the situation was critical, I wanted to ignore his weight. I didn't want this to be a barrier to our friendship. The essence of our relationship excluded his fatty tissue.

We had an easy night eating a healthy dinner. I cooked roasted veggies and a baked chicken. Paul ate slowly. At first, Joe was curious about Paul and his career, but otherwise didn't seem concerned about an old friend's visit, especially someone of his physique. Joe eventually got bored and went to bed. Paul and I stayed up until we decided to save more conversation for later. He was exhausted and acting brave—an obese man at high altitude. His body organs had to work harder than he had anticipated.

The next day, I was eager to show Paul what a beautiful place I live in. There is more than just the beach. "Wake up, Paul! Let's go to Washington Park. It's beautiful and only six blocks away. I want to show you a view of the mountains," I yelled down the stairs into the basement where Paul was staying. He was awake and appeared in his shorts with no shirt, showing his giant belly, complete with stretch marks. He was still the uninhibited Paul I loved.

He was ready for anything on his adventure in Denver. It was new and exciting, and just being together was fun. We walked slowly down the sidewalks of my neighborhood. I easily got ahead, and Indigo was eager to take off. I made Indigo heel next to me as I slowed down to Paul's pace and got the gumption to tell him, "I'm writing a musical." He was the only one to whom I could reveal what seemed like a preposterous creative endeavor. I knew nothing about the craft, but an idea came to me.

"What's it about?" he asked. He took me seriously.

"It's about a church that gets carried away with fundraising to the point they lose sight of everyday compassion. That's what I titled it, 'Everyday Compassion.'"

"That sounds intriguing. I can send you a program to help keep your script organized," he said.

"That'd be useful. I'm not organized or even close to done."

I proceeded to tell him the story. It was about an Episcopal priest who is African American. He is troubled with the mostly white congregation's obsession with money. He's not sure he wants to initiate change for fear of getting into a conflict so close to his retirement. The church guild, made up of the senior women, resists change carte blanche because "Why fix what isn't broke?" they often repeat.

There is a subtext to the story about embracing diversity. One altar girl is noticeably pregnant, and one altar boy knows he's gay and wants to tell his family. Another altar boy has tuned out the world as he submerges himself into video games that he enjoys during the service. I'm thinking the music will include a combination of hymns, spirituals, of course Handel's Messiah, and a rap song or two.

"That sounds like a great start, Jamie. These things take about seven years to birth, so you've got to get started now," said Paul.

"You're taking me seriously," I said as I grabbed his hand.

"Why shouldn't I, Jamie? He blushed. "I love your ideas. And being creative is serious fun."

The rest of the walk to the park was quiet. We absorbed the morning sun and the beauty of late season sunflowers and splashy orange chrysanthemums in the neighborhood yards.

Paul's stay was fraught with the tension caused by us wanting to hang out with each other like old times and my husband growing suspicions as my attentions became more focused on Paul. I couldn't get enough conversation with Paul about mutual friends and our inspired ideas.

Later in the evening, dinner with my mom was, as expected, delicious and amusing. Paul was disappointed that the evening was not "the three of us." I had to include Joe; he was my husband. Paul was used to living his life more solo than I was.

Lidi had to bring up the "inadequate" shtick as a matter of tradition, which was hilarious, given Paul's success in taking over his father's Hollywood business. When Paul left Colorado, we both were invigorated, wanted more time together, and promised to keep in touch. I was falling in like all over again.

He Shouldn't Have to Tell Me—
A Rant

Two tiny twin beds with a table in between.
He forgets our anniversary year after year.
I walk the dog, he stays home. Forget him. He would rather watch television.
He stays put, I go out. I'd like to go with him, but I don't pout.
He doesn't like my friends.
He won't make amends.
I like to travel. He'd rather change channels.
He brings home a daily dose of disdain from work. He hates his boss, who's "such a jerk."
His coworkers are "idiots." They don't like his sarcasm. Really now, would you blame them?
He likes the pretty assistant who brings doughnuts. (I don't care.)
He shuns my nightly meals. "They're too "spicy." He wants his food bare.
He yells when he comes home.
He wants sexual satisfaction to put him to sleep. He turns his back at night and shouts, "Don't dare wake me up. Don't make a peep."
He perpetuates condescending, rhetorical questions like, "What were you thinking?!"
He abhors Valentine's day and Christmas with my family.

"Why do you waste your money on these? he says, barely blinking.
He doesn't say thanks because "that's a given." I'm saying this isn't a marriage, this is barely living.
He loves me; I "should know that," he would say.
He "shouldn't have to tell" me anyway.

The Chicken Leg

I WAS EXCITED TO SHARE ABOUT MY PAUL VISIT WITH SOPHIE as she and I walked to the park. I wished she could have met him, but she was hesitant. "I'm not sure I want to meet him, because I don't think you know what you're doing," she said.

"He's a nice guy. The next time he visits, if he does, I'll introduce you. I love his Hollywood stories."

"Next time," she said. "Now let's walk fast. Where's your dog?"

"You don't like Indigo, so I didn't bring her."

"I like Indigo, I just don't like dogs."

"Will you listen to another one of my dreams?"

"If I have to …" I understood her reluctance about listening to other people's dreams, but I was eager to share it.

"So, Paul said … 'What's eating you, Jamie?' He was sitting across from my bed in one of my red floral chairs. He was chewing on a chicken leg from last night's dinner. Even from there he could see me grimacing as I lay in bed.

"What's eating you, Jamie?" he repeated

"What's eating me? By the way, do you like the chicken? I made it with a yoghurt marinade. My mind is eating me." I said. I scratched my head.

"What do you mean?" He placed his plate on the floor. The

dog didn't touch it. Then he rested his chin on his hand. He looked like The Thinker sculpture, deep in thought.

"I mean that I go to bed at night planning to get a good night's sleep with my 101 Dalmatians comforter on my twin bed, and I start to toss and turn. First, I think about the dog and her tags clinking, and that I should get up and take her collar off."

The dog had been scratching her neck. The summer was dry even for dog skin. "Then I think, I'm about to go to sleep. Then I lift my head. I see the television light from downstairs flickering and wonder what time my child got home from his friend's house and did he go to the friend who got busted for possession of large amounts of pot?   And why was he home anyway? I thought he was at college." I let out another sigh and started scratching my arms.

"Would you stop now?" he said. He put his fingers in his ears.

"Stop what?"

"Stop your mind from eating your sleep."

"I can't."

"Yes, you can. Paul leaned forward in his chair ready to give advice.

"How?"

"You need to slow down your racing mind," he said.

"How do I do that?"

He looked up on my bulletin board and read a prayer I had pinned on it and then told me, "You change the things you can and accept the things you can't do anything about."

"Can you tell me which is which?"

"You know the difference," he said as he stood up to comfort me.

"It doesn't work. I've tried it before"

"Well then you take two Motrin," said Paul

"What?"

"I'm serious. I read that in your health magazine downstairs when I got the chicken leg. Motrin works for mental pain too." He pulled a bottle out of his pocket and struggled in the dim light to open the top. "You can take two and let me know how it goes. I'm with you all the way."

I smiled. "Okay, I'll try—can't hurt, right?"

I sat up and looked around. There was no one there except Joe deep asleep in the other bed. I stumbled to the medicine cabinet, struggled to open the bottle in the dark and picked out two Motrin. Then I looked at my red chair with pink roses. There was only a pile of laundry that Joe had folded. I slipped back in bed and put one pillow under my neck and another between my legs. I sighed and entered a peaceful sleep.

"Well that message is clear," said Sophie. Now you just have to figure out what you can change and what you can accept. I could tell you what I think.

"That's okay, Soph," I replied. I wanted a listener not an advisor now.

A Warm Breeze … October

Colorado autumns can surprise you with summer heat and winter snow. It was a summer-like evening when Paul caught me off guard. Indigo was in the backyard, rustling through the leaves. The moon was full and tinted orange from wildfires in the mountains. I opened the windows, and the warm breeze encircled me as I settled in the dining room to write.

After Paul's visit in September, we emailed daily. I hadn't had this much fun in a long time. We wrote about our children, our jobs, what made us proud, and what we loved to do and dreamed of doing. Neither of us, unknown to our spouses, had ever stopped dreaming. We poked fun at each other, exchanged compliments, and made each other laugh. The belly laughs almost felt better than an orgasm. Maybe it had been too long.

Our spouses had long gone to their respective bedrooms. Mine retired before the 9:00 news. That's when I emoted all over my technology. Email had its deficiencies, but at least we could converse as fast as we typed. We became friends like before, but with more impetus to act on desires.

The dining room was dark, except for the moonlight on my shoulders and the computer light on my face. I was singing quietly. I imagined Paul's bedroom. He was alone in his "cave," as he called it. Disgusted with Paul, his wife had moved out of the master suite and put a lock on her bedroom door about five years ago.

"Can you hear my song, Paul?" I wrote.

"Obviously not, Jamie. What are you singing?"

"Look outside, up in the sky, and tell me what you see."

"Stars and airplane lights," wrote Paul.

"Anything else? Stretch your neck a bit."

"I just opened my French doors and walked onto the deck. Jamie, it's a perfect man in the moon. He's singing *Moon River*. How about that?"

"Are you singing with me, Paul?"

"Yes, I am. I love to sing. The wife hates my off-key voice, especially in public places."

"I get that reaction too. I embarrass my husband; I don't try to. It's spontaneous."

"I know what you mean," wrote Paul.

He continued, "About that song, it was a happy moment when my parents would put on an Andy Williams record. He was one of my Dad's best friends. Dad would pretend his beer bottle was a microphone. He would croon *Moon River* and then grab Mom and swing her around the living room. He would hold her close and dip her like in an old Fred Astaire movie. Each time they danced; it was as if they discovered their love again. I hung out on the couch and watched. I felt kind of weird, but I was intrigued."

Our emails flew back and forth as the moon inched across the sky; I stopped looking at the kitchen clock. Paul was supine in his giant nest in his cave. I could see his feet spread, in need of a man pedicure, with his technology perched on his chest. I wished I was there singing with him.

What I didn't want to see, but still felt, was his tall glass of vodka on the table next to him. He told me later that he needed to 'tone down' his drinking, but that vodka was a tough habit to shake.

He described his room and said his television was on his dresser. It was too big for the bedroom, but it kept him company throughout the night. In fact, "It was hard to sleep with it off," he said. His room made for a separate life from his family, even though his door was never locked or even closed all the way.

"I want love," Paul suddenly wrote me.

"That was something!" I said to myself. "Where did that come from?" Curious to see what happened next, I wrote back. "I do, too."

He wrote, "No, I want love and I need love."

"Is that a song? Or are you confessing your affection?" I replied.

"What do you think?" wrote Paul.

"Damn it, I don't want to think," my fingers responding as quickly as his comments appeared. "I can tell you have a buzz on, so how serious do I take this conversation?" These emotions are better expressed in person or by phone. Not emails. Emails lack *inflection*. "We could get this all wrong." I said out loud.

And then this message came: "Jamie, I'm *Madly* in love with you." He capitalized and italicized 'madly.'"

I liked the idea because I craved affection: *Love Parched East of the Rockies*. But had any man I cared for, ever said *that* to me? Especially the madly part? "Madly," meant his love for me was passionate and out of control. It must be a product of the full moon. And he hadn't *said* it to me. Email was too easy, so it didn't count. But I wanted him to love me madly.

Joe woke up and saw the glow of the computer and heard me rambling on. It wasn't normal for me to stay up late writing and talking. "Cut the noise! Who are you talking to so late, anyway? And what are you doing on the computer at this hour?" he yelled down the stairs. I didn't answer. I didn't have an answer for him. "Turn it all off, it's keeping me awake," he commanded. Then he stomped back to bed.

"Jamie, are you there? Did I overstep things? I'm sorry if I did," Paul wrote.

"Joe just yelled down the stairs. Anyway, about the 'madly in love' it's that it's email and you're drunk. What do I make of that?" I wrote.

"Tomorrow when I'm sober, I'll tell you the same. I love you, Jamie. It's a feeling that's lasted all my life. I'm finally telling you. I want to hold you by the light of the silvery moon. I crave all the good that you are."

I think I knew this side of Paul, even though he had kept such enthusiastic love hidden for over three decades. Something inspired him now. So I responded on this full-moon night: "You make me feel good, and that hasn't happened in a long time. I love you, too. But you better not fuck with me."

The emails stopped. It felt awkward. I was getting tired and needed some sleep. "Paul, are you there?"

"Yes, I fell asleep waiting for your email. I was dreaming about 'fucking with you.' Then my wife came in the room. She yelled at me for not cleaning up the kitchen, and was looking for the two dogs, which are cuddled up next to me. She kiddingly asked the dogs if I was writing to my girlfriend," he said.

"You're joking."

"About what?"

"About fucking with me. I just wrote you that I cared for you," I replied.

"I know. I got it." And then I fell asleep smiling. "I love you deeply and madly. Goodnight, Jamie."

"Goodnight, Paul."

The emails stopped. The full moon lit the staircase before traveling over the Rockies. I turned off the computer. I felt giddy as I made my way up the stairs and removed my clothes, piece by piece, while I sang The Doors' *Love Her Madly.*

Crumbling Marriages

OUR MARRIAGES WERE CRUMBLING. IT HAPPENED SO EASILY. What was good at one time became intolerable day by day. Too much neglect, too much disdain that led to too much alcohol and corrosive words. Inertia kept our marriages going long enough to accentuate all that was wrong.

In one email session, Paul and I convinced ourselves that it was "them." "We married accountants," I wrote. "They're practical. We're not. I'm sure we both promised we'd be faithful. But our needs are too great." Paul was the self-professed emotionally needy and I the sorrowfully sensitive.

"Every step of living with Joanne is a like tiptoeing across a field of hidden land mines," he wrote.

"I keep promising myself I won't get sucked into name-calling and put-downs. I don't like being defensive," I replied.

This was an appropriate moment to try to be good spouses, because Paul and I had our friendship and kind words as respite. This closeness was the safe house. Could we sustain this?

A few days later, Paul said on the phone, "I want to see you." He was insistent in a gentle way. I had stirred up a need that he thought could never be met. I hesitated. I was curious, but also cynical about love. My marriage was in a brittle state, and previous relationships had not been great. I still wasn't sure about the authenticity of Paul's love. Yet, I didn't want to let this opportunity go.

Love from a kind man sounded too good to be true. It almost didn't seem right. In my time, I had picked some scary ones. So scary that Joe seemed like the perfect fit. He was a protector and reliable. He gave me security.

I would have continued with the status quo if Paul hadn't contacted me in June. One of the first things out of Paul's mouth after that tipsy email declaration was, "I … I … I … *am* in love with you Jamie."

"How do you know you're in love, Paul?" There was silence. I picked at my cuticles. I started to perspire. We had very little face time, but a lot of emails. He couldn't really be in love with me. He didn't know the adult me. He stuttered because his professed love came from the heart. I had to be gentle.

I said, "I am in love with you, too." We were awkward because we were out of practice. We both wanted a partner who enriched our lives. What felt true was that we wanted to help each other conquer our weaknesses and be better people. We wanted to share our work and feel free to talk about our dreams.

"It was nice to see your family in September, but now I want some time with you. I wasn't sure I was searching for you as a friend or as a lover. I … I … I know I care a great deal. This may be difficult to hear. But I don't want to waste your time by not being honest," Paul said. "I'm trying to be more upfront at this point in my life.

"It's been over thirty years. I want you to know the grown-up Jamie," I said.

"Jamie, I know who you are. You're the one person who makes me content. I don't expect you to solve my problems. I can't seem to find a way that's not cliché, but I've been thinking about you for years. What we had as teenagers was pure love: no pretentions, just brain to brain love."

"I get it, Paul. After I got cancer and lived through it, you were the one I wanted to contact. I sent you a letter, but it was returned. I felt our business was unfinished. You made a difference in my young life that carried over into adulthood. Because of you, I was reminded that there were people out there who liked me the way I am. We were a calming pair.

"   I didn't expect this love, but I'm not surprised. I have been wondering about you and right now, if nothing more happens between us, I'll be content. I value your friendship and now I know your phone number," I said.

"Pardon me, Jamie, but you don't sound yourself," he said. "It's like you're waiting for the other stinky shoe to drop."

"I'm just a little scared. My feelings for you are real, even if it's complicated."

Planting Tulips … October

SEPTEMBER WAS NOT ENOUGH. PAUL PUSHED FOR MORE FACE time. I pondered right and wrong. Desire won out. We set a date for him to visit.

Paul's overnight stay in October was short, sweet, and productive. "If you plant plenty of tulip bulbs in the fall, your eyes receive a stunning treat after a long, dark winter. I like sunny yellow, bright orange and lusty pink tulips combined. It's kind of like that with exercise," I told Paul. "Make the investment, dig deep and you'll bloom. I have a personal stake you know."

"What's that, Jamie?"

"Well, you know." I gave him a wink. "Extended happiness if you get to a healthier weight sooner than later."

With that, Paul gave me the "Back off, Sweetie" eye and mounted the stationary bike with ease at the boutique hotel gym. He set the bike to "high difficulty" and started to ride. His body rolled back and forth, and his breathing increased. He kept going, looking around, hoping no one was staring at him. A foot fell off the pedal. He put it back on and kept going. Perspiration started to pour and would eventually drench his workout clothes. Out of curiosity, I breathed in deep to smell him—his sweat wasn't offensive, but somehow mildly sweet.

Paul grimaced over the pain of his right knee, an old baseball injury. It was swollen, but it would heal soon. He just needed to keep going.

He kept peddling. He breathed loud, like a bull looking for a mate. I liked that sound, but I don't think he did. Two petite young women were working their abdominal muscles while they watched this big man from their peripheral vision. They shook their heads. They felt his pain. I shook my head and said, "Harder, deeper, come on Baby, show me what you got, right here." His semi-serious glaring eyes let me know he found me only a wee bit amusing. His stomach inflated with air and barely contracted. He sucked in oxygen but didn't seem to exhale much. The clock was ticking. Thirty-five minutes had passed, and now his muscles started to burn. Fifteen minutes remained. His head rolled from side to side, trying to find comfort in this necessary pain.

"I'm an athlete," Paul whispered loud to himself. "I can do this," he said.

His lungs taunted him for "more air." He was especially in need because he was cycling for the first time at more than 5,000 feet. I expected his quads were screaming for relief and wanted to jump off—but it was a familiar experience, one he could survive. "I've felt this pain before," he huffed. "It's minor compared to getting into shape for football."

He eked out, "I love you, Jamie, but stop staring; I know what I'm doing."

"I know, but I want to help ... I'll be quiet." If he did know what he was doing, then why was he obese? Not a simple question to answer, I figured. I got on the stationary bike next to him to bring him home. I was only able to peddle at half his speed.

"My doctor says I'm healthy," he said between huffs and puffs. "All my blood tests are normal, really."

"Don't fool yourself. I adore you, Paul, but you and I

know there's nothing healthy about being as big as you are. I look forward to the day when your gasps for air are only in the bedroom. Just think what fun we could have if you were a few pounds lighter. We could perform half-gainers on a waterbed."

He restrained a laugh to conserve energy, but slowed down his peddling to say, "You're right, Jamie. I'm going to lose it, and I'll hold you to the unusual sex acts," he said, louder than he realized.

Paul hadn't seen the outline of his thigh muscles in probably 15 years. But today he felt them emerging. Motivated and dejected at the same time, Paul kept going, peddling with greater intensity.

"I want … a better … life. I need … a better … life," began his mantra between breaths. He reached for his water bottle, which nearly slipped out of his sweaty fingers. For a few moments he just peddled, no arms. He twisted the bottle cap and guzzled water. His Adam's apple jumped up and down in pleasure. He poured the remaining sips on his head.

I laughed. "You're working hard, but it won't kill you." He had enough energy to give me the eye again. Everyone in the small exercise room watched Paul. He worked the hardest. He had the most to gain and the most to lose. He complained the least.

Holding Out … October

AFTER PAUL'S WORKOUT, I KNEW I SHOULD BE HEADING home. It was getting late in the evening, but I didn't want our time together to end with just a good sweat. Joe was okay with me having dinner with my friend Paul. I didn't inform him it was going to be more than a hamburger. I had made sure I threw a cute dress and heels into my gym bag.

"Jamie, what happened to our so called 'good lives' with our spouses?" Paul asked over a candlelit dinner. "I want you to be honest."

"Only if you reciprocate," I said. "You've been holding out on me." I grabbed his hands and put them to my heart. I breathed in his clean smell. I detected a manly soap with a hint of lavender. Lavender was the calming herb. I kept inhaling to take in his soothing essence. It was my first course in this elegant restaurant. He watched in fascination and amusement. And I knew I was putting off giving him an answer.

"I gave you that soap, and I picked the right one," I said. A waiter came over and interrupted. "I'm sorry, it's getting late, and we need your order because the chef will be leaving after he prepares your dinner." He left us two menus.

We barely looked up. "You first, Jamie. I want to hear your story."

"I wasn't ready to be married, even by the time I made those marriage promises. I was damaged goods but I didn't know it. Lust is a great con artist."

"I hate to interrupt you love birds," the waiter said, and with that we let go of each other's hands.

I made a quick decision. "We'll both have the salmon special," I pointed to the menu, "with the steamed asparagus, and we'd like baked potatoes instead of the scalloped ones, no butter or sour cream," I took charge, wanting to make sure we ate well. Paul seemed happy to agree with my choice.

"And please bring us two glasses of your house white wine," he added as the waiter left.

"Now, I've lost my mind in love. I'm in a love maze that I can't get out of," I said.

"Me too, Jamie, and it's the best feeling I've ever had. You've given meaning back to my life. You had that spiritual thing when we were kids that always intrigued me, and I hope it'll rub off. But I'm not clear about your love for Joe."

"Well, there was love; maybe there still is. I loved the best I could, given my life experiences and his gruff personality, which he saves for me in private moments. At the beginning of our courtship, I needed to feel safe and know someone was taking care of me. During that time, I was convinced he was that someone.

"I believed I could be happily married and that he would be a great father, and he is. But I was shocked by his unpredictable verbal venom, which grew worse over the years. More than once, I tried to get him to take medication that might help calm his anger. But he refused. I thought I was realistic and understood his dark side and resolved that I couldn't change it. I often wondered if I was the problem. As time went on, his anger and anxieties became directed at me in a greater way."

The restaurant was almost empty when our food was served. Our discussion felt somewhat public. But we didn't let that stop us.

"I didn't think it was right to end our commitment, especially with young children, but he didn't seem to care how his behavior affected our marriage. At least he said so in so many words.

"I thought if I tried harder, I would make things better. At the beginning, I believed I could be a good mother and a decent wife. I assumed we would have many happy days together. Over the years, the cruel comments and sarcasm came more often and were harder to shrug off. At times, I would walk out the door and not return for a whole day.

On my side of the equation, I didn't realize that losing my father would have such a bad effect on my adult relationships. I remember just a few times together before he was gone forever. I think my marriage was an attempt to fill a hole in my heart. Joe didn't know what kind of emotional quagmire he was getting with me."

"And I wonder, Paul. You get me on the surface. But do you really get me?"

"I don't know, Jamie. You're complicated," said Paul. "I love what we could be, based on what we were and are now. I love the notion of us supporting each other to be better people."

My anxiety started to increase with this candid conversation. "I'm scared about your health issues; I can't lie. You know you need to resolve these if we're going to work."

"Jamie, everybody has issues. Do you think there's hope for me?"

"Of course, there's hope for you. If you don't have hope, all that's left is cynicism, and that doesn't get you anywhere. But you have some big things to undo, and it won't happen unless you face them head on. I've tried asking you, and you avoid me and give me the Bob Marley shtick '…everything's gonna be all right.' You know he got brain cancer and died."

"That's not encouraging, Jamie."

"Sorry. You've made careers for people based on your trust and confidence in their abilities. Now it's time to transfer that confidence to yourself."

"I love you, Jamie."

"You should. I'm one of a kind, and so are you. And I love you for many reasons, including your unwavering goodness. But the long jokes …"

"Yeah, my wife hates them."

"A marriage is full of the same stories over and over again. I think we need to leave the past behind. *We* need new stories," I said.

Goldie Fish ... November

PAUL ARRIVED IN THE AFTERNOON. HE COULDN'T STAY AWAY from Denver and me for very long. I was more exhilarated with every visit he made. Joe was starting to question the frequency of the visits. I wasn't always honest about seeing Paul. I wasn't ready to make permanent changes.

Paul told me that, as he stepped outside to his ride, he could see his breath. Still, it was another sunny day in Denver. From the airport, he had a view of the 14,000-foot peaks. I secured Good as Gold Limousine Service to drop him off at the Hotel Monaco downtown.

"This is your 'ocean,'" he said on the phone. "I can see why you like it here Jamie, the traffic is manageable, there's less pollution, and you can see your ocean from anywhere," he told me.

"Yeah, and people and cars seem to move a little slower. I like that, too," I said.

I tried to find unusual and customer-oriented places for Paul to stay. "You'll like the ambience of the hotel: sunflower yellow and tomato red wallpaper; small-town, friendly staff, and a real goldfish swimming around in a bowl to greet you in the room."

"Goldfish?" He was amused with my selection. "Inside that sophisticated woman, a part of you is still a little girl. I'm intrigued with the package," he told me more than once.

"I like that, Jamie. I guess the fish is my date tonight?" Paul was disappointed that his "just passing through trip" on his way from New York to L.A. did not yield more "Jamie time."

"Goldie," so named by Paul, "is circling a treasure chest filled with sapphire blue marbles. She swam to the top of the bowl to blow me kisses and beg for food."

"We're not all like that, Paul," I said, hearing him tap the bowl.

"Like what?" asked Paul. He sounded preoccupied and as if he was ready to grab his tablet to see his latest messages.

"Blowing kisses for food. Anyway, I'm glad you're here. I miss you. I'll see you tomorrow around nine."

"Oh, good. I like my pet. Can we take her with us in case you get boring?"

"Sure. Right now, I need to pay attention to the family."

The next morning, I knocked on the door of the Gold Room and Paul answered, wearing only a shirt that fell just below his crotch. He gave me a delicate kiss on my lips. My body tingled.

"Are you having a hot flash, Paul? What if I'd been the hotel service? You are the emperor with no clothes. But I shouldn't give you shit; I sometimes garden in my skimpy night wear, visible to my neighbors from their bedroom window. I just pretend they're not there."

He took the emperor comment as a compliment. "I knew it was you," he held me and we stopped talking for a moment. I sighed and stretched my arms around him and held him tighter, as if to squeeze the thin Paul out of the big one.

"We're a quirky love thing. You wear pink shirts in macho Denver, and I wear scuffed up cowboy boots in stylish Los Angeles.

"Yeah, and I like the quirky us," he said squeezing me back.

"Hey Jamie, look at my giant bath. Do ya want to take one with me?"

I was tempted, but I had taken a shower earlier in the morning. "Sorry, Paul," I kissed him. "Next time," I could barely look at his dejected face.

Sophie and Joe were in the back of my mind. I couldn't seem to get rid of either of them, when, at the same time, I was thrilled to see Paul.

On our almost daily phone calls, my friend Sophie asked whether Joe knew that Paul would be in town again. She didn't like my keeping secrets. And my conversations with her were becoming strained.

Joe knew only that I was going to breakfast with a friend. Keeping a secret was easy, since he never asked where I was going or where I had been. He was busy painting the inside of the house and was content to do that while listening to the radio full blast.

He smashed my aorta a long time ago. This isn't retribution, even though I'm in a constant state of heartbreak.

"I know you have justifications, Jamie," Sophie said.

"I love Paul, and that's it."

"Maybe it's time for some professional help. You know, with a marriage counselor you could gain more awareness of the reasons you've ruined your life …"

"Oh please, Sophie."

"… and the real motivation for Paul being in your life and, most importantly, how you can fix your marriage," she said.

"Paul and I need love and affection and a good laugh, not agitated partners who no longer tolerate us and, even worse, are indifferent. We've both stopped wanting to fix it."

Love Therapy

I TOOK SOPHIE'S ADVICE AND STARTED SEEING A THERAPIST named Michael, who was recommended by one of my fucked-up friends. I thought having a guy counselor would offer some balance to my female way of thinking. Previously, I had help to thwart depression, and knew it could make me feel better. With the right person, you feel like "Yeah, they get it! I'm not crazy."

This time, I was resistant to the therapeutic process. Was I doing this for Sophie and Joe, or for me? I wanted "love therapy"— help with moving forward, not marriage counseling that seemed retro. I didn't want to reflect on my years of hurt and rejection. I wanted to revel in love chemistry—emotions, intellect, the spiritual, and physical.

What I really wanted was for a professional to say, "That makes sense, and you deserve to be in love. It's your time, so go for it!" and "P.S. Forget the guilt." But this was the gist of the session:

"Tell me why you're here," was Michael's request at my first visit with him. "Because I'm in love." I said.

"Saying, 'I am in love' doesn't quite tell me enough. Would you explain a little more?"

I replied, "I'm mostly out of love with my husband and in love with another man."

"You must be hurting and happy at the same time … go on."

"Yes. It's good and bad. "Mostly good, I guess." Michael seemed to get it, but I'm not sure I was fully participating. I wanted validation, not questions.

Michael seemed to be a well-intentioned professional. He was sincere, and I could tell he had top training from all the certificates on his walls. But as the mostly one-sided conversation persisted, I wondered if he could talk love. While trying to answer his questions, I checked the books on his shelves, and saw no title with love in it. The closest was some publication called "Sex in Your Sixties."

"Go on," he encouraged.

"My friend Sophie says I need to be here to find out my true reasons for having a new man in my life and why I have quote, 'ruined my life.'" One could predict the next question: "Do you feel you have ruined your life?" I wasn't ready to answer that.

"You want me to put the stamp of approval on your new relationship," he observed. Oh, now he gets it, I thought. He understands, and I didn't have to ask for it.

Michael said, "You must be really hurting. Something must be terribly painful in your marriage for you to engage in another relationship. Do you feel like you're seen and heard by your husband?" I thought I was past caring about being seen or heard, though I mostly hadn't felt that for a while.

I was already convinced that my new love was real love. It all seemed so right. And I thought about Paul and his world of music, where love needs no explanation.

Love in a therapist's office doesn't seem to exist. I'm sure they understand and experience it, but they don't talk it. While I appreciated Michael's empathy to my situation, in later sessions, he seemed hesitant to repeat the word love.

But I stuck it out. Over time, I relaxed and delved into other issues. We talked about the sudden loss of my father and how it affected me. We talked about fear and procrastination and how they can defeat us. We spent time on my desire for safety. Most important to me, we talked about guilt as an obstacle to making decisions. That really hit home.

After several visits, I shared about where I saw myself in the triangle of relationships between victims, perpetrators, and rescuers. I have been all these.

He noted the "hostile communication" in my marriage and wondered how I had let this be a part of my life for so long.

Still, I dreaded any kind of analysis about my love for Paul. For me, it was pure, new and exciting. We thought alike, and we loved alike. We felt stronger together. We wanted to pursue creativity together.

I continued to see Michael, but it was obvious that, if I wanted to talk about "love," maybe I should stick to my friends.

Gold Leaf Frame … December

I LIFTED THE FIVE BY SEVEN GOLD-LEAFED FRAME THAT HELD Paul's photo. On this short visit to Denver, he had brought a piece of his past with him. I sat down with the frame and examined and touched it as though he was in there. I outlined his frame with my finger. He was wearing only gym shorts and tennis shoes with no socks. He was in his twenties. Those were the years when everything was possible and fears were something an old person had.

I knew this natural guy with wavy blonde hair and a strong chest. I held the picture to my belly to calm my churning stomach. I looked up at Paul. "Am I making a big deal out of this?" I said.

"I am that guy, Jamie. By the way, you *can't* have that photo," and gently removed it from my hands. "I keep it on my dresser as inspiration."

"That's the way I see you too, Paul. I see that athlete in you, that naïve, cheerful Paul, not yet tainted by life's disappointments. I want that photo." I grabbed it back. My look was plaintive, and he knew he wasn't going to get the picture from me right then.

"You've come a long way, Paul." He had lost significant weight.

"You helped me, Jamie. You make me happy, even long-distance happy.

"That motivates me."

"My part has been small. You did it yourself."

"Are we living a fantasy, Paul?" I said, changing the subject to my obsession about whether this love thing would work out.

"I'm not, Jamie. But you have to figure out your own stuff," he said.

"You say that, but when we take a drive, I'll have hard questions for you. Then I'll answer yours.

"I don't have anything to ask, Jamie."

"If that's so, then you don't know the whole picture." I didn't want there to be any surprises. I wanted us to know about the good and the bad. I have a theory that when we drive, you'll open up since you won't have to look at me."

"Oh, I don't have that problem with my twin girls—they tell me more than I ever want to know. It exasperates me, but I adore them. I'll do almost anything to keep the love flowing," Paul added.

I planned to test my theory on Paul, despite his fears of disclosing his less-than-perfect life. He was resigned. But flattering a woman is almost always a good way to divert a subject.

"You know your body hasn't changed since you were 18," said Paul.

"That's what you tell me. I try to keep in shape. It's more important now, don't you think?" I said.

"What do you think?" he said avoiding an answer to the question.

"I noticed that nice compact bottom of yours," Paul said. "I noticed you and had to adjust myself when you were walking up the stairs at your mother's house. Did you wear that sexy cowboy shirt and tight jeans just for me when I visited you?"

"I did. Just for you."

"I liked that," he chuckled.

California Poppies

HAVING LIVED SO LONG IN THE GOLDEN STATE OF California, I was partial to the bright orange poppies that lined the thoroughfares. Poppies can withstand desert heat and freeway noise. In the spring, they blanket drab freeway edges. California poppies are tough, and yet they're delicate. One bad weather episode could knock them down, but they pop back up with a kiss of sun.

"I like to think I'm a poppy by nature, bringing sunshine to people I love," I told Sophie over a cup of tea.

I was in a happy mood this winter day, enjoying talking with my good friend at our favorite coffee shop. We sat comfortably in cushy chairs next to a wood-burning fireplace, sipping our steaming drinks.

"You do bring sunshine. You're a good friend," Sophie responded.

"That's what I do for Paul. But he needs to know I have a dark side, maybe a little darker than average," I told her.

"Haven't you told him about your mood swings?"

"I've been hesitant to bring that up, especially since it's under control these days. When do you think I should tell Paul about it?"

"He should know what he's getting with you, especially now

in your life when there's so much to *lose*. I don't mean to be pessimistic; it's just safer that way."

Talking with Sophie brought back memories. In my early twenties, I thought my doldrums had something to do with California's coastal fog. Before moving to Colorado, I lived in a prime location, in a town just blocks from the beach. I rode my bike to work up the coast highway, past saltwater lagoons and pelicans gliding inches above the ocean. If I was lucky, some mornings I would see pods of dolphins surfing the waves.

Because I was not an early riser, this ride in the fresh air started my day right. By the time I got to work I was mindful of my peace and my appreciation of a being a coastal dweller.

Even living in ocean paradise, I was enveloped in a lack of energy and sadness that I tried to hide. Mood contradictions became a greater part of my life. I relished my meaningful work as manager of a primary care clinic and that I could bike to my job. Yet a lack of luster for life would last weeks to months with only brief interruptions of joy. I was a victim of something I had yet to understand, and that was my biological predisposition.

It wasn't until my late twenties that I believed my cure would be an adventure. As a teen in California, I listened to John Denver's songs and knew that the mountains were calling me. A Rocky Mountain high and attending graduate school in health administration in Colorado would be good medicine.

I loved Colorado from the start. The sun shines more than 300 days a year. People are friendly. But a dark fog followed me and affected my optimism, letting it out less and less.

When I would call home, my family heard the beginning of the sentences, "I'm happy here. I love this place. My life is good," but they didn't hear the end of the conversation, "I'm lonely. I feel hopeless. I'm a loser." I felt too much shame about my darkening thoughts. I really didn't understand my malady. To me, the phrase "I'm depressed" was what my mom said every

Christmas when she allowed herself to grieve for the loss of my father. Those words were for her, and no one else used them.

Like a cloudy day, I had no control over the grayness occupying my mind. Every morning I anticipated "having a good day." I put encouraging sayings on my mirror to live in the moment. The guilt that nothing worked almost overwhelmed me. "I am fortunate," I would say. Still, I had fantasies of doing myself in.

I wore bright colors, thinking other's smiling faces would rub off on me. I had a whole collection of feel-good T-shirts. As I entered my thirties, I couldn't imagine being anywhere else but in colorful Colorado. Joe and I had created a beautiful family. I worked in an exciting career, flying around the country, consulting with elected state leaders on innovative health policies.

Then one day I experienced an awkward time at work. I couldn't stop crying. In between sobs, I would tell myself, "My life is good and, I don't know why this is happening." My staff and coworkers witnessed my breakdown. They didn't understand. It was the ultimate humiliation. Before long, I took leave and then left my job.

I was finally diagnosed with bipolar depression that, for me, included long periods of sadness, hopelessness, guilt, and lethargy. These periods were coupled with brief moments of high energy when I would run up my line of credit and extreme irritability. I would experience normal moods in between, but they came less and less. I tried professional help and many medications didn't work. I felt engulfed in misery until I started lithium, which made the mood swings recede. But it also toyed with my memory and gave me hand tremors that affected my self-confidence.

I probably didn't have to leave my job, but I needed to get better and it took a while. I did improve. But it was shame and embarrassment and the length of time it took me to feel good again that kept me away. During those years, I didn't know how to handle it. That wouldn't happen again.

I owed it to Paul to let him know about this. I wasn't sure about the timing, and it wasn't that urgent because an even newer medication had made my life much better. I didn't know why I was so afraid to tell him. I knew he would be understanding, and my fears would be for nothing.

El Chapultepec … December

PAUL'S LAST-MINUTE VISITS TO COLORADO REQUIRED QUICK planning and calling in favors from friends. I couldn't wait to see him, but I still wasn't ready to forsake family commitments. I was protecting myself in case something didn't work out.

I told Paul about my friend Laney, who would show him the town.

"You'll like her. She's intelligent and still has the body to carry off skimpy and sexy. I hate to walk my scrawny behind next to her voluptuous one," I said.

"What's the catch, Jamie?"

"I have family obligations. My son is coming down from college. Joe and I are having dinner with him at his favorite Mexican restaurant to catch up and hear how his studies are going. I've arranged to have Laney show you downtown and take you to a legendary bar."

"I need to be with you, Jamie," he said with a heavy dose of disappointment in his voice, I'm coming there to see you. I miss you terribly," Paul said during a phone conversation the night before his visit.

"I know, but we need to make a Plan B." This was the down side of living a secretive life, which I don't recommend for those prone to guilt.

"She'll pick you up at 8:00 p.m. at your hotel," I instructed him.

I made a quick call to Laney. I asked her to show him a good time. I knew she would. I suggested she take him to El Chapultepec because he would love that place for its dive-like ambiance and current live music. She assured me that they'd have fun, and she'd tell me all about it.

When Laney called me the next day, she filled me in about their night. She told me at the precise hour, Paul squeezed into the front seat of Laney's mini coupe with no complaint and they drove around downtown for a quick tour. They passed by the Christmas lights that outlined the City and County Building.

"For a small city, it's got a lot going on. Can you take me to Five Points?" Paul said.

"Why do you want to go there?" Laney asked. "It's really only a place for the young crowd."

"I read in the hotel magazine it was a hot spot for jazz back in the day."

Laney drove her mini coupe like she was competing in the Indy 500. Paul said nothing but gripped the dashboard a few times as if it made a difference in Laney's speed. Laney pointed out Cervantes and a couple of old-style blues bars in Five Points.

"Now I am taking you to El Chapultepec. We're going to have some fun, and I won't say any more," she said. Laney made a hard left onto Larimer Street. Paul's eyes opened wide. He felt a pressure on his bladder and feared he might lose control of it.

I thought *I* should actually pee in *my* pants when I drive with Laney just to get her to slow down. This was no freewheeling L.A. This was Denver, a bit more law-abiding and happier.

Laney parked across the street from the bar. Paul pointed. "Is that it? I was expecting some swanky disco place." They crossed the street. Sidewalks were filled with swaying bar patrons. They had to perform the Saturday night sidewalk dance, dodging left and right. When they entered the bar, Paul grimaced when he saw a place he didn't expect.

"El Chapultepec doesn't make a good first impression," she said. Bulbs are bare. Seats are scarce. The naugahyde in the booths is torn. The bar is said to have the worst bathrooms in lower downtown. The guys don't care much. The women are disgusted.

"I like it," said Paul. He warmed up to the place when he saw the eight by tens on the walls capturing famous musicians playing impromptu gigs in this dingy bar. And there were old Polaroid shots of the many lesser known but popular locals. These were the people who rocked the roof off the place on weekend nights.

Paul eyed the band across the bar. It looked like a bluesy group. Tonight, the bar must have squeezed in more than its legal limit. "I get it, Jamie." Paul smiled. "This is perfect, Laney."

"Jamie thought you would take to it right away. Want a beer?" Laney surveyed the perimeter for young well-dressed guys.

"How about some vodka?" Paul asked.

"They only serve rot gut here," Laney replied.

"That'll be great," Paul said. He tapped his fingers on the bar. "I wish Jamie was here with us," Paul kept saying.

"You'll have to settle for me."

One couldn't help but talk to strangers, since they were up against your body. The band played for a while and took a break. Paul bought a round of drinks for the band and learned about their musical backgrounds. He told them just enough to get an invitation to sing with them.

Paul took up a big part of the small stage. "I need audience participation," he said. With a quick check with the band, he started slow. "This is for you, Jamie," he said into the microphone that he seemed comfortable holding."

"I thought that was sweet," Laney told me.

The loud audience quieted. "Who is this fat fuck on the stage?" someone asked.

"That was so rude," Laney commented as she progressed through the events of the evening.

"Hey, what would you guys do if I had a bad voice?" Paul asked the crowd.

"Get off the stage!" yelled someone from the crowd. For an instant, I could almost see Paul wondering, "Where was the friendly Denver that Jamie had told him about?"

Then he sang, the Beatles, *With a Little Help from My Friends*. The band played slow and kept the beat with their heads. Paul moved side to side looking graceful for a big guy, as he continued the ballad.

By this time, the bar goers stopped heckling and joined in with this gutsy emperor with no clothes. They loved it.

Paul had a little trouble with the high notes. But the room responded to the song's questions. Paul and the crowd shared the love back and forth.

"We're having fun now. Thank you very much," he said. Turning to the band he said, "Thanks for indulging me."

"It's cool bro, it was fun," the leader said.

"So, Jamie, now you know about our evening. We really wish you could have been there with us," said Laney.

She wasn't quite finished with her account of the evening. "Paul was pretty drunk by the time we left. I don't know how many people bought him drinks. The girls loved him," Laney had to tell me.

"I know," I said.

"I kept him close, not that I was worried, Jamie; he's so smitten with you."

"How was his voice, Laney?" I knew the answer.

"Awful!"

"But the crowd sang along, clapped to the beat, and hooted and cheered when he was done. 'One more! One more!'" they screamed.

"What did Paul do?"

"He gave the microphone back and ordered vodka on the rocks. We probably danced another 45 minutes. Your friend is a great guy. And he actually has rhythm."

"What did you think of your date?" I later asked Paul.

"Laney showed me a good Mile High time. But she is a crazy broad."

I knew he would have fun with Laney despite himself. I was a little bit jealous, but more appreciative of my friend's date with Paul.

"There's nothing wrong with a night out with a tight-bodied lawyer who can maneuver her way around town. And it's even more fun in her cherry mini coupe."

"Yeah, she drove fast through those city streets. But we had a good time even though I wished it was you I was rocking with."

The Top Drawer ... December

COLD, SNOW, RAIN AND EVEN SEETHING HEAT DOESN'T deter Laney and I from walking. Twice a week we take our dogs around the park and back to my house. That's when I hear about Laney's gentlemen. She dates men twenty years younger and wears four-inch heels after she hangs up her lawyer costumes. She looks darn good and all her body parts are originals.

"Men my age are just too old and worn out," she said as we started our cold evening walk around Washington Park. "It's a mind fuck when a guy I'm into can't get it up," she declared. She wondered if it was "lack of feelings" for her or if it was "his problem." What a condom conundrum, I wanted to but didn't say. This day my mind was focused elsewhere.

She wanted to tell me about "Claw Man," her latest. Laney had nicknames for all her lovers. This one, she told me, lifted weights and so he had a hard bottom, bulging biceps and one of those rare-in-real-life muscular bellies. "And this guy could perform," she emphasized.

"I've been dating him for a month, and yesterday we finally had sex at his place. The way he tore off my skirt and blouse was such a turn-on. I didn't care that he had popped all my buttons. But his kissing was a bit overdone—a little sloppy like a dog cleaning his master's face. And the butt slaps might have been exciting, but they made my bottom sore. Perhaps that was the point. I'm open-minded, but sex with him is extreme. 'Forget the cuffs,' I told him."

She continued, "Later that evening Claw Man got up to use the bathroom. 'I'll be right back, my sweet,' he said. Calling me 'my sweet' was cute. While I waited, I decided to look around, first in the top drawer of his bedside table. I was looking for clues about his private life and fantasies."

"What did you find?" I was very curious.

"A whip, some metal balls, a double rubber penis with bumps and a real bear claw."

"A bear claw, what's that for?" I, too, tried to keep an open mind as I kept listening, but none of that paraphernalia was a part of my sexual repertoire. Maybe I needed to spice things up with Paul; maybe I should have with Joe. I didn't consider myself prudish, but more of a "natural" woman. Still, I liked hearing about Laney's romps.

She didn't have a plausible answer about the bear claw. But she said, "He's such a nice guy, even though he can't carry on a two-way conversation, and you know I like to talk. I've had so many interesting experiences with men. I was thinking I should write a book. What do you think?" I waited for Laney to pause while I took in our surroundings. Not every neighborhood has a park with two lakes, a mountain view, some 70 different kinds of trees, pelicans, egrets, an occasional bald eagle high in the trees, and toned athletes of all ages performing their daily workouts.

Finally, I said, "That's a good idea. Write that book, but I think someone has beaten you to it about the kinky sex. Anyway, I wouldn't want to read it. I've already heard it." I was glad she laughed. "I'm happy that you had an eventful evening with Claw Man. Can I tell you about mine?" I cut Laney off sooner than she wanted.

"Your what?"

"I'd like to talk about Paul," I grinned widely.

"Do you have to?" Laney had prejudices against extra-large guys.

"I've been listening to your bump and grind accounts with men almost half your age. I can't imagine the pubic coif you require. Now, I have something to say. This is a big topic," I said.

"Tell me *everything*."

I ignored her sarcastic tone. "I believe few men are focused on pleasing a woman. They give up too soon. Read those men magazines. They try to convince their readers to keep it in first gear to give women time to warm up. I've been disenchanted. Once I had a boyfriend fall asleep in my crotch. He was snoring, too."

"That's pathetic."

"He had narcolepsy. Joe used to be good, but he's been taking short cuts for a long time."

"Second-rate sex. That's what happens in a marriage. I won't get married again," said Laney.

We continued around the park, Laney walked faster. I had to breathe harder.

"You know Paul's last visit in December wasn't all talk and no action." I said. I knew Laney was skeptical when she thought about me being with such a big man.

"Before things got started, I asked Paul what kind of lover he was."

"You can't just let things happen?!" Laney reprimanded.

"Quiet Laney! I'm telling my story now."

"Paul looked up at the ceiling. I waited."

'I'm passionate,' he said staring at me with his big blue eyes. I blushed. 'It's getting hot in here. I waved my hand across my face.'

"Already, Jamie?" He laughed.

'I thought you would say 'I don't know." Could you open the windows?' I asked.

'The windows don't open. You're going to have to get sweaty with me, Jamie.'

"After years of boring sex, I thought I was out of commission, but when I think about Paul, my body heats up. I was excited about this big man. He is my Santa, my Happy Buddha. How could I not enjoy making love with a man like that? He delicately removed my outer layers and placed my clothes on a chair in a neat pile. He felt my lacy bra and panties between two fingers. He looked at me as if he was taking inventory of long-lost possessions. He spoke not a word but shook his head.

'Is this good news or bad news Santa?' I asked.

"You're pretty much the same as you were as a teenager, except more beautiful." He let out a "Sheesh."

"That compliment was difficult to accept, but with such sincerity I had no response other than 'Thank you.'"

He took my hand and we rested on top of the giant hotel bed. His belly easily met mine. I inhaled his minty breath. He kissed me on my nose. He knows I don't like my nose. He kissed my forehead and combed my hair with his large fingers.

Our lips met, and we closed our eyes. I could smell the soap he used from his last shower: a manly frankincense and myrrh that I gave him. My body shivered as he moved his fingertips down my spine. He buried his face in my neck, saying he enjoyed my natural fragrance.

His lips were soft, but certain. I could taste the mint I had detected before.

Instinct led him to start to move his body over mine before he realized the impact of well over three hundred pounds on me. He held himself over me in a shaky push up. "I think I would crush you if we went any further," he said. I didn't want to think such practical thoughts, but I realized he was right; his weight might bruise me.

Laney and I continued walking around the park. She looked behind us to see if anyone was listening. "Don't worry, most walkers have ear phones," I said.

He caressed my breasts with hesitation, as if he had not been intimate for a long time. 'You're soft,' he said as he slowly touched me. We untwined our arms and legs. I thought he was getting up to turn off the light, but he kneeled on the floor and pulled me down to the bottom of the bed." I looked at Laney to see if she was still listening.

"I'm listening, but finish soon," she said. Laney was walking as fast as she could, hoping that I would run out of breath and be quiet.

"He was slow and deliberate, and then moved faster as he sensed my enthusiasm. My body tightened. My back arched. My muscles went limp. "Thank you, Paul." I whispered. We lay next to each other for a long comfortable calm, me in his arms.

"Are you finished?" she pleaded. "No offense, but I'm just not into hearing about fat guy sex."

"For now." But I added, "Don't ever underestimate the tender passion of a big guy, Laney."

We completed the rest of our walk in silence.

Extra Extra Large

PAUL WANTED TO GET SLIM, SLIM AS HIS BASEBALL GUY friends who only had small beer bellies. It was achievable. He had to maintain a steady course of none of that and less of this.

Every day he would eat a salad and a chicken breast and a whole grain something for dinner. He would drink protein shakes with fresh fruit for breakfast and enjoy hard-boiled eggs and rice crackers for lunch. No more 2:00 a.m. bowls of ice cream with chocolate sauce. No more pizzas with extra parmesan cheese for breakfast. No more gulping whole milk from the container. But lunches with friends at the latest in restaurant didn't count. He would indulge now and then, but not every day.

Paul had to exercise four times a week for an hour or until his gym clothes were soaked with sweat. The gym rats became his new best friends. Friends were essential to Paul through this life-changing process.

It would be easy to stop drinking. And it was important. He knew there were calories in eight ounces of vodka. At least he wouldn't bring the bottle to bed. "It really wasn't a habit," he said. And I was happy to agree. "I can quit any time," he would say. I tried to believe him. The three drinks he had at the Gifted Guys bar, Paul's favorite L.A. hangout, somehow didn't count.

It still stung that his close buddies intervened to stop his habit. They said, "It was love" but it felt like bullying to Paul. No one brought up that awkward time again. After all, he was the boss of a multimillion-dollar business. "I know what I am doing," he would remind them and me.

He didn't have to be extra, extra large like his father. But he already was larger than that. I don't think they sold clothes in his size at Macy's. Paul would admit that his father, who loved his own image, almost destroyed his shining star son. Paul did it, Dad took credit for it. It eroded his delicate self-concept, which translated into a hidden consumption of an outrageous amount of calories.

There was no atta boy dad in his house. No "Son, you've done a great job."

Not once," Paul once lamented when I prodded. It wasn't good enough that Paul toiled long hours, stayed up nights, sought out experts, read volumes, charmed funders, and knew it was his and no one else's splendid creation. He was the creative bottom line, not dad any more. Now Paul was the one who could make an artist's career soar.

Every son yearns for his father's approval, and when he doesn't get it, he fills that emotional hole somehow. Paul consumed.

Why didn't Mom protect him from Dad's narcissistic poison? It was too late to get the full story; his mom was gone. Later, Paul would write in his journal about his billboard father and his passive sweet mom, as well as what he ate everyday and his exercise regimen. It was time to end the self-flagellation. He found love, his own, so he could stop hurting himself now.

The Gifted Guys ... January

I WANTED TO BE AN INVISIBLE BYSTANDER AT THE GIFTED Guys. The patrons were like the blokes at the local bar. But their paychecks were bigger. They could afford to be liberal philanthropists because, even after taxes, they still had enough cash to play with.

They drank a lot of the hard stuff unless they were "on the wagon." Then they drank only wine.

The next best thing to being there was Paul's retelling of conversations he had with his buddies, especially this recent one with his old friend and mentor, Oscar.

He told me, "The first thing you need to know, Jamie, is that the Gifted Guys is a sacred place where the deal makers in 'the biz' divulge their secrets and share jokes. I didn't name the group, by the way," Paul said. "We get together almost every night at the country club pub to get things off our chests. We don't have to look over our shoulders. We can count on our guys to keep our secrets from the press and to give each other unsolicited advice. The unwelcome counsel is bestowed with love and often has a shred of truth that is worth listening to."

"I thought you would be amused with my conversation with Oscar. Oscar is a semi-retired producer of some the hottest HB0 shows of the '90s and an entertaining cynic."

"I hope I'm amused," I said.

"Well, don't be offended."

"I'll try not to." (I wondered if I should be hearing his conversation with Oscar.)

"We were talking about you, and Oscar says, 'How well have you thought this through?'"

"I wrote about her in my journal," I told him.

"You have a journal?" Oscar chuckled.

"Yeah, it started as a way to keep track of my weight loss and to fight off cravings. It was Jamie's idea. It made me realize other losses, too. I loved my wife, Oscar, but our marriage was doing me more harm than good," I told him.

"What makes you think this new one won't do you more harm than good? In my 75 years and three marriages, with expensive girls in between, I found that they all can beat you down. They dole out guilt. You feel shame, and it's a mess that Dr. Phil can't fix. Just say 'yes' to everything and then go hang out with your buds. Make the broads happy and everyone is happy," said Oscar.

"I've tried to work it out, Oscar. I don't want to wait any longer."

"Oscar grabbed my shoulder and stared straight into my eyes. He said, "Next time, we need to talk about those dark circles under your eyes. I'm concerned about your health."

"I haven't been sleeping well, Jamie," Paul interjected, "thinking about all these big decisions. But you know I'm going to work it out."

"I'm not too worried but go on about Oscar."

"Oscar sniffed and still a large droplet of clear fluid was about to fall out of his nose. I tried to concentrate on the messenger and was relieved when he wiped the drop with the sleeve of his purple Armani shirt." A storyteller like Paul remembered these details.

"You know we're doomed to have boring marriages after 25 years," said Oscar. "Mine got boring after fifteen. I have children ages 53, 35 and a feisty 18-year old just ready to go to college. She's a kick. I had to wait this long to get one most like me," he snorted. "He lifted his whiskey to his lips and waited for my reaction. I smiled."

"Our wives get bored with sex after the first child. Breastfeeding and diapers ruin it. They become the rug rats' tits, not ours anymore," explained Oscar.

"I yawned and bought two more vodkas each before the happy hour was over," said Paul

"What about the new one? Can you trust her motives?" asked Oscar.

I'd had enough of Oscar's pessimism and wanted to call you right then. But I knew you'd be disapproving of me being tipsy.

"Don't we all have ulterior motives? Paul replied to Oscar. "The idea of sex with a long-legged, big-boobed, blonde who still fits into her high school bell bottoms *motivates* me. Is that legit? I thought I'd approach Oscar's argument from his sensibilities."

"That's legit Paul." Oscar nodded with sincerity, like a supportive friend would.

"By the way, she has many qualities. She's funny in a cutely odd kind of way. She laughs at my jokes, most of the time. She's sharp, there's no bullshitting her. She's caring and humble—a rare commodity around here. She has a spiritual side that intrigues me—a relationship with God and good that I am trying to soak up. She's fun, and I like fun. I'm happy, and I haven't been that way in a long time. I love her. I have for over 30 years," I said.

"You make me blush, Paul," I said. He couldn't see, but my cheeks flushed to a hot red. "By the way, go light on the God and goodness description. I don't feel like I am so good right now," I responded.

"You are to me, Jamie."

"So inquiring minds want to know your plan?" Oscar pressed.

I took a gulp of my drink. "Vodka is made with potatoes," I said.

"That's old news," retorted Oscar.

"I thought it was time to change the subject," Paul told me. I didn't blame him. Paul was hesitant to share his thoughts unless he could guarantee the friend's loyalty and, even then, he might retreat when confronted with the hard questions. "You had to be that way in Hollywood if you wanted your own life," he told me.

"So, what do you think, Jamie?" Paul asked.

"I don't drink vodka. I did for a while, but it made me depressed. It took many years for me to catch on. Now I am a one glass red wine drinker, on occasions. I was taught to be moderate. So boring."

"You're never boring, Jamie."

"Thank you. But I have to tell you what I read, Paul. If you're serious about shedding your tonnage…"

"Do you think you could use a more compassionate word than 'tonnage'?"

"…you will need to stay away from the alcohol and have no more than two or three drinks a week. Alcohol adds calories."

"Yes, Jamie," Paul said as his voice tone raised, anticipating, or dreading my commentary.

"But I read that liquor makes you store fat. Your body sees the alcohol as poison and tries to get rid of it. So if you're eating, too, the liver stops processing all the other calories until it has dealt with the alcohol. Anything else you eat while you're drinking will turn into fat. I know you don't want that, so I thought I'd better tell you."

"Are you finished, Jamie?"

"Yes, I am, my sweet thing. I just had to share. It wouldn't be right to keep valuable information to myself."

"Thank you, Jamie, but I read the magazines and books, too. I'm the big one, remember? And I'm losing weight, slow and steady, and I've curbed the alcohol," he said. He was annoyed, yet still calm and kind, if you can be all that after a judgmental lecture. That's what I love about him.

"I shouldn't have ordered two more drinks just because it was happy hour. Thank you for helping me be aware,"

Paul knows he has a vodka fixation. He's gotten help a few times, but not because he was enthusiastic about it. He is now. But he still hangs out at the Gifted Guys almost every day and is tempted every day.

As with many of us in this world, as he aged, a part of Paul's desires, like playing baseball, had slipped through his fingers like Malibu sand. Sometime vodka became his pacifier when life threw those curve balls.

You should have seen the velocity of Paul's throw to second base in high school. His whole body lunged into the speed of the ball. It's hard to tell when he stopped being an athlete. Maybe it was after his Dad had "the talk" with him. He discouraged his son from his "useless pursuit." Dad's "bird in the hand" convinced Paul to join up, with hesitation. That happens.

Paul resisted having the family business handed to him. It had strings attached, including a father who needed all the credit, even if he wasn't due it. On the other hand, it was an exciting, great-paying life, and Paul was good at show business even with all its stresses. Paul was good at everything, except controlling what food and drink went in his mouth, getting along with his wife, and singing in key.

He couldn't part from his drinking friends at the Gifted Guys, but he could rid himself of alcohol. In his past, alcohol consumption digressed from being a comfort, to becoming a depressant and a nearly unshakeable habit.

Just once, I would have loved to show up to the Gifted Guys and surprise Paul. I would have dusted off the shoulders of my short black dress that had been hanging in the closet too long, and I would have worn some sexy black heels that I could've walked on without wobbling. I would've snuggled up next to him to listen to the guy chatter. I would've been quiet, so they would forget I was there. I would have switched his happy hour drink orders to "two fat free milks on the rocks" and whispered words of encouragement in his other ear.

I would have been his scintillating coach in his one-man race for good health. Maybe I already was that.

Emails ... January

IT WAS A COLD EVENING IN DENVER BOTH INSIDE AND OUT.
I had made a stir fry dinner that Joe and I ate together, sitting in
the family room and watching the evening news programs. Joe
said, "thank you" for dinner, and that was about it. We cleared
and washed the dishes in silence. Joe answered my "How was
your day?" questions brusquely. The television stayed on as we
both worked on our laptops. I was looking forward to having Joe
go to bed early, as he did on week nights, so I could catch up on
my emails.

Joe reached for the channel changer and turned off the
television. This was unusual. He never turned off the TV until
he was ready to go to bed.

"I was suspicious about your so-called friendship with Paul
and his visits to Colorado. I looked through your emails. I know
what you are doing," Joe said.

"Oh," was my insufficient response. I needed time to think.

His eyes seemed to bulge with the stress of confronting
something he didn't want to know about.

"You invaded my privacy. I don't like that." My stomach
gurgled, and my breathing got shallow.

"What are you going to do?" said Joe.

"I don't know what I'm doing," I said. "But I've had enough of your anger. It feels overwhelming. You have forgotten how to love." I was prepared for this moment, but this was unscheduled.

"Do you even love me?" I asked Joe, feeling my stomach turn.

"Do I what you?" he said.

"Do you love me?" I persisted.

"Of course. I shouldn't have to tell you that," he said.

"Yes, you should. And I don't remember the last time you did tell me." He had turned the TV back on and didn't bother to turn down the volume as I continued.

"You do nice things, like change my oil, but you have forgotten how to be loving. You don't seem to care or notice me. You don't care about my interests."

"That's true," he said.

"You're often embarrassed by the things I say to strangers." Joe nodded his head in agreement.

"You get angry every day that I don't wash the dishes by the time you come home."

"That's the least you could do."

"And further, you don't like to walk with me and our dog. You say you are too tired."

"I am, after a long day of work. You know that," he replied.

"You don't like to travel, you don't like my family— 'The Christian Alcoholics,' as you call them. So rude and not true."

Joe laughed.

"You don't like my cooking most of the time. All your sarcasm and put-downs add up to contempt," I said. He acted as if he had stopped listening. I kept going.

"You only like sex your expedient way, and you have polluted our computer with viruses that hitched a ride from your favorite porno sites."

"Don't you think these are petty complaints, Jamie?" He said smirking. "Besides, I think you are the one that likes expedient sex."

"They may be petty, but they add up. Over time, the negativity chips away at me until I wonder what part of a loving marriage is left."

Joe pressed, "What are you going to do?"

"I'm leaving you, I think," I said. My stomach turned again. He didn't move from his seat or look at me or even change the channel.

"I didn't expect how I reacted to Joe looking in my emails," I later told Sophie. I was mad, not shamed, or embarrassed or caught. A part of me knew I would be found out. I think that's what I wanted—for him to know I was in love with another man.

Like Paul's, my marriage had gone askew. We appreciated our marriages for their longevity and raising children. But our spouses had little interest in us as feeling beings. It had taken its toll. We had little left to give, but still they were spouses, even with the years of marital neglect. I wasn't ready to be decisive. I was unsure about leaving Joe and breaking up our families. I also felt dependent on Paul's decisions, which were not forthcoming. And I was afraid of the unknown.

Caveman ... January

"It's been too long since I've heard from Paul," I said to Sophie over the phone. Even though she lived across the alley we spent more time on the phone than in person.

"How long would that be?" she said.

"Oh, one day. He's in London attending the opening of his new musical. I didn't sleep well last night. I had a dream that disturbed me."

It was a cold night outside. I was freezing because I had kicked off the covers. I ate a bar of dark chocolate before I went to bed, and the caffeine made me toss and turn. After fighting with my bed and waking Joe from his deep sleep, I finally succumbed.

This married couple lay under a down comforter and a wool blanket. He was hot for her. He wanted sex. She didn't. It was too cold. But earlier they were so heated mad that they had to turn down the thermostat in the middle of their screaming—it began about money and ended about sex.

For her, the thought of shedding flannel pajamas was like dancing naked around a campfire at the North Pole. One side may get hot, but the back side would freeze. She wouldn't do it. He would do it any time.

His body was as hairy as a Neanderthal, and his primitive brain was programmed for copulation at all costs. This intense caveman and temperate princess were mismatched. But she had to appease him or he would be angry.

He felt like sandpaper against her body as he grunted and dripped large drops of sweat onto her face and breasts. He didn't bother to wipe the sweat that fell from his protruding forehead. She breathed in his putrid odor. If she smelled that way between her legs, he didn't care or notice. She was less diligent about her hygiene these days.

He grabbed her hand to stroke his penis. It was one of the few parts of his body that wasn't hairy. Then he tossed her on her belly.

"I love your ass," he growled.

She didn't care; at least his briny sweat wasn't dripping in her mouth any more.

"This is gross, Jamie," said Sophie interrupting my dream.

"I know…"

The ice princess stretched her head back, looking around the room as if she wasn't participating, and then turned her gaze to her right. She noticed the small can of unused mace on the top of her dresser. It was meant for an intruder who would take away their confidence in the neighborhood. Mace would destroy her marriage as fast as a bonfire would destroy his magazines.

That was an idea. The magazines … they should be incinerated. It was their fault he was grunting behind her.

"So, what do you think that dream was about?" I asked Sophie.

There was a very long silence. "I think it means you don't like having sex with hairy men or your husband," she said.

"Yeah." We said our "goodbyes" and I quickly hung up. There were things I just didn't want to analyze to any great extent.

Aunt Marina ... January

In late January, I visited my Aunt Marina to help her recover from a painful knee operation. Those are the worst. I would hate to be in her situation, recovering all alone, so I offered my help. She lived in a suburban town south of Los Angeles. After a few days of cooking, knee exercises and massages, I convinced Aunt Marina that an hour's drive north to have lunch with my Hollywood "friend" Paul would be a good diversion from her aching knee. I was ready to slowly let my family know about my relationship with my illicit man. I'm not sure why.

We picked Paul up and decided to go to his favorite Mexican restaurant in Santa Monica. I expected authentic, satisfying food, since the familiar smell of pork green chili greeted me at the front door.

The small cafe was filled with a long line of tables at which Paul's staff and colleagues were seated. They were celebrating a successful show. Upon his unexpected entrance, they stood and clapped and cheered. Paul responded as if this adulation hadn't happened before. He reciprocated with a shy smile and shrug. He took time to chat and joke with the young staff. Their faces relaxed as Paul acknowledged everyone. I was prouder of his humanity than his recent accomplishment.

Honestly, I didn't know all that goes into his career, even though his entertaining anecdotes gave me a sense of his more-than-pedestrian job.

He is "Mr. Hollywood," to my girlfriends back home. But the artists know him as Mr. Sutter. Their respect acknowledged their symbiotic relationship and gratitude for a gentle, inspired leader.

Paul wasn't put on this earth so much to be entertainment but to know it and make it thrive. Because of his parents, he grew up with famous artists, so he loved them but wasn't star-struck by them. Paul can't necessarily direct, act, write a script, perform stand-up comedy (though he's never afraid of telling a joke), play an instrument, dance, or sing on key. He really cannot sing on key. But he has an eye and ear for the exceptional artists and understands their idiosyncrasies and insecurities and can find ways to inspire their creativity. He encourages greatness and will smooth over any faux pas his coddled celebrities might commit.

He fixed a rough situation the afternoon before a live program. Trapeze artists high up in the theater threatened to walk out of the show right before its airing when a rapper called Small Change referred to the women acrobats as "bitches," which they overheard. Paul had to explain that the artist meant no disrespect and that it was Small Change's way of saying "beautiful young women." It was a hard sell and a narrow escape.

Paul has a skill for recruiting new best friends to contribute to projects, whether it's a television or Broadway show. And the friendships seem to last far beyond the project's life. All the while, he is disciplined about adhering to a show's budget. A few years ago, he thought Lady Gaga had enough talent to do without her entrance in an egg.

He complained it was an unnecessary expense. He lost that battle in favor of artistic expression.

He's not big on producers and other behind-the-scenes folks grabbing attention. "If they perform their role well, the result will speak for itself," he tells me. It was clear by the standing ovation in the restaurant that he had done his job well. That's my publicity for my producer friend, whether he likes it or not.

Back to the meeting with Aunt Marina. We sat down in a cozy booth separate from the partiers. The two alphas, Paul and Aunt Marina, faced each other. If they had met before in our young lives, no one remembered. I squirmed in my seat, put my arm on Paul's shoulder and watched my aunt's reaction. It was noisy at this restaurant, but it was painfully quiet at our table. Aunt Marina leaned over and picked three pieces of lint off my black shirt.

Paul pointed toward Aunt Marina as if he was ready to make an important statement. He opened his mouth and nothing came out. Aunt Marina looked straight at him, beyond his pointing finger. I helped myself to a chip with salsa. I looked over at Paul, whose eyes were wide open. I didn't join in the exchange. I was not included.

Aunt Marina is one of the matriarchs of the family, even though she is only nine years older than I am. For me, she plays the dual roles of loving sister and discerning aunt. "Your hair looks poufy," she said to open the conversation. I put my hands to my head. "You're making it worse. Maybe you should check it out in the lady's room," she said. Paul gently rubbed my back and gave me an encouraging nudge. I excused myself.

I noticed the carved wood calla lilies in ceramic pots that framed the back entrance. I thought I might escape.

The bathroom was a haven. I enjoyed the colorful artisan pieces decorating the peeling walls that probably hadn't been painted in thirty years. Even cognizant of California's drought, I let the warm water run as I washed my hands in the ceramic sink. It was easy to linger.

Neither Aunt Marina nor Paul looked up at me when I returned. They continued their conversation about the varied careers of Marina's grown children. Paul leaned against the hard back of the booth.

"You look worried," said Aunt Marina. "You're such a worrier. Paul, look at those two lines between her eyes. She should get Botox, don't you think?"

He ignored her critique. "I told your aunt that my intentions are genuine and that I love you," he said.

"Oh, God. Well good, I guess. I'm glad we got that over with. Shall we order now?" was my response.

Aunt Marina seemed satisfied, but somewhat disapproving. The news of my relationship would now spread throughout the family and I suppose I was ready for that.

"By the way Aunt Marina, I wanted to say, we don't do Botox in Colorado."   This was my dismal defense.

"Sure, honey," she replied with gentle sarcasm, seeming always to have the last word.

Common Grounds ... January

I SMELLED THE MYRIAD OF ROASTS AS PAUL AND I ENTERED the busy coffee shop full of happy chatter. This was Paul's favorite place to hide and think in Santa Monica. I was taking the morning off from taking care of Aunt Marina.

"I think she approves of us," I said to Paul. "It sounded tentative to me," he said.

"Well, as I drove her home, she got a little philosophical, 'You know Jamie, orchids live in many places but blossom in only a few,' she said." I took that horticultural observation as a thumbs up. Paul was glad to hear that, but ready to move on to more important discussions.

I loved his favorite place. It was homey and friendly, but it looked like business got done there. Paul wanted to show me the hangouts he knew I would enjoy, enticing me away from Colorado. It was difficult to think about leaving Denver. I was proud of my adopted city and its outdoor fun and down-home friendliness.

We found a small table in a corner where we could talk without being overheard. "What's the family doing today, Jamie?"

"I don't know, I haven't heard from the boys lately. Joe has stopped talking to me. We've got to do something, Paul. I told you he's read my emails." I blurted impatiently.

"I know... I know you are waiting for me. But I need you to let me do this my way and in my time. I'm committed to the gastric thing, the alcohol thing, and the Jamie thing. I wouldn't be talking to you during my every free moment. I wouldn't be telling half the world about you either.

"I know you love me. But he read our emails and maybe it's time he did. I'm not good at secrets."

"What happened after he saw them?"

"There was no explosion. It was underwhelming. He just confronted me and I said I was leaving him. (I didn't tell Paul the exact wording.) Joe almost seemed relieved. But with no full-time job, there's nowhere I can go, except to the basement. I'm really frustrated by our delays. And today, I only have a little time with you. Then I'm going to back to Laguna Beach to help Aunt Marina with her knee recovery."

"I adore you, Jamie, but what am I doing? I am taking away another man's wife."

"You aren't taking me away. If my marriage was satisfying, I wouldn't be involved with somebody else. There are no cheaters in a happy marriage." I looked at Paul then picked at my cuticles. "And furthermore, I'm taking another woman's husband." He nodded.

"What's your mom saying about all this?" He asked because he always cared about Lidi's opinion.

"You'll like this. 'We live too long. We should be able to shift husbands every 25 years,' she quipped."

Paul laughed. "We are good for each other, Jamie." He put his arm around me then rubbed the back of my head. This was the affection I missed in my marriage.

"Our methods have different time frames. But the outcome will be good. We'll work this out, Jamie, I promise." he said.

I knew that we hadn't had the test of time. I didn't want to wait to find out the things that might color our love. I knew my intuition about Paul was right. Don't experience and wisdom count for time?

But were there invisible forces that led me to what Sophie considers is "questionable judgment?" Shake it off, Jamie, and seize the moment, I told myself.

Before we get to the important business, can I show you something?" I asked.

"Sure," he could tell I was excited. Here's my first draft of my Everyday Compassion play. It's rough. I hoped that you would look at it." I put it in his outstretched hands. "It's hard to have someone look at my creation, but I know you will be gentle." Paul had a huge smile on his face.

"Your encouragement in September inspired me," I said.

"I would love to check it out and will be tender with your baby. He thumbed through it then tucked my manuscript in his brief case. "You should be proud of yourself, Jamie. Isn't being creative fun?" I agreed and was relieved that he was so enthusiastic. Since I reconnected with Paul, my imagination had been energized. I was writing a play and poems and even thinking about a music video.

Then Paul said in a more subdued tone, "Now I want to show you something." Paul lay a green notebook down on the table and asked me to look in it. I thumbed through drawings of the stomach at various stages of surgery and lists of healthy foods and supplements. It was a thick inch of technical information. I smelled the Sumatra roast being ground, hot chocolate, and fresh baked goods, too.

"This is more information than I can digest, Paul." He smiled at my pun.

"That's exactly what it's about, a new way to digest. Your opinion about the gastric bypass matters to me."

"I don't think I'm qualified to give an opinion, but I think it's all wrong."

"I'll be operated on by some of the best doctors in the country. These are the guys who do the fat celebrities. It's the last resort in weight loss."

"That's a lot to chew. I had to break up the seriousness of the conversation. "You don't need the last resort."

"My doctors want me to get this done as soon as possible. They're concerned about the burden of the weight on my heart. They say every day I stay so heavy I take chances with my health. I understand that, but I just have a few business matters to tie up. And there is a part of me that is terrified with getting this operation."

"Me too, Paul. I'm really scared. You could die. I've heard this procedure called medical malpractice. Will this solution work for the long run? And what are the side effects? Even if the guy on the early morning show turned out all right, he's still getting pudgy. What are the complications? Don't you risk getting blood clots? How many of these surgeries has your doctor done?"

"One question at a time, Jamie. And anyway, I don't have all the answers."

"You seem convinced it is the only way to get the dramatic weight reduction you want, even though you already have lost a lot on your own."

"I prefer to call this quest 'a weight drop,' because weight "loss" means finding it again. And I never want to go there again, never," he said.

"Well, I don't think you should do it. You should drop it the old-fashioned way, the safe way.

"I need your support. But there's no other way to get healthy. Nothing else works for me for very long. What I'm doing now is not fast enough."

"It's fast enough for me." I was getting hungry. I started to notice the buttermilk scones and apple turnovers on people's plates. "I'll eat chicken and veggies and protein smoothies alongside you forever. How's that?"

"I love you, Jamie, because I feel loved by you."

We changed the subject and left before we could order some delicious carbohydrate.

Love Makes a Long Life …
February 14

IT WAS A CHILLY MORNING WHEN I WALKED DOWN THE stairs to let Indigo outside. It was Valentine's Day.

Joe had long ago gone to work. He yelled at me the night before. He resented the implications of "VD" as he called it. "Maybe your *boyfriend* will give you a card, but don't expect anything from me."

"At this point, Joe, I don't expect, nor do I want anything from you," I told him after he had turned and walked out the door, slamming it behind him.

This living situation was humiliating. But I couldn't blame Joe for his disgust at my slowness in figuring out my future.

I hovered over my laptop on the dining room table, keeping some distance like it might bite me. I didn't want to be eager to check for emails for fear there would be nothing there. I took my time. I heated water and made myself a cup of tea. I held the cup with two hands and breathed in the soothing steam.

After a satisfying kibble breakfast, Indi stretched and curled on top of my feet while I sat in front of my computer. If she could read, I would have given her a Valentine. I pulled off my slippers and caressed her back with my toes. She turned over to expose her belly. It was mutual love. There were few conditions.

Joe did leave a card on the kitchen counter after all. It was one of the Scooby Doo punch-out cards from the kids' arts and crafts drawer that I had yet to clean out. It said, "I Ruff You! From Joe."

The card was a nice, last-ditch effort. In his briefcase, I left him a dark chocolate bar with almonds. Though repeatedly hurt by his insults, I felt some obligation toward the relationship. I reckoned I would always be in debt to him. He was a good father, and we had put in our time as a married couple with moments of family joy.

I plugged in the computer, then lifted the screen and pressed the buttons to bring up my emails. It was from Paul Sutter. The email title was "You Fill My Life with Love." The message said, "5:00 a.m. Hi, Jamie, I wanted you to receive this email first thing in the morning. I woke up thinking, 'I have a Valentine—someone to whom I want to send a gushy card and red roses.'

Before you, my reason for living was lost. Everyone, including Joanne, saw the results of 'a man who stopped caring'—my big belly bursting through my golf shirts. I don't know why I let myself go off the deep end. But today I feel blessed."

I read on. "Others may have known that I was hiding my vulnerability behind my fat, but you are the only person with the guts to be straight with me. Not that I asked for that, but I needed it. I was looking for you for a long time, Jamie. I wanted to feel the simple joy and acceptance that we had as kids or maybe the love we have now. I don't remember ever having a friend as close as we were. We understood each other, and we were only sixteen."

That was the end of the email, but not the end of his thoughts, I figured. So, I sipped my tea some more and waited. I heard nothing around me except my own breathing and the dog scratching herself. Near the sink, I saw that the sun had started to shed a golden glow on my orchid plant, which had not bloomed for a long time.

Paul sent another email: "Luckily, before you arrived in my life, I was becoming aware of my self-destruction. I couldn't stomach it any longer. (Bad joke for your sense of humor.) Many times, I tried losing weight."

"You have made a difference in my life. I will be forever grateful. Few women would love a fat man, but like you said, you see me as Paul. You remind me of what is good about me. I am grateful for you, Jamie."

"I created this ditty while taking a shower. I count my blessings that I have a woman like you in my life.
So, here's my Valentine poem for you:"

Love Makes a Long Life

Love makes a long life, Jamie, and that's what I'm aiming for with
*   you. Love makes my blood pressure low. It curbs my midnight*
appetite. Love keeps me asleep at night. It reminds me to breathe in
deep. Love makes me forget the bottle. Love makes dark days shine.

Love's not perfect and neither are we, but
Love with you will make a healthy long life with me,
I am yours, Paul.

Paul was right. Love keeps us healthy. But I wondered, "How can I tell him what I feel?" He dared to tell me. "Get brave, Jamie. You love this kind man. Don't waste time," I told myself.

I looked around my dining room feeling vulnerable and elated and trying to avoid the thesaurus.

Dear Paul,
Your early morning words embrace me. I can feel you close. Did you know I love Valentine's Day? I love to glue hearts on

doilies and send them to my boys with the hope they will enjoy the day.

So here is my Valentine for you.

My Heart

You are my heart
Better than the one I have in my chest.
You are the passionate heart that I forgot,
That I left in a place I don't remember.
You are my heart and my love … returned.

You have brought passion back to my life, passion for you and for living. I guess we have done that for each other.

And I ended there. The computer was silent. He didn't write back. I figured he took a morning nap. I wrote another email.

Your love has given me the courage to be myself. I will be there for you.
Your Jamie

Sorry for the pause, Jamie. I fell asleep. Before I start the rest of my day, I want to say … I know all about *your heart* Jamie. And that's why I love you—madly.

Happy Valentines Day, my extraordinary woman.
Paul

New York City … February

As I opened the door to room 1201 at the Leonardo in the theater district of Manhattan, I was amazed by a golden suite that sparkled and dazzled me. I was a traveler of two-star motels. A silver bucket overflowed with miniature champagne bottles. Under the bucket was a linen with edges of pink embroidered roses. Nothing in this room was made in China, not even the bath mat.

I turned to Paul, my eyes wide, as I put my hands together over my nose and mouth like I had just won the lottery. I tiptoed around the room to inspect it not wanting to leave prints on the plush vanilla carpet. There was so much to look at in a first-class room. Paul laughed.

"Come on, Jamie, you've been to places like this in your travels," Paul said.

"Not like *this* Paul. Never," I said.

"Can we set our stuff down? It's been a long day. We've taken a train ride and seen a Broadway show all in one day. Not to mention a great dinner. I'm tired, how 'bout you?" Paul said, as he scratched himself and yawned.

I kicked off my cowboy boots and took off my socks to curl my toes in the ultra-thick, soft carpet. "I was going to say thank you for the great day. But I think 'thank you' is an understatement. I want to be careful that you understand that this isn't what our love is about."

Paul took my hand and brought me to the white couch in the sitting room. He sat me on his lap and held me as he lightly scratched my back. I would have purred if I could. I tingled from my toes to the top of my head as I felt Paul's small but meaningful gesture. It counted, and it added up. The down-filled couch was big enough for the two of us to stretch out and lay our heads at opposite ends.

"Paul, give me your feet. I know it's been a long day. I'm going to give you a foot massage to make you drool," I said.

"You can't touch my feet, Jamie, they're too calloused."

"Yes, I can touch them. Give me the right one and let me show you my stuff. I love you, Paul, and I loved this day. Thank you." He reluctantly put his feet in my lap and let me knead the tension out of them. We were still operating in secret from our spouses, and that knowledge hovered over our fun now and then. I was on a "trip to see my best girlfriend Gracie," and Paul was "working."

"Look at me, Jamie, please. You don't have to tell me thank you again on this trip. I'm needy, but this isn't what I need. I need you to share your bawdy sense of humor with me. I need you to text me that you are thinking of me. I need you to wear sexy black dresses that show your beautiful legs when I take you out to nice places. I hope to do this often without threatening this health kick I'm on. I need you to hassle me about my bad habits. I just want to feel loved. That's easy, right?"

"Right, Paul." I put my arms around his neck and kissed him. I got up and then started to help Paul get up. But I realized I couldn't do that. He had to do it on his own, but with some difficulty. I hated to see him struggle as he tried to lift himself off the couch, but such struggles weren't for long.

"I know, Jamie, and we both know I'll be in a good place soon." He grunted as he repeatedly tried and finally succeeded in standing up.

"Yes, I love you, Paul, more than a pig loves slop."

He laughed and returned, "I love you like a pig loves slop, or something." I laughed too, and hugged his diameter with my long arms.

The separate king-size bedroom looked out on the lights of the cityscape. It didn't seem so long ago that New York was under siege, smoke and ash carpeting the streets for 100 blocks or more. Now the city sparkled from a gentle snow.

I turned around. I stared and then I pet the velvet pillows and slid my fingers across the gold satin bedspread. I immediately threw the bed décor to the side to caress the sheets.

"These are 600-count, at least," I said, as I brushed my fingertips back and forth on the silky fabric. Paul watched me while he scratched his belly. "Come on Jamie, let's go to bed."

I threw my clothes every which way while Paul placed his neatly on a chair. We crawled into bed and held each other. I wondered if any of this could be sustained: love, secrets, and mutual admiration.

Paul fell asleep first, until I shook him. "You're snoring like a freight train," I said.

Oh, no, I thought, he has sleep apnea. How could he not? It's a common problem of big men. I knew about it. I'd been diagnosed with it five years ago. (Skinny people can have sleep apnea, too.) I'd been using a CPAP—a machine that pushes air to open your blocked airway—ever since. You wake up refreshed instead of exhausted from haphazard sleep. Even with all its benefits, I'd been reluctant to pack this sexless sleep aid in my luggage. I wasn't sure how a nose hose would be received.

We both needed a good night's sleep. The only solution I could think of was to share the CPAP. Paul let me strap a rubber mask over his head and fit it on his nose. He looked at me as though he had been humiliated with this unbecoming elephant trunk. I tried not to laugh. The tiny mask on his big head was hilarious. But it worked for now. He stopped snoring. "Paul, we'll deal with this in the morning," I assured him.

"Huh?" he replied. "That sounds good, Jamie." He didn't mention how the television (his night-time mistress) was turned off and I didn't mention how I hated the curtains closed. We had several decades of sleeping habits to sort out if we were going to make a go of this.

In his sleep, Paul pulled off the mask and settled into the bear-like snore. I put a pillow over my head and was ready to put it on his face to end the love affair right then. Not really. "I love you, Paul," I whispered.

"I love you, Jamie," he said as he interrupted his struggling slumber. "Good night, and we'll work this out," he said. I believed him. I smiled, folded the down pillow to cover my ears and pushed my bottom up against his back. After a few deep breaths, I fell asleep.

My Face Began to Itch … February

I HAD DREAMED ABOUT IT. BUT THE IMAGINARY REHEARSAL was futile. This New York party that Paul and I attended was to honor one of his colleagues. It had all the accoutrements of a celebrity festivity. We stood together for a photo before a backdrop with the sponsors' names written all over it. I tried to pose at an angle so my nose looked aquiline instead of a little bulbous. My cheeks blushed a subtle mauve, my lips shone, my neck was as smooth as a Rodin sculpture, I hoped, and the bags under my eyes were somehow hidden by good makeup. The lighting was perfect for a vain woman. I thanked Lidi for a confident natural smile due to years of braces. And I fantasized I was the "Who is she?" that night.

No, this wasn't a dream. I'm sure Paul's acquaintances wanted to know who I was and what I was doing with this big shot Hollywood guy. We held hands and stayed close. We were having fun watching people and flirting with each other. I felt smug—like I had foiled the glitterati. New York was the venue to dress up, and to feel beautiful and important.

I felt so very good in the dress I'd bought at a high-end consignment shop in Santa Monica. The staff recounted that Stevie Nicks came in one day wanting to donate all her old dresses that didn't fit her any more. I'm not sure I believed the story, but I was a sexy, witchy woman in this form-fitting, off-the-shoulder black dress that had flowing sleeves and a flowing skirt.

We were seated at the second row of tables in the center. Two beautiful middle-aged women joined us with their dates. I should have known it wouldn't be old friends from high school or current ones from Paul's neighborhood. He didn't really warn me because it was normal for him. It was an everyday thing for Paul to chat with Stevie Nicks and Bonnie Raitt. It was like a reunion. They greeted Paul with enthusiastic hugs.

Please, please don't introduce me to these people! I felt horribly shy and inept. My face began to itch.

"Hey Jamie, I want to introduce you to my friends," I heard Paul say, as I ran to the bathroom, the back of my dress flowing behind me. Somehow, I managed to run across slippery floors in my four-inch heels that were kept on only by thin straps around my ruby red toenails.

When I got to the restroom, I noticed that my arms had started to itch. I figured it must have been something about the nylon in the dress. I usually wore natural fibers. Even tags on the back of clothes bothered me.

I paced back and forth in front of the bathroom stalls, looking in the mirror to adjust my hair, not aware that my breathing was shallow and fast and that I was depriving my extremities of oxygen.

"I can't talk to these people," I said, as I sat on the toilet. "I'm going to text Paul."

"Excuse me, is that you, Jamie?"

"Uh …Yes, to whom am I speaking?" I replied, polite and unsure.

"This is Bonnie, Paul asked me to retrieve you," she said in a genuinely kind and very recognizable voice.

"Shit!! I mean, so nice to meet you." I was still on the toilet.

"That's so considerate of you. Would you please tell him I'll be right out?"

"No problem," she said, "And so nice to meet you, Jamie."

"It's such a pleasure, Bonnie. I'm a big fan," I added.

"Uh … well … I don't see a big fan switch."

"No, I'm a big fan of yours," I said, now doubly embarrassed with the assumption that she must have made.

"Oh, I appreciate that," she graciously replied. "Well, I hope to see you soon." And she left. We still had become acquainted only with one another's shoes.

"It was sweet of you to send Bonnie in after me. She's a nice person. But what the hell am I going to say to these people?" I texted Paul.

"Calm down, Jamie. They're looking forward to meeting the woman I love. You look gorgeous, by the way," he texted back.

"I keep thinking about the lyrics of a crude punk rock song from my college days where the singers blurted out, 'Sit on My Face Stevie Nicks!' It keeps going through my head. I'm sure she didn't like that tribute," I texted.

"LOL" he responded.

Sitting on the toilet, I regressed to an unsophisticated mom and wife from somewhere in the very middle of the country where the closest I come to celebrities is People magazine at the checkout stand.

"You're going to have to get used to this. First breathe and then get your cute tush out here," he texted.

Of course, we had a great time, with me drinking a little bit too much. I may have laughed a little too much, too. One could understand that, I hope. Paul did. He didn't drink this night because he was trying his best to taper off. He stuck with soda water and lime. He kept his left arm around my left bare shoulder much of the night, while he ate with his right hand. In this position, it was difficult to lift my fork, but it didn't matter, since I had lost my appetite.

At one point, Ms. Nicks winked and subtly pointed up and down at my dress. She mouthed, "That looks good on you." I acknowledged with a nervous nod and smile. Did she know? She must have.

I squeezed Paul's left hand. I was in seventh edgy heaven.

Barbra Streisand … February

THE NEXT DAY OF OUR NEW YORK TRIP, WE TOOK A TAXI TO A
Brooklyn high school. "This is one of my favorite things to do,"
Paul said. "You're going to enjoy this Jamie."

Paul gave an animated and self-effacing talk about the life of
a producer. I was proud to see him doing his shtick: telling jokes,
calling on the kids for questions, and appreciating their interest
in his work. He told humbling anecdotes about his interactions
with famous people. He gave credit to all his young staff who
were crucial support for producing shows. He made it sound
like anyone could do what he did if they wanted to. He told
his young audience that if they were "ever in the neighborhood
and interested in being producers, to get in contact." He had no
props (but his lively hand gestures) and no slide show.

After the speech, one of the students ran up to him and
asked if he knew Barbra Streisand. I was in the front row of the
school auditorium, so I could hear the conversation. Paul said he
had met her a few times. "I love Barbra Streisand!" the student
gushed. He wanted to know about the performer's personality
and whether she was happily married, of all things. He grilled
Paul for gossip about other famous "old school" singers, as he
called them.

As we drove from Brooklyn to the airport, Paul had time to
reflect on his time with the student. "That kid was so enthusiastic.

When I get home, I'm going to call the principal of the school to find out if she can tell me more about the young man," he said.

Later, Paul told me that the child was well-known and loved in the school. He was the first African American president in a mostly white school. He's one of the best voices in the school choir and a talented thespian, too.

In that same phone conversation, Paul said, "I know this is selfish, but I felt that in doing good I would feel good. I offered to bring the young man and his mother to Los Angeles and pay for their hotel and their tickets to Barbra's concert next month. I phoned his mom to invite them. At first there was silence. And when I said, 'Well??' they both screamed 'Yes!' into the phone. Jamie, this is the best thing I've done all year."

Paul was so excited about the response, like it was he who had been offered the experience of a lifetime. He said that the student's neighborhood is making a big deal of it. There was an article in the local paper. The mom, who's a single parent, is getting a free hair styling, and people are contributing to purchase a gown for her and a tuxedo for the young man.

"It's hard to contain myself, but my family can't know," Paul confessed. "Joanne doesn't like me spending what she calls 'frivolously,' especially on other people."

"I love the way you spend frivolously, Paul. But why are you so afraid of that woman?" I pressed.

I was proud and thrilled for him and annoyed that he couldn't stand up to his wife.

He didn't have an answer, or chose not to answer. I noticed that was what he did when I pushed about uncomfortable topics like his marital situation. I was ready for him to tell her about us. I was anxious for us to be a legitimate couple, and not fugitives of marital law.

"But there's more to the story," Paul said. "Joanne oversees our finances and got suspicious when she found some bills for round-trip tickets between New York and Los Angeles."

She also questioned his trips to Denver. She usually didn't pay attention to his travel or care much about it, for that matter. But these charges piqued her interest.

"Tell her, Paul, tell her about me. I'm losing my patience, and I'm tired of living in limbo."

"I'm sorry, Jamie. I concocted stories that she accepted with some skepticism. I love you and understand your eagerness, but I'm not ready to tell her about us. There're a lot of things to consider, like my children and my finances."

I wanted to end abruptly what started out as a happy conversation. "I have to go, Paul." There was a pit in my stomach when I began to wonder if he would ever be ready to tell his wife. I wanted to trust him. And I was desperate to believe that everything was going to work out, but that pit just didn't go away.

My Closet ... March

"IT'S TIME TO CELEBRATE WINTER ALMOST BEING OVER WITH a hearty dinner and wine," I said as I texted Sophie. Being of Italian descent, I knew she would appreciate my pasta putanesca with heirloom tomatoes, capers, green olives, and red pepper flakes.

Sophie embraced her heritage—large family parties almost every weekend, good wine and a loyalty to friends and loved ones. Her choices had disappointed her and so had her parents. But life was like that, and somehow, we couldn't let dysfunctional families bring us down.

"Hey Soph, I've been doing all the talking these days, and I want to hear about you," I said.

"I've been thinking about my mom." She turned the stem of her wine glass. "It's hard to have her living so far away, since I'm the one who takes care of her. I wish I could get her out of her funk." Sophie's mom had suffered depression for much of her life. Her dad worked hard and loved his cigars. Like many people during those times, he didn't know how to deal with his wife's lack of interest in life and indecisiveness. He just went about his way and died early from lung cancer.

"I take charge," Sophie continued, "and I make decisions before I finish my first cup of coffee. But my choices haven't always been the best. You know me, always looking for a solution or, at least, action. I'm attracted to men whose personalities are the opposite of mine, which isn't going well. Those introverts are nice, but I have to initiate everything."

We sat at our worn dining room table. Joe and I were attached to our scruffy relic. There were divots where Jason banged the end of his baby spoon against the table and Justin followed along.

"This is delicious and spicy," said Sophie. "Just like I like it. You always say you can't cook and look, you made this."

"How about we sit by the fireplace and have some more wine," I said, trying to reverse the mood of the moment. Joe had gone to a friend's house to watch football, so we had some girlfriend time.

"Now you have to tell me about your trip back East. How did you manage to pull that off and leave your Joe behind?"

"He's not much 'my Joe' these days. I got to see my old friend Gracie J. And this was an opportunity to see Paul in his element. I wonder if Joe notices I'm home or not." I took a sip of my wine. "If you come up to my closet, I'll tell you the rest of the story by way of my haute couture."

"Jamie, are you sure you want to go down this path?"

"No, but I do want to go upstairs. What I'm most proud of is that I outfitted myself with just about all secondhand stuff. Can I show you? I want to brag about my brief rich and famous lifestyle. I hate keeping all this to myself," I said, hoping Sophie would play along.

"I'm not big on your sordid life, Jamie, but I'm curious." She groaned and lifted herself from her curled-up comfort, at the same time trying not to spill her cabernet.

"Sophie, indulge me. I need someone to show and tell to." She grudgingly agreed.

"First, that little black dress you lent me? I felt so good in it. I transformed into a sophisticated woman when I wore it.

"I know, girl. That's why I am giving you that dress. It's time for you to get stylish. But you can't make your life such a mystery."

"We all have our mysteries; even if it's the bizarre things we search for on the internet. I just saw two provocative "celebits" today. One was before-and-after- photos of starlets who 'didn't age well.'"

"Could you stay on topic here? You go all over the place, and I have trouble following."

"Sophie, you're fussy tonight, drink your wine. So, when I looked at the internet pictures, I didn't see 'bad aging,' whatever the hell that is. I saw the needless use of plastic surgery on young bodies. It made me wince, Sophie. Can't we women just get along with our own selves?"

"Go on, Jamie, please go on, and try to keep with the point. How did you get through college with that maze-like mind of yours?"

"I call it creative, and so does Paul. You can imagine what Joe calls it."

"I don't blame him, Jamie."

I was so excited about my February trip with Paul that it put my mind in a constant state of brainstorming. But I could focus. I showed Sophie my closet, with clothes recently sorted per colors and seasons, and tasks like work and play. I reminded her that much of it was secondhand. But the girls, Sophie … bless their damaged hearts. Who told these women that they needed melon-size breasts to match plum-size cheeks and inflated lips that look like a cartoon character? Really, I wonder what they did to their crotches."

"That's enough."

"It *is* enough Sophie. I feel for these women, because I'm not sure that they feel so good about themselves. They're raising the bar too high, and us poor mid-country girls can't keep up.

"None of us ages perfectly. For most of us, it's our self-love that needs the lift, not our breasts. Still, maybe I wouldn't mind getting rid of these drooping eyelids.

Trying to get back to the clothes, I said, "I want to wear that little black dress again," I pointed to it on a hook on the back of my closet door. "It shows off my legs and hides my stubborn belly fat in a masterful drape."

"You don't have any belly fat."

"Enough to annoy me. You know most of us women, especially after children, have some. But we're bombarded with tacky pop-ups of women grabbing their belly chub. It seems like every issue of popular health magazines includes articles about secrets to lose stubborn belly fat, complete with photos of blondes who are too young to have it."

"It's not that simple, Jamie. I know," said Sophie as she looked down at her well-toned body with its slightly bulging waist. "I don't want to talk about fat. I've been working on mine for months. I'm discouraged. Cutting down on wine at night will get rid of this," she said and grabbed her barely excess tummy. "Right now, I'm not in the mood to let go of it—the wine that is."

"I get it, Soph. I'm not the only one with life complications."

"Check out these fishnet stockings. I need to wear them to neutralize white legs. That playful addition was the icing for a glamorous evening with Paul at Al Pacino's favorite café—the Lime Twist. I proceeded to describe the evening.

We left the limousine waiting out front on 71st Street with the other shiny black pumpkins. I wondered how many Cinderellas were inside this upscale bistro trying to score their perfect Match.com sweetie? I was a well-seasoned one in my sophisticated second-hand attire. I hoped that the evening wouldn't end too soon, and that I wouldn't lose my man to early slumber from a long day's travel.

When I walked in the door with Paul, heads turned. I did my best to exude sophisticated calm that was spiced with an inner laugh all evening. Paul was somebody, a respected behind-the-scenes somebody. He didn't need gratuitous attention. Well, not much. I was Nobody with a capital N-O, wearing a short sexy dress. I was Paul's high school friend from many years ago, but still showing off my long legs. I could get away with this at least while wearing the fishnets that I last wore at a Halloween party.

I was enough of a 'somebody' for Paul and me. He made me feel better than famous. His eyes twinkled. He was pleasantly amused with my outfit. While we waited to be seated, Paul said in a stutter that happened sometimes with a tender comment, "You, you, have grown into such a beautiful woman." I squeezed his hand and lay my head on his heart.

"Thanks Paul, you know how to make a tomgirl feel good." I was cognizant of the slit in the back of my dress. I asked Paul to remind me not to bend over, even though I had stockings on. "Hopefully, they will camouflage my barely-there undies," I told him.

"Sheesh!" He rubbed up and down on my backside to feel for panties then pulled me close. "What do you mean cute black nothing, I want to see. Oh … it's a thong … you nasty thing," he said. Nothing passed this perceptive man unless he let it.

"Look Sophie, see this lonely pair of thin-strap heals?" I pointed. "They are there between the hiking boots and the comfort pumps. I put those designer shoes on in a consignment store and said, 'These babies are going on a ride to New York.' You see the complete outfit, Soph—not overdone and just right for a dinner with the rich and famous." I continued the story.

We sat at a small table with Paul's two friends. We seemed in the middle of the waiters' traffic pattern. Nothing stopped the laughing and loud voices from bouncing from one end of the café to the other. I strained to keep up with the conversation and responded as if I knew where the dialogue was going. My hearing is compromised from those arena rock and roll concerts.

Behind our table, male servers in lime green jackets and black bow ties swarmed, waiting to pounce. "What can I get you to drink?" one asked. Paul answered, "We'll have Chandon please." When was the last time I had Chandon? Never. Behind the servers we could hear the clanking of pots and yelled orders to sous-chefs.

"Paul, there's nothing intimate or secluded about our table," I observed.

"Jamie, it's the opposite. This is the table where you sit to see and be seen."

"I don't see anybody, Paul," I said in a low voice.

"Here we are, Jamie."

Paul's friends were stimulating: a man who was CEO of a giant mutual fund and a woman who owned a premier acting school. I wondered if she could see that I was acting like I was comfortable?

I whispered to Paul, "Please don't let me embarrass you, and bump me if I start to spice the conversation with expletives."

"Jamie, you're fine. Be yourself. I love who you are, and, by the way, you look dazzling," Paul said as he combed his fingers through my just-washed hair and looked me in the eyes.

"What were we saying?" Paul asked his friends as he rubbed my back. His friends noticed and smiled in encouragement at our public display of affection. From bits and pieces of conversation, I sensed our dinner guests were happy for Paul's new happiness because they had known him to be successful but sad and lonely for so long.

"It's so good to see two people in love at this point in our lives. You have so much affection for each other," said Mr. CEO.

"I'm fortunate that Paul found me. We were great friends when we were kids."

"I wanted to be more than a friend, Jamie," interrupted Paul.

"Yes, I know, Paul. I was shy, but you made such a big difference in my life. I was damaged, and you made me feel whole. And that's something I never forgot all these years. And you know what Paul? Not to embarrass you in front of your friends, but you still have the kind soul you had then. You really haven't changed much."

"You either, Jamie."

"Enough of the mutual admiration." I was apologetic to his friends. "I guess you are party to our public display of gratefulness. It's a romantic evening being here and in the most amazing city in the world with two people I know Paul is very fond of. With that, will you excuse me?"

I have a habit of using the lady's room in every restaurant I've ever been in. The toilets were unusual yellow-green porcelain. A chandelier sparkled with crystals in the shape of leaves, and swirling green stone surrounded the sinks. On the wall hung a Seurat-style painting of John Lennon and Yoko Ono standing next to his memorial in Central Park. The bathroom was worth the visit.

There was no escaping. Paul's friends were protective of his gentle spirit. After I returned from the green restroom, they scrutinized me for his benefit and seemed cautious but optimistic. When I first met Mrs. Dorman, the acting school owner, she said, "Oh, you have laugh lines. Those lines around your eyes are good. They show that you love to smile and laugh and that you are genuine."

"That, I am, Mrs. Dorman," I replied.

At the dinner table, Mrs. Dorman concluded that I was good for her Paul. "Not anyone would be right for him. He deserves a woman's kindness, affection, and loyalty. He's the most gentle and sensitive person I've ever met in this business. In my line of work, I've known a lot of people, and not a whole lot are down to earth. Paul's one of my favorite people, so you can understand how I must protect him," she said.

As we were leaving, she took another look at me and grabbed my shoulder to twirl me around as if I was auditioning for a coveted part in a movie. Damn. I wondered how perceptive she was. Was she going to see my crumpled professional failure? Some of those lines were crying ones. I was once the rising star. I published the papers, traveled, and consulted with politicians, then I let it all abruptly end. That wasn't supposed to happen. I was to be an independent, successful woman. I couldn't do it. I wouldn't do it. At the time, my mental condition, coupled with my strong mother instincts, wouldn't have me do it.

Almost finished with my New York reminiscing, I continued my closet tour with Sophie. "Hanging on the door hook is a black cowboy shirt with bright red and blue embroidered flowers. See the tag? It's a Rockmount from one of the best cowboy fashion stores in the West. I got this one from a friend who got tired of it, and I wore it to a Broadway show.

We went backstage to meet the actors. They loved my shirt and were deferential because of my date. 'What do you play?' asked one of the actors because I was admiring his musical talent. Oh, God, what a question. I didn't play a damn thing, not even solitaire. But Paul chimed in, 'She's a rap artist. She gets down with her mama rap self.'"

'Very good, said the esteemed actor. 'I would like to hear some.'

'Maybe sometime.' I grabbed Paul's hand, 'So nice to meet you. You must be very busy getting ready,' and pulled Paul along before he suggested I perform one of my profane songs."
Sophie enjoyed my closet journey and now was satisfied that she'd caught up with my life. She yawned, and then I could hear Joe unlock the back door.

"I'll be going and leaving you to your husband," Sophie said as she reminded me of my reality.

That night, I rolled out of my bed and put this little rhyme to paper, so I could get it out of my head.

The No More Belly Fat Rap

Spare your wheat; for a treat.
Move your ass, move your feet.
A tiny glucose is OK, but skip the O.J. every day.
Eat more fiber: your colon will know.
Have no fructose. It can blow.
Eat your veggies, dairy, fruit.
Feel your best. You'll look cute.
Don't disregard essential protein. Build that muscle. Make your
butt lean.
That's enough, don't you think?
Oh yeah, go light on liquor drinks.

Uh huh.

Dear Abby … March

THE BIGGEST PART OF MY RELATIONSHIP WITH PAUL TOOK place on the phone during late-night walks with Indigo. Indi and I needed outside time after she spent the day barking at passing hounds and leaflet carriers while I scored hundreds of kids' proficiency tests.

It got more difficult to keep the spouses out of the equation. We had to be up front sometime. And my husband was already aware and angry.

Our next step weighed on our thinking and our sense of duty, though duty may be hard to believe. A fair share of fear made me hesitate—fear to leave after twenty plus years of a secure situation. At least our marriages were predictable. It's what we knew, even if we didn't like it.

"You know my wife lost her affection for me a long time ago," Paul said by phone while I was walking Indi.

"I know you're unhappy and that you blame your weight in part on her."

"God, I love you, Jamie, but can I finish? You wouldn't believe how the wife and I got into it."

"Are you calling me from your hands-free phone?" I asked, because I figured he was driving. I didn't acknowledge the wife conflict. Really, I was trying to avoid it. But I was concerned about him driving and talking while he was upset. He assured me he was safe.

"Where are you?" Paul asked.

"I'm walking Indigo."

"Give her a pat for me. Hi, Indigo!"

Indigo's ears perked up. She looked around and barked once.

"Do I really want to hear this?" I said.

"I'm not sure. It's not my best moment. But I just want to show you how bad it is in my house." He seemed eager to tell me what was wrong with his life and his wife. I'd just as soon not hear about his confrontations with her. I tried to keep our conversations on the positive side. I wanted to move forward, not regurgitate the past. And I preferred not to be exposed to Paul's shortcomings. But I didn't blame him. I wanted to justify my angst, too.

Paul seemed embarrassed about this moment, but needed to talk out his conflict. "I need empathy. There's no one else to talk to. And you're my friend," he said.

I was his adoring friend, but not his Dear Abby, I thought.

Paul said, "Well, this morning's conversation was tense: 'Can we stop this ugliness?' I asked Joanne at the breakfast table after we shared a pot of coffee. We only eat breakfast together maybe once every four months. Before long, Joanne stood up, her eyes squinting and her lips squeezed together. It was a sunny day outside. Inside, a storm was brewing. She picked up a marking pen and doodled a frosty the snowman with a sad face on the refrigerator pad."

I interrupted Paul's account, "I'm not prepared to hear this," I was wincing on my end of the phone.

Paul continued. He was determined to tell all. He told me how Joanne said he was "the ugly one" last night. That he scared her because he had never talked to her "that way" before.

He didn't spare the details. He told me Joanne turned and gathered her hair to tie up into a bun on the top of her head. Then she faced Paul with her arms holding her body tight.

"I'm sorry, and I want us to stop being mean to each other," Paul told her.

Joanne spewed forth: "Why suddenly do you care?   I'm done having sex with you. Do you really expect me to find you desirable? Look what a sight you are." She glared at him.

I continued to listen to Paul as I let Indigo romp off-leash. It was a difficult juxtaposition: happy dog, sad boyfriend.

"Tears dropped from my cheeks. I'm always the first one to cry in the family," Paul said. "I miss having a wife," I told her.

"Oh, shit," I whispered to Indi.

"You have one, Paul, and she's right here," Joanne replied. She was not happy with the direction of the conversation.

Neither was I happy with the direction of his account to me. "Do I really need to hear all this?" I interrupted again. This was going to be a long walk with Indi.

He wanted me to be party to his thinking because it was his last effort to see if anything good was left in his marriage. He felt he owed that to his family. And he wanted to be honest with me. I guess I appreciated his honesty, but it was hard to listen to him. It was disturbing to hear an intimate clash between Paul and his wife. It was difficult enough to be involved with the war of words with Joe.

Paul didn't answer my question and kept talking about how Joanne came back unsympathetic. She told him that he "disgusted" her and to "stop the whining."

"Can't you stop being so calloused?" Paul said to her.

"I'm not calloused. Everybody loves me, except you," Joanne replied. "I won't talk to you about this."

Then he said that the family dachshunds, Andy and Chuck, slinked into the kitchen as if they were hoping that the atmosphere had returned to their favor. "Come here, puppies!" Joanne's voice increased two octaves to greet the pets. "Mommy and Daddy are finished arguing," Joanne said. Andy and Chuckie rubbed their rears against everyone's legs waiting for a doggie massage." Paul reached down to scratch their heads.

Paul's love for animals made me wonder where our dogs would go when the families split up. Maybe it was too soon to worry about that.

"The discussion really didn't get better, so I eventually grabbed the keys off the kitchen counter and revved up the Lexis. I love that svelte sedan, Jamie, almost as much as I love you: like you, she's beautiful and she's got a hot engine."

"Thanks for the comparison." Though sarcastic, I was happy for him to interject his love for me in this sad account.

"Something made me head north on the Pacific Coast Highway past the coffee shop where I meet my neighborhood guys," Paul continued. "I can't believe I didn't stop by. Mornings with the Batter Ups are fun. Our surface conversations are our man therapy—few questions, just acceptance. But today, I wasn't ready to talk, even at a superficial level.

"My wife dislikes so many things about me. But I'm a good provider. I'm proud of that. I meet the financial needs of the family, keep the vacation homes available, and have an address near the ocean."

"The beach has good memories," said Paul. "And my beach memories of you have lasted my whole life, Jamie."

I'm glad he's still thinking about me, I thought.

Still, it didn't matter that people laughed at Paul's jokes, loved that he was easygoing, warm-hearted and gentle, and that they wanted to work with him. It didn't even matter that his kids adored their father. And for him, it didn't matter that Joanne was loved by all who worked with her in the industry. She aggravated him. He disgusted her. It was bad chemistry.

Paul wanted to tell me the rest of what happened. Was it going to get worse, I wondered?

He said that Joanne hated when he tried to enter her bedroom when her door was locked. She said, "Couldn't you see that I wanted privacy? Work is getting me down. I hate fucking Hollywood and its fake tits. "But it loves you," Paul tried to make peace.

He told me much more than I wanted to hear: "She keeps her closet and bathroom locked. She doesn't want to think about my hands on anything of hers. She doesn't want me to touch her. Over the last couple of years, she would cringe when I would give her a New Year's hug. I don't get it, Jamie."

Paul admitted he would try to open the door to her bedroom when he was drunk. He resented being locked out of her life. Last night, when she wouldn't open the door to talk, he said he got mad. He confessed that Joanne was always afraid that she couldn't stop him from knocking the door down if he pushed against it, which he said he never did. "At worst I would cuss," he said. While this separate bedroom situation caused a lot of tension in the household, Joanne wasn't going anywhere.

"I'm really more afraid of her than she is of me," admitted Paul. "And she knows it."

"I don't know why she locks you out. But it sounds like she's annoyed with your antics," was my unsolicited observation.

He continued the story. "I came home a little drunk from the Gifted Guys."

"I don't like that," I couldn't help but say as he continued his sordid story.

"I know, I know, Jamie… Just listen … Please? I feel utter shame. I'm confessing my sin."

"'Bitch, let's have some sex,' she said I slurred. I swear I don't remember ever saying that, Jamie. And if I had had sex with my wife I would have been thinking about you."

"That's real nice, Paul." He couldn't resist kidding even when things were serious.

"I know I banged at the door for Joanne to let me in. I wanted to talk things out. I shouldn't have done that."

"Yeah, that's not foreplay, Paul. That wouldn't work for me."

"Hush, Jamie."

"She countered something like, 'Are you kidding? No way are you coming in! You're repulsive. You should be embarrassed with yourself. Get away from my door and don't come back … ever!' It was a chilling voice."

He wondered how his family had come to this. He told me that the festive wedding photo on top of the fireplace mantel was a sham. But that was twenty-five years ago. Now, he said that Joanne feared that the worse parts of Hollywood were rubbing off on their girls. Private school and tutors had not insulated them, but instead had spoiled them. One of his twins wanted a boob job, and the other one couldn't wait to get her nose fixed. "It's ridiculous," he said, "I hate thinking about my little girl cutting off the Sutter's nose," said Paul.

Apparently, the girls were eating cereal for dinner in the television room. They could hear through the walls. Morgan yelled, "Stop it, you idiots!" at the top of her voice. Hunter yelled at Paul, "Dad, take your vodka bottle and go to bed. Quit bothering Mom."

"They were furious with me, but they thought their Mom could be a control freak and a nag. Their mom insults me in front of people at dinner parties—the few that she would attend with me. The kids can't stand being around us when we're both home."

So that was it. Paul wasn't proud of what he did. "I need to get out of there," he concluded. "I know I have made some bad mistakes, and it was shameful for my kids to hear. The whole situation is unhealthy. I was anesthetizing myself through the bottle. A psychologist would be better, but it doesn't seem to be enough and I don't trust those guys. I've had enough."

I wish he had enough of the bottle. But he said he was working on it.

Remembering the Amusement Park
... March

It was another night sitting on Sophie's kitchen stools drinking red wine and catching up. Now and then, we stretched our legs.

"Have you heard from your daughter?" I asked Sophie as I looked around the room at photos of mother and child during happier times.

"No, but I follow her on Facebook. And I see her flying around Colorado Boulevard in her Dad's cherry red truck. It looks like it's become hers." Sophie said.

"So, she's safe, more or less."

"Is a teen ever safe? I think I'll exhale when she hits 25 and is less impulsive, hopefully. For now, it's better that I don't know what she's doing. She wanted her Dad. He can handle her. I don't talk to him; email is easier," said Sophie.

"Watch out for the ambiguities of email," I warned her.

"Oh, we're way past ambiguous and into confrontational. What's up with Paul?" she asked to veer from what hurt. I was always happy to talk about Paul.

I told her that we spoke more often the closer he was to having the gastric bypass. "I'm not so sure about this operation, but that's what he wants, and a speedy weight loss is appealing." Sophie and I put the wine glasses to our lips at the same time.

"We'll have more fun, and his aching knees should feel better when he's carrying less weight. The extra pounds have burdened his joints. The bad knees are from college baseball days coming back to haunt a huge middle-aged man. His doctor wants him to use a cane, and he refuses.

Paul said his wife is apathetic about his operation. He told me the wife doesn't want to have anything to do with it. "Hire a health aide," she said. She said she was too busy, and it would be too gross.

I didn't blame her, I told him. I was irritated. He wanted her to want to help, but he didn't really want her help.

"Let her be. After you get the gastric bypass, I'll nurse you back to health," I said to him.

"What the heck were you thinking, Jamie?" Sophie questioned.

"I wasn't thinking. Can't I take off for California to tend to my email boyfriend and leave the grouchy hubby behind? Yes, that's what I'm going to do. I'm going to help him. There's nothing romantic about replacing bandages. Joe can't stop me. Besides, I'll only be there for a few days.

"If Paul and I don't end up being together, I want to be there after he leaves the hospital and needs someone. Nothing bad will happen when I'm there … this time. Besides, Joe doesn't seem to care much about what I do anyway."

"Then why haven't you left Joe?"

"I'm being strategic. I have to wait for Paul to leave his wife," I said.

"Anyway, I couldn't help Paul when we were kids. I can do something now."

Sophie finished her glass and poured another. She seemed a bit troubled with my "strategic" answer, which I admit sounded cold-hearted. But she was willing to save that discussion for another day.

I considered the deep red of the cabernet we were drinking and began to summon up that time at the amusement park. "It was gruesome, Sophie. Paul was stabbed six times in his stomach and I just froze and watched in horror. Blood was everywhere. It was smeared on him from his bare feet to his soaked hair. His shirt and shorts were drenched."

"Sophie, your face is white," I said interrupting the story. Sophie said nothing and signaled me to go on as her right hand circled the rim. I licked my dry lips and got myself a glass of water. I kept my head down and my eyes closed and continued.

"No one lives after that, Sophie. Paul was lucky. What could I have done to prevent it?"

"Nothing," she said.

"Funny thing is, now he won't talk to me about the stabbing."

"He lived. Everything is all right and everything will be fine with his gastric bypass surgery," Sophie said.

At that moment, Paul called. I picked up the phone on the first ring. Sophie heard this part of the conversation: "Oh, Sophie and I are talking about that summer in San Diego … I know, I know, I will stop worrying," I said. "Paul says 'Hi, Sophie.'"

"Hi, Paul," said Sophie.

"I love you very much. I'll talk to you later," I said. "Goodbye."

"I want to help. He lifted me from my teenage angst. Now I want to return the favor and make sure he comes to no harm," I said to Sophie.

We continued our conversation about anything but blood. In the meantime, I lost my taste for red wine. So had she.

The End of the World ... March

At 8:00 p.m. Joe was engrossed in a detective TV program and tucked under a fuzzy throw. I grabbed my fleece hat, mismatched mittens and my parka and headed for the front door. A late winter storm had left a pile of snow and surprised the budding trees.

Indigo started barking. The leash gave away my intentions, and she pirouetted twice with a giant dog smile. By the front door, I yelled toward the back family room, "Bye, Joe! I'll be home soon." He didn't reply.

"Come on, Indigo, let's walk!" Indigo growled happily.

Gone were the zero-degree nights, the kind where your nose hairs freeze instantly. Now the snow was wet and heavy, and the night temperature hovered around a balmy 32 degrees. The snow would probably be gone from the pavement by tomorrow evening, and we would have spring again.

I looked up and saw Orion's belt twinkling in the sky. "What if one moon-sized meteor crashed on the Earth? We would vanish, Indi. And we wouldn't know it. I think that would be okay," I said as we strolled along the slushy sidewalk.

I stuck my Blue Tooth in my ear and kept my dumb phone in my pocket. I shouldn't be so critical of the phone. It never broke when I dropped it, and it was easy to use. But texts had to be brief.

I let Indigo off the leash to play. What a treat for the furry girl. No one was out in this cold weather, so there would be no encounters with startled walkers. Indigo barked as she jumped over snow piles on neighbors' yards, ran back to check on me, then plowed through more snow hills.

"Let's walk two miles, Indigo. We need the exercise." The phone rang in my ear. Before I could say anything, Paul said,

"Hi, Jamie. How are you and Indigo?

"She's happy. I am, too."

"How was your day at 'school'?" Paul got the questions in first before I had a chance to make a more challenging query.

"How many tests did you score?" he asked.

"Maybe 600."

"That's your best, isn't it?" "It was a pretty easy math question. I managed to distract myself by thinking about the end of the world," I said.

"Where did that come from?"

"Indi, come! She runs away from me sometimes. Sorry for yelling in your ear, Paul. The end of the world thought came from the dead cornfields around the office and the tractor rolling the cornstalks into giant bales. It was a live vista of a Van Gogh painting. It seemed like the farmer was wrapping it up for good."

"I don't know how you got there, Jamie, but I'll follow you to the end of the world, baby."

"Good timing. That's what I want: You and me in the same place when the world ends. Indeeee!" Indigo ran back and jumped on my legs.

"I'll be there, Jamie. Just hope that our phones work, just in case."

"Would you sing me a song, Paul?" I asked.

"And she's gone anytime she goes away," he sang.

"Indigo, Indigo! I have to go Paul. I love you." I hung up. I didn't wait for his reply. I already knew what it was.

Nurse Ratchet … March

"Will your family help with the bandages or do you need a professional?" I asked Paul during a recent phone call. "What's it going to be, them or Nurse Ratchet?" I was apprehensive about this drastic surgery he was about to have, one that would instantly shrink his stomach and would require that he change his eating habits all at once. I worried that he would minimize his post-surgery needs and end up alone with no support. Maybe I was overly concerned, but between Paul's bravado and his wife's contempt, things could turn out badly.

"Nurse Ratchet sounds kinky. I'd go cuckoo over her, if that's you," said Paul.

"If I help, there'll be nothing kinky about the gastric weekend, Paul. All business and bandages."

"No, I guess no kinky acts. But maybe we could try something? Would you wear a bikini? I'll lie in bed recovering, and you could run around looking sexy. It'd help me heal faster, I know it, Jamie."

"What are you going to say to Joanne?" I asked, ignoring the bikini comment. I knew he didn't want me to approach this subject, but I asked anyway.

"Oh, God, Jamie. I love you. But let me take care of my thing. And you can take care of yours."

I wasn't sure either of us wanted to think about these kinds of "things" or even take care of them.

The Staircase ... April 1

I WAS ALL BUSINESS THE DAY I LEFT FOR NURSE DUTY. I descended the stairs of my house with a carry-on suitcase in hand. The wheels of my suitcase banged down the stairs and the heels of my boots punctuated each step. Joe tried to ignore my percussions. He didn't offer to help with my luggage. Why should he? It was all very uncomfortable, but I was determined.

I dusted the staircase rail with my empty left hand. The staircase was the best part of the addition to our home. Its artistry and detail made the rest of our original bungalow seem self-conscious. The staircase led up to the master bedroom and total privacy. Joe and I had made additions to our house some years ago, and neighbors advised that we "leave the kids downstairs. A master bedroom by itself will keep the marriage sacred," they said.

The master had the memories: Two boys were conceived. There, we could scratch where we wouldn't in public. It used to be a room where Joe loved to watch me dress and undress. It's a sunny room, but we had lost our cheer and stopped talking when we were in there together. Hoping to make our marriage better, we traded in our queen for twin beds, so Joe could get a sound sleep away from my restless legs. Maybe we shouldn't have done that.

"You look comfortable, Joe," I said when I reached the bottom of the stairs. I was standing above and behind him. My top lip was curled up in that way when one smells rotting turkey slices in the fridge. His back was turned to me as he watched television in the family room.

Joe didn't seem to notice that I was on my way to California. He was slumped in his favorite chair, drinking a Pabst Blue Ribbon. He had slid down to where his butt was almost off the seat and his head was in the middle of the back, his legs stretched his stocking feet to the middle of the coffee table. Indigo's head was perched on his lap. He looked like he had settled in for the Final Four.

"I'm leaving, Joe," I said.

"I'm watching some basketball. Where are you going?"

"You're kidding me, right?"

(Two weeks prior, during an uncomfortable dinner, I had explained my plans to help Paul with his recovery and just a few days before I reminded him of my trip.)

"Yup, I'm kidding. Have a good time," he said.

"I'm not going to have a good time."

"Huh?" he looked up. The television was blaring.

"I'm going to help my friend," I said louder.

"Who may be your future second husband. Where did you get the nerve to walk out the door and expect it to be unlocked when you came back?"

"I don't care if the door is locked." I had a simmering anger that overwhelmed practicality. "I finally have something with someone who understands and appreciates me. *You* just loved me for my bean burritos and boobs."

"You loved me for my boobs," he mimicked. "Cut the crap!"

Thank God no one else could hear our conversation. It's almost as if he gave up and let me go. It would be hard to understand our marriage. No one can understand another's marriage.

"I'll be home in a few days."

"You're going to go off with Paul, and in a few years or less you'll realize what a good guy I am. You'll be back. I'll decide if I want you then."

If I had turned my back to him to hear that statement, he might have been intriguing. But not so, squished in his giant chair like a crotchety old man. He didn't bother to stand up to address me eye to almost eye.

I wasn't sure what was happening with Paul. All I knew was that he made me feel good about myself and no one had done that since my children were born. Was it such a social crime to want your partner to make you feel good?   Conventional wisdom says you ought to learn how to make your own self feel good. I do that; I've got my vibrator.

I don't dispute a lot of Joe's good-guyness, but the basics aren't enough to counter a negative attitude and biting sarcasm.

In front of me was kindness and someone who was amused by my idiosyncrasies. I craved an intimate relationship where the other honors your ways. Who could dispute thirty-dollar shopping sprees at a second-hand store?" Who could find fault with a woman who struggles to be on time but doesn't always succeed?

I just want someone with whom I can be myself. I want to be in a situation where we encourage each other, not bring each other down. Like me, Paul is a restless sleeper who snores loudly and scarily. We could fill the bedroom with double the white noise of CPAP machines. And he wouldn't bang his leg on the bed to startle me. Joe would.

Flying Fun

Sophie and I sat at our favorite coffee shop—she was sipping "the darkest roast possible," and I had black tea. We lucked out with finding two chairs next to each other facing the fireplace. There was just enough ambient noise to feel comfortable with our sensitive conversation.

"I think you need to see beyond that long nose of yours, Jamie. You will regret …"

"Regret falling in love for the first time, Soph?" I said.

"Please, Jamie, you loved Joe once."

"Love and in love are two different emotions; you know what I mean," I said.

"I feel crazy in love with Paul, the kind where you stop making sense and stop being sensible."

"You better not lose yourself, Jamie. It's only been emails and phone conversations and short visits," she said.

My wordless stare in reply said I was going ahead with my plans, and Sophie knew it. "Okay, okay, get on with Nurse Ratchet. Do what you're going to do. I'll wait. Joe may not," said Sophie.

The next day, I looked forward to my flight to California. My carry-on bag was packed for a beach vacation: a few changes of tiny underwear and tank tops, my bikini swimsuit, shorts and sandals, and a toothbrush thrown on top. I was flying across four states to change Paul's bandages.

We spoke a few times, for brief moments, while he was in the hospital. He didn't tell me until later that he had had some complications. His family didn't visit. Paul was disappointed, but relieved to have quiet recuperation time with his Smartphone.

I planned to eradicate my flying anxieties and fears about my nursing abilities by making the most of the first-class flight Paul had booked for me. I had no idea how to deal with gastric recovery, but I would do my best to help heal him—or at least to take his mind off his oozing incision.

I was eager to reach my seaside destination. The hotel already was emailing me, thanking me for my reservation, even after I had asked for confidentiality.

What is confidential on the internet? "Nothing. You should know that, Jamie," I said to myself.

Here's my prescription to overcome boredom and worries while flying: Never mind the "in case of a water landing" instructions, especially when you'll be flying over the desert.

If you get to fly first class, push the oversized leather seat way back like a lounge chair and take a short nap. Then get up at least once and look over the shoulders of your fellow flyers to see if they are writing anything interesting on their laptops.

If you're flying west, look out the window when they mention the Grand Canyon. You will see a river on the sandy bottom of the giant hazy canyon with pink and orange walls. It looks majestic, but not quite real. Imagine something is happening down there, like a group from Minnesota is rafting down the Colorado River in shorts and T-shirts and no sunscreen. Ouch.

Read a funny book, like Nora Ephron's *I Remember Nothing*. Paul gave me that book. Watch an old love comedy like *When Harry Met Sally*. Nora Ephron wrote that story. Laughing helps relieve anxiety.

Sift through the airline magazine and look for the wrought-iron giraffe that doubles as a paper towel holder. That's my favorite object that I never buy. Read *People* magazine cover to cover. There usually is not much violence in there, just engaging gossip.

Drink a glass of wine; eat a cheese plate with grapes. Use the toilet at least once. The business one is the least used and is less likely to be drenched with pee by those who neglect to lift the seat. Don't fly airlines that charge for baggage.

Chat with your neighbors about their careers. Maybe they are anxious flyers, too. I've held hands and offered soothing words to terrified strangers while riding out roller coaster bumps. Giving makes you forget your own concerns.

Ask the attendant for a second cup of Diet Pepsi or, better, request the whole can and some water and more snacks. And that's how I make my flight a mini-vacation.

Bloody Love ... April

AFTER HIS GASTRIC BYPASS, PAUL NEEDED A PLACE TO recuperate for a few days. Home was not an option, since the spouse was not interested in being a caretaker. I was. I wanted to ensure Paul was going to get through this surgery all right. His wife may have cared, but she was too busy with her career to tend to a man who she had watched get into this predicament all by himself. I didn't want to think about what she had been through in her marriage with my loved one.

I arrived at the Los Angeles International Airport on a breezy afternoon. I rented a car per Paul's instructions: "Whatever you want." I was used to Hondas for the decent gas mileage. Joe would appreciate that prudence. But Paul would want me to have one of those glistening cars in the exclusive part of the rental agency. I filled out the paperwork, confirmed my worthiness with proper identification, and sped out of the parking lot in a bright white convertible Mustang with the radio blaring Steppenwolf's *Born to be Wild*. My scarf and hair blew in the wind. This Mustang angel of speed and L.A. culture was mine.

I reached the hotel in 30 minutes. My now-frizzy hair from the humidity was not the look I wanted for Paul, but Nurse Ratchet tied her hair back and was ready for bandage duty. The cute bellguys at this luxurious beach hotel were eager to help me out of my rental. I gave the sun-bleached blonde my keys, and the angel screeched off around the hotel driveway. Another guy wanted to take my bags, and he used the aging term "ma'am."

I said, "Please call me 'Miss,'" and I gave him an ample tip with a "thank you" and hoped he would remember the lady who liked to be "a Miss." He took my small carry-on case. "Is this it, Miss?" he asked.

"Yes, I'm a minimalist," I said. Why did I need to give any justification?

"A what, Miss?" he said.

"Please just let me stand here for a moment to breathe in the ocean air before I go in," I said.

"You go right ahead, Miss."

"I suppose you can call me 'Jamie.'" I sighed.

"Yes, Ma'am."

"Please ... Call me Jamie."

"Yes, Ma'am ... Jamie," he said. I felt like I was part of a vaudeville act.

The beach seemed cooler than the Rocky Mountains in the spring. I was glad I had dressed for beach springtime with cowboy boots, jeans, a fuchsia turtleneck, and an orange rayon scarf with giant dragonflies. When the sexy me stepped out of the flying angel I looked around at the other guests. I had transformed into a tourist with bad fashion judgment. But Paul wouldn't notice my overstated ensemble.

I stood outside the hotel's front doors. The beach was so close. I could hear the waves crash and see the water race up the sand. It was high tide. The last time I slept so close to the ocean was when Joe and I were on our honeymoon. We hadn't taken a beach trip since.

I could smell the salty fish scent of the kelp beds not far past the breaking waves. The saltwater was healing. Paul would get well soon. I breathed it all in and then turned to find my patient.

I was looking forward to seeing my friend post-op. I just needed to find his room, and I didn't want to ask for help to start this unusual tryst. I tried to maintain maturity as I sauntered past the pool and Jacuzzi while I looked for room 110.

"Hey, beautiful," he said in a low voice when I entered the room. "I love your colors." How could I not love a man like that?

"Don't move," I whispered as I looked around the large suite decorated in white beach retro. It was tasteful—white wicker furniture, plush white towels, and prints of palm trees framed in bamboo.

At the foot of the bed covering Paul's feet lay a fluffy comforter covered in a white duvet. "Hey, Paul, it's beautiful here. I want to go for a walk and a swim and I want you to come with me." Paul said nothing. He tried to push himself up in a sitting position from the side of the king-size bed, but couldn't.

With his large index finger, he signaled me to approach him, as if he was the Godfather post-appendectomy. I did what he said. You do that for the Godfather, especially if he is incapacitated.

As I leaned down to touch him, because he couldn't hug me, he placed his hand on my cheek. He had left the hospital just three hours earlier and was weak and very tired. I hadn't seen him tired like this. He was always strong. Now he was getting used to the notion of being on his own without a team of hospital staff encircling him. I'm sure he told his share of hokey jokes to keep the nurses returning.

Now, it was just him and the nurse with the white Mustang. In an improper medical moment, nursie and patient kissed. No one was around, so I kissed his soft lips again.

"Did you lose any weight from that surgery, Paul? I'm keeping a journal of your daily weight loss from here on out," I said.

"Really, Jamie?"

"No, not really."

"I don't know, Jamie, I will see in a few days. But let me ask you this … Will you still love me tomorrow?" There was always a song ready for the moment.

"I will love you for the rest of my life. I have loved you through space and time. I have loved you through awareness and delusion," I said.

Paul had maintained his trademark silly and musical sense of humor despite the operation. I didn't think it would emerge so soon. I didn't care if he had already lost weight. I wanted him healthy and pain free. That's all. And that was hard to gauge, since he didn't complain.

Taking care of Paul and his bandages in the swankiest Southern California beach hotel was like the movie *Carrie meets the Ritz Carleton.* The metallic sweet smell of blood and body fluids distracted me. I had yet to see his incision, but I still felt my blood leave my head. I needed fresh air, so I opened the door to the balcony that overlooked the ocean. I could see the beach and windy waves and couples holding each other tight as they were walking.

Blood and Love: Was that a song? I couldn't think of the tune, if there was one. We had to get down to business. He slowly lifted his shirt and winced. The incision—and moreso the insides of his belly—hurt because of scar tissue from the stabbings he survived as a teenager. This varsity football player was reduced to a fragile, smiling Howdy Doody. But unlike the amusement park incident, at this point in life, I could make a difference.

I would listen, and I would try not to fantasize about blood rituals nor taste his blood as I was tempted to do. I'm kidding. After a day of throwing bloody bandages into the trash, rinsing out stained shirts and boxers, and accidental spills on the linens, we were suspect. Housekeeping told on us after visiting our room to freshen it up.

Inside Paul's body, fluid gathered and exited his large belly through a tube into a small plastic bottle that needed to be drained at regular intervals to prevent spillage. Bandages around the tube became soaked and needed changing. When we didn't time it right, pink fluid drooled everywhere. This was a round-the-clock job. Nights were difficult because we both were tired. But Paul remained optimistic.

In the middle of the first night, I was startled awake by a sexy crimson nightmare—the one where the illicit couple rolls around in the king-size bed, embracing each other and kissing with abandon. Blood oozes from their pores and orifices and drenches the bed and pillows. The shining white Mustang, their get-a-way car, leaks blood from its leather seats and headlights. The angel cries bloody tears as she flies overhead.

After what seemed a half-night of this gruesome scenario, I woke crying while I hugged my pillow. I needed to hug Paul, but I couldn't. It would hurt him. I grabbed a towel and lay it in a pool of bloody fluid in the middle of the bed. Paul was sound asleep, so I turned away, dreading the morning cleanup.

By 6:00 a.m. the bed looked like a passionate murder scene. He needed immediate attention. There was no one else who could help Paul, but part of me would have delegated the morning shift.

After changing the bandage and sopping up the red fluid on his belly and bed, I cleaned his shirt and let it hang in the bathroom as if the perpetrator was proud of the recent horror he had committed.

There was a perverse humor in the situation. Only we couldn't laugh hard for fear Paul would pop open. This time together moved slowly.

"Paul, I understand your wife," I said.

"I'm sorry, Jamie, I know this is a mess. But you offered to help, and now I need you. You're giving me a new start on life.

There's no one else that can do that for me. I love Nursie Ratchet almost as much as I love Jamie," he said.

That's all I needed to hear. But I was sure housekeeping would think I had had a menstrual period from deep down in vaginal hell where tampons were ineffective. Like a classy hotel would, the front office wrote a delicate note to let us know we would have to pay extra to cover the cost to sanitize the sheets, white bath towels, and hooked cotton rugs.

"It wasn't me!" I yelled as if the front office were the schoolyard bullies telling me I peed my pants. I wanted Paul to set them straight. When we left the room to meet a friend for a glass of wine (Paul had water), I imagined that management invaded our privacy to make sure there were no victims. Just in case they did, I left a note on the bed saying, "It wasn't me!!" signed, "The Woman."

Later that evening, Paul and I visited the front desk to reassure them. It was a busy place. The British concierge said in a somewhat disgusted but polite voice, "Mr. Sutter, when the cleaning staff went to freshen your room they were horrified by the bloody mess in there."

"That sir, is not a bloody mess, it is *bloody* love," I interjected. I looked at Paul to see how he reacted to my nerve. He stared and mouthed "Nurse Ratchet!" I walked away to avoid causing any more trouble.

Paul wasn't defensive with the hotel staff. He explained the situation while I looked for a drink and sat next to the lobby fireplace. I sat close to the fire so that the crackle of dry wood would mask Paul's explanation about us painting the room red. A shot of fine whisky warmed me, and the ocean view soothed me. All seemed well again. I had faith that Paul would sort out things and compensate the hotel for the biohazard.

Neither of us could have anticipated the amount of fluid that would drain from his belly and how difficult it would be to keep up with it. Paul may have known, but probably hesitated to warn me for fear I would change my mind about helping him.

I looked over at him as he chatted and laughed with the British guy and realized it was time for the bandages to be changed again. I could see a pinkish liquid slowly leaking through the bottom of his shirt as he stood at the front desk.

Although we had become vampire lovers, this was a love rendezvous I hoped never to repeat.

I Should Lose My Appetite

AFTER A FEW NIGHTS OF ROOM SERVICE, IT WAS TIME TO
venture out for a longer period away from the claustrophobic
hotel room. Paul and I sat down to what I hoped would be a
romantic dinner at the hotel restaurant. The table was set with a
crisp white cloth, fine china, and crystal wine glasses. We could
see the lit-up beach and breaking waves. I'm not sure where
I got the notion that anything would be romantic under the
circumstances, but I was looking forward to a date with each
other outside of room bloody 110.

I knew dinner for us would be lopsided, and I didn't know
how to fix that. I was hungry for a good meal, and Paul was
abstaining from most food types. During the early days after
the gastric bypass surgery, Paul could have only clear broth. His
new stomach needed to be introduced gradually to complicated
foods. I wanted to fill myself with a medium rare steak and baked
potato stuffed with sour cream and a spinach salad. How could
I be a glutton while he looked on? I should lose my appetite.

"I don't see anything on the menu for me," he said.

I didn't, either. But I knew if restaurant management
sympathized with him, they would make what he needed. "Tell
them you just had gastric bypass surgery to lose weight and now
you can only eat certain things, so could they kindly bring you
a bowl of clear chicken broth. Every restaurant has that basic

ingredient. Perhaps even talk to management, and they will become your new best friend. They won't be able to refuse your sweet, vulnerable self," I told Paul.

We tried it and the waiter said, "Yes, sir, whatever you want."

"Thanks, Jamie," Paul responded with a crooked smile.

"You're welcome, sweetheart. This is my kind of restaurant, Paul," I said as I tucked my napkin into the top of my shirt.

He laughed.

Our candlelight dinner was a bit strained. I had quickly eaten just a few bites of each part of my dinner before I saw Paul salivating and pushing the aroma from my meal toward his nose. I had the waitstaff remove my plates and settled for a large bowl of chicken broth and crackers, even though I was a famished nurse.

Pheromones … End of April

After my nursing duties, it seemed like too long a spell before we planned to see each other again. I rid myself of self-consciousness and inhibition to write Paul poems. The words were more from my heart than any schmaltzy card I could have sent. Sometimes the poems encouraged discussion.

The Lair

She's tossing and turning over love,
While the bear snores, unburdened in his cave.
What's he dreaming of?
Being in his lair all day.
Does the bear know she's there?
She lulls him to a greener place.
He can't see.   He can't touch.
But her pheromones give her away.

Paul was quick to respond. "I liked your poem, Jamie, the one about the pheromones and the bear," he said in a phone conversation.

"You motivate me," I said.

"Am I the bear?" he asked.

"Of course. What did you think about it?" I was eager to know.

"I told you."

"I know, but I want more."

The sentiments in the poems were from a part of me that had lain dormant. I hadn't written love poetry since I was an angst-ridden teenager. It wasn't from my waking life. That was a life of paychecks, bills and due dates.

A new life full of love and kindness was fueling my creativity and desires. My body yearned for him. I reminded myself of this new passion just by touching myself. I felt my breasts and my belly in front of the bathroom mirror. I looked pretty. I never thought like that before, or at least I hadn't for a long time. But Paul made me think so.

When he and I were away from each other, I thought about his strength and determination and pretended my body was curled up next to his.

"Did you make me a bear because I'm big?" he asked.

"Well, yes, and because you're strong. You don't give up," I said. "Even at your worst times. Even when your smiles were just to placate your people, there was a part of you that never gave up. That was the part of you that set you in motion to search for me."

"I just wanted to feel love again, even if it was the last time," he said. "Why was she there when the bear was asleep?"

"That's how she found him," I said. "The bear was in a long hibernation. That's the way he coped with the sparseness of his emotional life. Even before he knew it, her pheromones made her irresistible."

"Then what?"

"Well, the bear is coming out of hibernation. And I'm not sure what happens next. All I know is that he has a thing for musk perfume."

The bear smiled, I figured, and then said "Goodnight."

Two-Story House ... May 1

It had been over four weeks since his laparoscopic surgery, and Paul was feeling energetic. We decided on a trip to a Colorado hot springs while Joe traveled east to see his relatives. But before our mini-vacation, Paul seemed ready to take the "next big step," he said, in us being together. This entailed satisfying his curiosity about what his "new home" with me would be like. Maybe this was a bit too soon to consider. But I was happy to give him a preview of my tastes in decorating.

Our two-story house with its popped top is in a charming neighborhood of 1930s brick bungalows. When you walk through the front door you're greeted by warm colors. Red dominates the small living room with tomato red throw pillows and burgundy leather chairs.

I love my Mario Cespedes giclée over the fireplace, which I got by flirting for a good deal in a bad economy. The print portrays fantastical animals in the Amazon. The low price almost included a coffee chat, but I was too timid to accept. Solid color figures dance on the walls. They are reproductions of Keith Haring paintings. He's the famous graffiti artist who died from HIV infection. He went too soon.

There is just one framed photo showing our two grown boys, Jason and Justin, with their big white smiles. The picture almost looks like an orthodontist's advertisement for braces.

Iron figurines from Peru are perched on the mantle. My favorite is one with a naked female chief on one side and a nude male chief on the other. In a male-dominated house, it's important to display the female.

Each part of the house was updated to keep things current and bankable, according to Joe. For me, it was more about aesthetics, trying to feel good in my home, and make it welcoming for guests.

Bright watercolors from Santa Fe artists and hand-sewn molas from Panama artisans hang on the dining room walls.

From the living room, we went into the dining room. Paul touched the dents on our table. I told him that my toddlers hammered those long ago. Joe, a sentimental dad, cherishes this worn piece of furniture.

The kitchen is small by today's suburban standards, although it's updated and functional. At a typical gathering, almost everyone hangs out there. Guests surround the cook and help themselves to whatever they want from the fridge. The irony of our friendly house is that Joe dislikes entertaining. With Paul, I could count on lots of neighborly get-togethers.

Paul liked my house, which was a big change from his giant Mediterranean perched on a cliff overlooking the ocean. He was ready to downsize not only his body, but also the rest of his life. These were both choices and necessities.

Catholic Guilt ... May 1

Paul and I drove to a hot spring just a few hours south of Denver. Mountain vistas surrounded the resort. The sulfur in the water made it smell like rotten eggs. This didn't deter us.

We had entire pools to ourselves. It was nighttime, so it was okay to go naked.

The full moon allowed me to look at Paul's body carefully, yet with discretion. He had lost more weight than I had imagined. Paul was more obvious when he looked at me. "I'm glad you don't wax your pubes," he said.

"That's an indiscreet compliment," I replied with a red face. A tall peak behind us wasn't the only thing looking up.

We could have stayed in the soothing water all night long. The bubbles surrounded us almost like those in the ocean, except these were therapeutically hot. Our bodies relaxed.

We watched the moon move across the sky. For this moment, we exhaled peacefully and caressed each other's faces. I touched his back and shoulders gently. He sighed.

The wind blew, but the 104-degree pool kept us comfortable. A bit of perspiration ran down our faces. This was a rare moment when we shared the outdoors and each other's company without interruptions.

"I have a game, Paul. Will you play along without knowing what it is?" I said.

"For you, Jamie, yes."

"This can be fantasy or reality. Deep or shallow thoughts."

"Tell me what you want."

"That's it, Paul. The name of the game is 'Tell Me What You Want.' What do you want out of this life if you could click your fingers and you'd have it?"

"Are there any parameters?" he asked.

"Nope. That wouldn't be fun."

"Well … I already told you what I want, Jamie. Think about it."

"No, Paul, you tell me about it."

"I want love. I want your love," he said.

"That's it? My list would be so much longer. And you know you have my love. Haven't I proven that? How many of your girlfriends clean up your blood?"

"Just one more thing. I want to be skinny enough to make love to you and not worry about squishing you," he said.

"I'm liking that." My already flushed face turned a deeper red and I smiled. I squeezed Paul's hand.

"Your turn, Jamie. Give me the list. This has to be good."

"I want to laugh every day."

"I like the first one," Paul said.

"I want to be appreciated and understood."

"I can do that for you, because I already do," he said.

"And when I am tired of all that, I want a king-size bed and pretty white comforters like they have at this resort. I want our bodies to be healthy enough to exercise and … you know. And I want you to kiss me."

Our lips met. The kiss was not an urgent 'I've got to have you' kiss, but a loving 'I can treat you right' kiss. Not too short, but not too long. Maybe it was 10 seconds.

"Oh, yeah," I said. "I want to travel around the country with you in one of those streamline recreation vehicles. Let's go to every major-league baseball stadium and see a game."

"I like that, Jamie. I like that you are thinking about me."

"I want a sexy new black dress and three-inch heels to wear to a fancy restaurant in New York. I couldn't do the six-inchers."

"Six-inchers, Jamie? If you can't walk in them, would you wear them to bed?" I jumped out of the hot pool to show him how I would walk in the over tall ones. Steam from my body created a halo affect. My wobbly, dripping walk brought tears to Paul's eyes and a laugh that hurt his belly.

"What are you doing out there? Please get back in before I take a picture."

"I want your children and my children to be healthy and happy."

"Santa must have stiffed you, Jamie, because that's a long list," said Paul. We laughed for a while and I sat on Paul's lap. The hot springs had cast its spell, and we were teenagers again, only this time we weren't afraid of each other or anyone else.

"Can't you still hear our parents telling us the 'shoulds' and 'shouldn'ts'?" I asked.

"My parents didn't tell me much. They were busy, so I was on my own."

"Well, my mom did," I said.

"What *don't* we want, Jamie?"

"Oh, I have a short list for that—guilt. Is there a way around it, Paul?"

"The only way I know is to renounce our Catholic upbringing," said Paul.

"We both have Catholic in us. Did it do us any good?" I asked.

"I don't think so," Paul said. "I remember the giant bleeding Jesus at the front of our family church. As a child, I imagined that everything I did wrong made more blood spurt from Jesus' hands and feet. I would scream if my parents tried to make me sit in the front pew close to the gore."

"As I grew up, religion seemed to get in the way of my decisions. Religion was the reason I never kissed you as a teenager," said Paul. Maybe I shouldn't blame it all on Jesus."

"Religion was the reason that I wouldn't look you in those pretty eyes with the lust I felt in my teenage heart." I said.

I guess we have Catholicism to thank that we weren't teenage parents.

Catholic guilt is good for something. I could do without it now.

Invalidated … May

Now and then, I passed my creative writing by Sophie to get her reaction. I was eager to hear what she thought.

"What's it about, Jamie?" said Sophie. "I wish I could write poems, and it's great that you do that. The last poem I wrote I was in the fifth grade. It was about Abraham Lincoln."

"Mine is about validation," I said. "It's about me and my needs," I said, as I got up from Sophie's couch to hand the poem to her. Her fireplace crackled. The smell of the burning mesquite was soothing. We continued to sip our red wine on the rainy spring evening.

Validate Me

I say something, you say nothing. It's unrequited conversation.
I get no validation.
I ask a question, you answer it. I ask another. You call it,
"interrogation."
Still no conversation.
But in the end, when I look back.
It's more than nothing and less than something. Do I like that?

Validate me, don't recreate me. Make me feel about myself. I can't
do it alone.

Validate me. Am I pretty, am I smart? Am I good?
Make me feel like I know I should.

Validate my being, myself, my trouble.
Validate my hunger for you.
Validate my parking ticket, or two.
My needs never stop. Let's go eat at IHOP.

You know when you validate me I wake up on a cloud.
Then it wears off and I float back down.

Be my mirror, am I asking for much?
You know me. Show me, what I already knew.
Can't seem to hold on to me without you.

I watched her eyes move back and forth across the page, then fixate at certain spots.

She shook her head once without being aware of her effect on me. I changed positions from sitting back on the couch to sitting with my feet on the ground, my body leaning forward, and my hands held over my knees.

The crease between Sophie's eyes deepened and she squinted as if the print had become tinier and almost unreadable. She heaved one deep sigh and finally looked up at me. "It's fine," she said.

"You wench!" I said half in jest. "I reveal my feelings and '*It's fine?*'

"This is how you feel? It's an attempt at humor at your own cost. I think more of you than this. Don't send it to Paul. I don't want him to know how being in love makes you desperate," said Sophie.

"Desperate??!" I was perplexed by her critique.

"*Can't seem to hold on to me without you.* Do you really think this? Well, your poem is the truth. I will give you that," said Sophie.

"I like the poem. Give it back to me you uber-critical friend," I said. "After all, why should you have to like my poem? But did you at least get the humor?

Anyway, it's how I've related to the opposite sex."

In short order, Sophie and I moved on to more mundane conversation. I wasn't sure Paul would see this poem. But it did explain my perspective, however invalidated it was.

Joanne ... May

I PRACTICED A FEW OPENING LINES BEFORE I CARRIED OUT what was the most outrageous act of my life: to meet with my lover's wife.

At first, I thought I would try the direct approach: "Thank you for meeting with me Joanne. I thought it was important to chat with the ex before I decided what's next. My mom didn't before she married my stepfather, and that was a big mistake. He ended up being a jerk."

Scrap that.

I did say, "I just wanted to meet you, Joanne. I figured our paths would cross, and I hope we can be civil."

"There's no way you and I will be friendly," Joanne said. She smiled, showing her bright white teeth. She reminded me that Paul was not her ex-husband yet. "But he will be your ex-whatever very soon. I'm still married to him, and you're not. I don't know why I'm sitting here talking to you. I had a stomach ache, diarrhea, and insomnia thinking about this moment,"

"Me, too. Paul doesn't know about this meeting, and I don't plan to tell him. I know you have twin girls in high school, and I have two boys in college. Are your girls acting crazy like my kids did?" I said in my meager attempt to change the subject and relate.

"You're a bitch." Joanne responded. I flinched, but I tried

to look composed and attentive. "You've attempted to steal my husband and steal my life. It won't happen. It's half my business, too. I hate that man. I mean, I love him. I've worked hard in this business. My dad was a mailman, and my mom stayed home to take care of us kids. They sacrificed for us and we just got by. I worked my way to where I am now. I did it all by myself. I'm not going to lose my life to some crazy impulsive yee haw from the Midwest who doesn't know what Hollywood is really like."

I listened as best I could and re-crossed my legs while I held my coffee cup tight. I was prepared for the tone of the conversation.

She continued, "I didn't get married to have it fall apart this way, and now look, I'm talking to you. My dead mother would die again if she knew I was being interviewed by my husband's lover." Her pretty face contorted as she said, "lover."

I waited for an uncomfortable while. I looked at the design on my coffee cup then smelled the dark roast as the cup warmed my hands. I met Joanne's striking green eyes to show I wasn't afraid of this meeting that *I* had arranged. But I was surprised that Joanne even agreed to it.

"This isn't an interview. This is a chat over coffee in your territory. I came all the way from Colorado, which is not the Midwest, to hear what you had to say." Bullshit, I thought and so did Joanne as her eyes rolled to the sky and down. She huffed.

From another table, an over-delighted male colleague of Joanne's approached us. His curiosity about this female stranger was obvious. Joanne was not going to introduce me. He was wearing a white shirt unbuttoned to show a shaved chest, and tight jeans with no crotch privacy. He had sculpted one of those beards that made him look like the devil. "You look gorgeous," he told Joanne. She clearly was annoyed by his obsequious comment.

Joanne stood up to fend off the intruder. While the

colleagues chatted, I checked out Paul's wife. She must have a lifetime membership to a premium gym, by the looks of her tight bottom and developed biceps. She had no belly fat. Her body was the opposite of her husband's. So was mine, but not so refined. She wore her black hair past her shoulders with streaks of light brown. She must be getting grey. She used a shampoo with a pleasing fragrance. I forgot the adversarial moment and wanted to get closer to her hair to get a good whiff. Maybe it was jasmine. It was an odd time to have that feel-good sensation.

She was careful with her looks, but not excessive. I liked her pink lip gloss, which seemed to stay on for multiple sips of coffee. I noticed as she lifted her mug that her nails were precisely manicured. I looked at my own self-tended nails.

At some time in her life, she stopped laughing and smiling without a care. Did it happen to Paul and her at the same time? For him, their life was unbearable. For her, it was the hard knocks of marriage. She never thought of leaving him or her lifestyle.

Paul said her looks were "okay." "She was nothing special," he told me, and shrugged. But I would have liked her, for her looks alone, if we hadn't wanted some semblance of the same man, just very different aspects.

There were questions we forgot to ask, like: "Do you regret taking up with my husband?" she didn't ask. "Not at all, but I am sorry for your pain," I didn't say. Or, "Joanne, how can you hate him and love him?" I knew this answer: "I don't know." How could it be any other way but confusing?

I wanted her to tell me anything I didn't know about Paul. We didn't get that far before I thought it was best to end our meeting, even though this was only an imaginary conversation.

Hardships Lead to Greater Truth …
May

"Sophie, I have the house to myself," I said. I peered out the window of my second-floor office and saw Sophie across the alley in her kitchen as we talked on the phone. I could see the side of Sophie's face as she rearranged photos on her fridge. All the lights were on in her house, as if it were full of people.

I imagined that Sophie's daughter was yelling from the bathroom "Mom, get me a clean towel!" I could almost see Sophie yelling back. She is annoyed, but happy, because everyone is safe and warm. Her dog was barking at the front door warning a passerby not to get too close. But there was no dog. No daughter, no husband. They didn't tell her what they wanted; they just left. Her first husband left her for another woman when their baby girl was only two years old. The second couldn't handle the "out of control" teenage daughter.

After the husbands were gone, her daughter ran away, not far, but far enough to hurt Sophie so badly that she would wake up in the middle of the night moaning and hugging her pillow.

"How about some Malbec wine on this breezy evening?" said Sophie

"You can come here, Soph."

"That would be great. My house feels empty," she said.

I couldn't say I was sorry, or cheer her up or any other trite bullshit. She had been through enough. She crossed the alley and came through the back door; there was no need to knock.

"Let's just hang out, Sophie, and drink until our teeth turn red. I'll call you a cab home."

"That sounds perfect, Jamie, you know me."

We hugged and patted each other's back. It was the kind of affection friends who know each other very well can share.

"I wanted to show you some stuff from my school days, if you're interested."

"I'm always interested, Jamie. I'm writing a book about your life."

"Leave the parties in, but keep the men out."

I love having my friend the width of an alley and one dumpster away. It's fun and convenient. It was almost like college.

I handed Sophie a good-size glass of the Argentine wine, and we got comfortable at the dining room table.

"Here's my scrapbook." I handed her a large, yellow over-filled repository of memories, some worth documenting, others too boring to care about. It smelled musty from corsages that had dried to brown blobs. I kept odd things so as not to forget. There was a Christmas card from Paul saying he was paying me back, and it ended with a "Love, Paul." I can't believe I lent Paul money. He was a rich kid.

"I'll be your docent through a tour of my life," I said to Sophie. This is a picture of Paul and me. There are very few of these."

"Jamie girl, you guys make a handsome beach couple. Paul is tan and muscular, and I love that big smile."

"Yeah, I don't think he knew he was cute. He put his arm around me to pretend we were boyfriend and girlfriend. That was okay, because we were such close friends." I remember the conversation that day:

"'Do you see the girls playing volleyball?   And that one super-tall guy?' I asked

"'Yeah, that's Wilt Chamberlain,' Paul said.

"He was a regular at the beach and loved to play volleyball with the pretty beach bunnies. Paul and I were voyeurs—quiet observers. Wilt spiked without effort. He placed the volleyball so that the girls had to extend their reach and show their cleavage. Beach volleyball has always been a sexy sport. The next couple pages of the scrapbook fast-forwarded through time.

"Here's a group picture from our 20th high school reunion. That's me and there's Paul," I was quick to point out.

"Are you kidding?   This is disturbing. You look great but what happened to Paul?" said Sophie.

"For Paul, it was more than time that happened. This was a troubled person self-destructing. We really didn't talk at the reunion. I was sad. The sweet guy had turned into an overfed beast with a large 'notice me' complex. He acted as if I wasn't there."

"He was drinking tumblers of vodka and whatever. I think they were Sex on the Beach. You remember those with cranberry juice?   He laughed loudly, and people wanted to be around him. Some people. His Hollywood career was about to take off or maybe already had. And it seemed to take a toll. He hadn't figured out a becoming haircut, and his pants sagged. His eyes were bright red from who knows what."

"What happened to your friendship, Jamie?"

"I'm not sure he even knew I was there. I hung out with my girlfriends. I was probably intimidated by him and disgusted. I had kept in touch with only a few friends from my past. He brought an outrageous date—somebody who didn't seem like a good match. She was a curvy woman with big platinum-blonde hair and lots of cleavage.

And here's a picture of Paul and me now. "Holy shit, Jamie, this is the man you are in love with? Not that tanned muscular beach babe, but a very large guy—and you actually look happy with him and he with you."

"There was always an attraction to the personality I knew as a teenager. I'm ashamed that I stayed in the women's bathroom where my high school chums were snorting white powder rather than venture out and find out what was up with Paul."

We both had our fair share of hardship. Hardships lead to greater truth and wisdom. Paul had that wisdom when he was young and when we met again in middle age.

We're bound to make mistakes in love a second time around. Maybe we wouldn't succeed. Maybe we shouldn't. But we are compelled to try love again.

Pushing the Issue ... May

Sophie was pushing the issue. "Jamie, tell me about that trophy over there. You know, the one behind your computer screen?" she said. She lifted her chin as to soften the pointing. I didn't think the trophy with the musical note was noticeable.

"You're damn observant, Sophie. When were you snooping in my office?"

"You don't tell me everything, and I want to know. I'm concerned, and I want to be fully informed. After all, you don't talk about much else except Paul, and I'm pretty sure it's from him."

Sophie smiled after that comment, hoping to prevent a conflict. There was an unwritten code among friends that you can push only so far. We all know we are adults and we'll figure things out one way or another. We never wanted to give up friendship for a mothering role.

Sophie liked to kick back in my sunny office. It was the weekend hangout for us. There was a chaise longue where she would relax.

"See, right there?" Sophie bent her finger to indicate it was around the corner of the computer screen. She could have gotten up, but didn't want to push that hard.

"Okay, it's there and I hide it, sort of," I said. I like the award's message. I like to be reminded.

"What does it say?" said Sophie.

"It says, Most Inspirational."

It was sunny, and the walls were painted yellow. I was fortunate. I had no room to complain. Sophie heard too much about how my life was incomplete. A discreet role of her eyes let me know how annoyed she was.

"Please, Jamie, how could you complain so much?" Sophie said under her breath.

"What did you say, Sophie? Don't you love that chair? I'm content when I'm sitting in that chair. That's my favorite piece of furniture in the house. It's where I talk and write and feel good," I said. "And I'm letting you sit in it now. So be gentle."

"Tell me about Most Inspirational."

"First of all, I didn't ask for this. But anyway, it's just a joke between Paul and me," I said. I picked up the award and swiveled in my office chair to address Sophie. I gave her only bits and pieces, almost enough to look justified in my arrangement with Paul.

"What about Joe and the boys and Paul's wife?" Sophie said. She couldn't resist breaking the "Don't Be My Mom," rule. "I'm ready to speak my mind. There are things that bother me." Sophie was ready to spill her ill will. "Doggone it, Jamie, do you deserve Most Inspirational?"

I didn't expect this question about *deserving*. I just wanted Sophie to go along and be agreeable. I wanted Sophie to listen and nod her head yes.

"I do deserve this award, Sophie. But I won't be in the Hall of Fame. It's from this one friend. Can't you say his name, Sophie? Yes, for Paul I'm inspirational, somehow. I don't do much but encourage him. Every human needs some of that." I started peeling at my cuticles as Sophie listened with her brown eyes wide open.

"We all want the people we love to help motivate us to do better. In Paul's case, to get healthy. Other people in his life are too busy. They overlook how this powerful but vulnerable man might need as much help as anyone else. All I do is speak the truth: 'You're working hard. You're doing your best. I love you and I'm proud of you.' It's simplistic, but it's what he needs and wants. And I do, too. Is something wrong with that?"

"I want your inspiration, too. I hate feeling controlling, like the one who bears the blame for my divorce," Sophie said.

"You did your best with your circumstances," I said. "And I think it's time to move on and find another handsome bastard. I feel for your sadness, but it will go away." Sophie couldn't help but shed large, quiet tears that landed on her sweater. I can't say that I was feeling empathetic at that moment.

She stopped asking the questions for a while because there really was no need to know more. But then she broke her silence.

"What about your own husband, Jamie. Doesn't he deserve that treatment?" said Sophie.

"He does."

"Why don't you give it to him? Is he the 'has been' husband and Paul the 'have some' boyfriend?"

"Some of that, Sophie. You're asking me to do 'the right thing,' right?

I continued, "I don't want the finest real estate in America with manicured gardens on one side and rugged trails, creeks and trees on the other. But I want to live my life with pizzazz. Is that so wrong? I mean, I don't want to change anything about me, but I just want to have a little more fun.

I fantasize about the grand parties. The dresses. Saying 'No, these are my boobs,' and 'yes, this is my face.' I like myself at 50-plus. I'm growing into my beautiful feathers."

"I'm asking you to think about it. Joe may not be Hollywood glitz, but he's loyal. He works hard, and he's fucking reliable and a great dad. How often are they all that? Is Paul that?"

"As far as I know he is, and he is loveable." I said.

I wrote this while at work and texted it to Paul.

Tender Rhyme

How many love poems can I write in one day?
Good, bad and you … so far away.
Long or small, that's pretty much all.
I sit on this throne and wait for your call.
(I need you to write me a love letter, Paul.)
Short and sweet on this toilet seat—that's where I form my tender
rhyme.
Cherish this small one that stops in time.

An Email from Paul ... May 29

DEAR JAMIE,

With each passing day, my love for you gets stronger and more passionate. These are feelings I don't ever remember experiencing. It has taken me a long time to really figure it out. But it's true and it's real and it's not going away.

For some reason, you have filled a void in my life, and our daily communications help make my life complete. Not that there is anything profound in them. It's just the comfort of knowing you love me and care about me and that you want and need to see me be healthy.

I love your personality. You are very intelligent and, most important, funny. I'm not sure everyone around you understands your creativity and sense of humor, but I certainly do. You are also beautiful ... you always were ... too bad you didn't have a daughter.

God works in mysterious ways. If we had gotten together when we were young, who knows if it would have lasted. Now we are older, smarter, wiser, and, hopefully, have learned from any mistakes that we have made along the way.

Anyway, I love you. It's the BLT—The Big Love Thing, you know.

Yours,

Paul

Paul,

I just breathe a big happy sigh. It is a BLT. Now will you go to bed … with me? I need to sleep … with you. ILY, Jamie

Jamie,

It's just how I feel. I guess it's easier to write than to say. ILY2, Paul

Clair de Lune … May 31

PAUL WOKE UP EARLY TO GET READY FOR HIS TRIP TO Denver. Two days before, he had written what he considered his first real love letter. It seemed like a long time away from each other. Technology doesn't replace touching.

Clair de Lune, a melodic piano piece, played on Paul's mini stereo. He set it to repeat six times to usher in the day in a calm way. A classical piece seemed like an unusual pick, but Paul liked all types of music. It was a break from rock and roll.

He smiled. He couldn't stop smiling. Seeing me after what seemed like a long time sparked the thrill of the first date and the desire for the newness to never end. I was the first woman that "fit," he would say. Loving came naturally for us. Now we were ready to make plans.

Paul and I had options. But we needed to decide and go with it. We needed to be brave. There would be emotional victims. We didn't want anyone to be hurt, but we weren't clear how to accomplish that.

He thought over our recent conversation: "I worry about my kids," Paul said on the phone last week.

"Me, too." Our voices were accompanied with deflation-like sighs. But we were either acting or stagnating.

"We've had long marriages with our spouses," Paul said.

"They are long, sluggish marriages. We've been stifled. We tried, because marriage and family are important to us. We both tried, over and over. But we were bamboozled," I said.

"What *bamboozled* us? I like that word, Jamie."

"Feeding our fears and delaying our desires," I said.

"I made mistakes, Jamie."

"Me, too. I've learned. There's a cost for our love. The status quo might be safe, but it's dreary."

"I want more face time with you, Jamie."

We needed a list of considerations. Paul was organized and offered to make that list. He relished the challenge. Everything was up for grabs. Decisions might not have been that hard, yet Paul worried about losing his unraveling family. He put that out of his mind. I was "worth the risks," he said.

Even with the worries, the newness of the relationship was scintillating: more exciting than pulling off the perfect music awards program on television. His body tingled in anticipation. We were moving beyond all talk. We were "taking action," he had told his friends last night.

Paul looked at my picture on his phone—the one from last fall when we were at Red Rocks—one of the most awesome natural concert settings. He put his hand to his chest and could feel his heart thumping on his fingers. He laughed heartily and cried.

The night before, he toasted with his friends. Each was undertaking a new life; one was starting a new business, and another was moving in with his girlfriend. After dinner, he checked in with his family, informing them where and why he was going and when he would be back. No one was happy. The family was coming undone before he shared that information. He was a big part of that. Still, he was moving forward to a "healthier" life, he called it.

"I really hate to go to the doctor, Jamie. I don't want to hear any bad news, and I don't trust a nurse to hook me up to the stress test. I want the doctor there. Besides, you know, my doc says I am pretty healthy for a big guy," he said last night.

He ignored the fact that his leg had been bothering him since his operation. It could be something fixable or something more serious. I worried.

Paul didn't want to consider serious. I told him, "It might be something to do with your gastric bypass. I know you can take more pain than most people, so you could overlook something."

Paul continued to get ready for his day. He felt a little tired and nauseous after staying out late drinking shots with the boys and then talking to me on the phone. Still, he finished his work with clients in New York and Atlanta by 7:00 a.m. Already ten emails had arrived between the time he fell asleep and when he woke up at 6:00 a.m. He called each contact and had a cheerful chat. He had a knack for making mutually beneficial business deals.

"Marketing is like making love. You have to change positions now and then to keep it fresh," he told his consultants at a recent meeting. (He noted how all the women nodded in agreement.)

Paul took a shower, careful to lather his face and all the creases in his body and then rinsed with warm water. He didn't want to move. He picked up his soap bar and smelled the fresh lavender that I had described in detail. "Paul, here's a little stress reducer while you shower, and you can think of me, too. I grow lavender in my backyard. In the summer, I comb my hands through it and then breathe it in for a serene moment."

Paul noticed the extra skin on his belly. He was halfway to his goal, and there would be more loose skin, but he shrugged it off. He would deal with the aesthetics later.

Paul loved taking showers. Being self-conscious about his girth meant this was the only way he experienced a total hot body massage. And showering was his time to create without the demands of technology. He looked at the water draining in the shower. Now he could see past his stomach the way a woman may experience her belly after childbirth. He had lost a hundred pounds in the last twelve months.

"This was for Jamie. No … she's right. This is for me," he said.

Paul noticed that the music was more intense as he walked out of his aqua-tiled shower. It had a sheer glass door, so he could peek at the television on the opposite wall.

He dried off while he hummed to the haunting sweetness of *Clair de Lune*. Paul hummed to anything. In the mirror, he was pleased to see that he was a smaller version of his former self. He checked his phone for my messages. He loved my tiny communications. They were "like mini-Hallmark cards," he said. Nothing yet, but he would see me soon.

He pressed his belly just below his sternum to relieve a twinge of indigestion. "Blarrrr!" Out came a huge burp. "Luckily, she didn't hear that. Do ya think she would still love me? I'll have to break her in slowly. Maybe I will even try to stop them. But she's no dainty flower. She's Shrek's Fiona. God, I love that woman!" he said to the puppies sleeping on his bed.

Nothing stimulated him like his friendship with me, he told me that more than once. He "couldn't wait to hear" what I was thinking. He "thrived" on my support. But I reminded him that his big changes were his doing. *He* oversaw the good he was delivering to his life. No matter, I planned to be there to cheer him on.

"I'm blessed. Our thing is too good to be true, and I thank God," he said aloud and shook his head in gratitude. Paul basked in the goodness of love. He said I "inspired" and "amused" him, and I made him feel "manly after a long spell."

He had not had such adoration from a woman in a long time, he thought. This was mature love and puppy love both. This was the kind of love found, by chance, after a marriage had dissipated into the practical world of career, chores, and exhaustion. This was love lost and found.

Paul couldn't ignore that he had once been excited about his wife. When he married her, he loved showing her off to his friends. She was the best thing that had happened to a rich kid with a disheveled existence. He was excited about what the future would hold. They shared the work they loved, raising children and living in a home near the ocean that they decorated together in rock and roll memorabilia. Joanne did her best to keep him organized.

Paul embarrassed Joanne by how he cavorted when he was with his friends. For Paul, being embarrassed was being alive. But Joanne was pragmatic and aggressive. "I knew she would be a great asset to my career," Paul said. Besides, my parents liked her, and I guess pleasing them was important to me."

But love, like summer in the Rockies, can end with one snowy day. For Paul, it was when Joanne said she and the kids were moving to Santa Fe and he wasn't invited. She wanted her children far away from the narcissistic effects of Hollywood. She wanted a break from their marriage. It wasn't an idle threat; Joanne and the kids packed up and left for a few years. Paul and Joanne stayed married, but lost intimacy. Their mutual affection had withered when raising children highlighted the difference in their values. People sometimes can weather that, but they didn't.

With Paul and me, it was compatibility. Our habits and values were similar. We looked forward to projects together and giving life to each other's goals and dreams. We looked forward to having partners who treated each other with kindness and respect and could overlook small foibles like leaving dirty dishes in the sink and sticking your foot in your mouth. We looked forward to tender love every day.

We weren't dumb about what we had to overcome. We were both worldly enough to see the issues that life had wrapped up like dog shit in a pink Victoria Secrets box, almost keeping them disguised and hidden. So much living equaled so many boxes.

We were more alike than dissimilar, even though we had married opposites. Paul didn't think of our togetherness as a precise fit like an Armani suit, but more like a Life is Good T-shirt—soft and casual. Doesn't it sound like a fun way to go through the rest of our lives?   There was no stopping this romance, since these soul mates had been sanctified as teens.

After drying off, he stood naked and pushed through the pictures he had of me on his Smartphone. He had gloated when he showed them to his friend Sally during his work-related visit to Austin two weeks ago.

"Would Jamie leave her husband?" he asked Sally.

"I don't know, Paul. It's a big move for her. But I believe she will for you," Sally said.

"But she has two boys."

"They're in college, and they aren't stupid."

Paul paced in his office with his earphone. He'd had this conversation with Sally more than once.

"I'm not quite convinced."

"About who?" Sally asked.

"About either of us having the courage to leave the comfort of the known."

Paul stood up from his giant bed and came back to the present. He shaved, flossed and brushed his teeth, and combed his hair. He dressed in his "Best Dad in the World" boxers and his favorite pink shirt and baggy jeans. It was time to get new pants and a belt. He was downsizing. "Maybe Jamie and I could shop together," he thought aloud.

Paul surveyed the top of his dresser where he kept his valuables. The house was quiet. The wife had already gone to work, and the twins, home for the summer, were sleeping. He looked at last year's Fourth of July picture of his petite redheads.

They looked like American Beauty dolls in his large, bear-hugging arms. He rubbed his jasper heart from me for good luck and placed it in his right pocket as he did every day.

His favorite part of *Clair De Lune* played. The building melody brought intense feelings. He let a few large tears fall down his cheeks to land on his pink shirt.

"Life is good," Paul declared. He was overwhelmed with a full, happy heart. Moments with me began to flood his consciousness.

"I love your sentimentality," he remembered me telling him.

"I love that you tell me these things," he replied.

Paul was content with life for the first time in many years, and his peaceful face showed it. He held both his slimmed-down hands to his heart. He hadn't noticed in the mirror that his skin had turned gray, as if the blood in his face had raced to more needy parts of his body.

Paul gasped and quickly sat on his bed. He moaned and fell back with a smile. With eyes wide open, he saw a yellow porch light. "What's this? The light is so dim." Then it grew brighter. "Good, someone changed it and that's plenty bright now," he said to himself.

Thoughts of his family faded in. They were at the ocean. They hiked down a narrow path from their house. Paul was in his bare feet, carrying two folding chairs and bags of food and towels. The family headed through the dry vegetation of the beach cliffs, their destination that clear blue water ahead with the kelp beds dancing back and forth under it.

"Come on, Daddy, let's race!" the girls screamed. The sea looked like a giant aquarium in this protected cove.

Paul was proud that this was the backyard for his family. It was an ocean where they could see small fish swimming around their bodies as they waded on this perfect, calm day. Seals laughed and clapped as they floated on their backs.

Joanne was wearing a tropical-patterned blue and white bikini. Her tight, tan body excited young Paul. He grabbed her, hugged her with his powerful arms, and kissed her a sloppy one on the lips. She laughed and wiggled her petite self out of his grasp.

Paul was tanned and toned, with just a hint of a beer belly. His blonde, wavy hair was past his shoulders. "Life can't get better," he said to his wife. The kids giggled, watching their parents' affection and grabbed their legs. Paul picked up the "big twin" and Joanne "the smaller one." They swung the girls around as gentle waves encircled them. They walked down the beach to say hi to neighbors. Paul's mom and dad waved and yelled, "Hello, son!" His dad's giant belly shook as he laughed.

Paul saw his friends from high school, whom he calls now and then. "That's curious, why are these people here today?" Paul asked Joanne. She didn't answer. Paul noticed the warmth of the sun on his back. He laughed while his daughters tried to catch the surf in their small hands.

"There's nothing better than this!" he said to his wife. Paul looked up at the bright sun, glad he had worn polarized shades. Then he took off his sunglasses.

"It was okay. The light was pretty." It made his body feel loved. The warm ocean splashed on him, and he dove under the waves and wanted to swim as far as he could see. He saw me waving and laughing from a small sailboat. I called over to him excitedly. He kept swimming, and then gave in to the ocean. His body relaxed. "This is really great!" he said with enthusiasm. He heard *Clair de Lune* ending. It lulled his heart to a slower beat. He swam slower, then the music stopped, and he made his final exhale ...

The dog walker barged into his bedroom through the slightly opened door yelling, "Paul, couldn't you at least feed the dogs?" She was almost a part of the family and resented the neglect of the dachshunds by their busy owners. He didn't say anything. She was annoyed. She saw Paul still on his bed, and screamed, "Paul! Paul!" She retched and held her hands over her nose and mouth to prevent herself from throwing up.

His close friends told me that he was found dead with a smile on his face.

Succulents

I HAD TEXTED PAUL AND CALLED HIM IN THE MORNING, expecting to hear from him. No answer. I began to worry. Paul always called me back.

I stopped calling during the day. I figured he got my message. But it was too silent. It was an uncomfortable silence, like when no one laughs at a joke.

Later in the day, I sat fidgeting and making small talk with my therapist Michael during my weekly counseling session.

The sun highlighted the geometric patterns of the succulents on his windowsill. I could see the foothills and the snow-capped mountains. It was a beautiful afternoon, and I was looking forward to picking Paul up at the airport in a couple of hours.

My phone rang. I apologized. I hoped Michael didn't mind if I answered the call, since I hadn't heard from Paul all day.

"Hello?"

There was silence.

"Jaaamie?" the woman's voice said in a slow deliberate southern accent.

"Yes, this is Jamie."

"I'm Dena, Paul's assistant." I had heard about Dena. She was that assistant who doted on Paul, who would irritate him with her hovering.

"Yes, I know who you are. Paul has spoken about you. Is he okay? What's wrong?"

"I'm terribly sorry … Paul passed away this morning," she said. I dropped the phone on my lap.

"Jamie?"

"Nooooo! God, no!   Please. He wouldn't have left me without saying goodbye," I shouted.

I picked up the phone and reluctantly put it to my ear.

"I'm so sorry; I know you were close to him. We're all sick here. Everyone loves Paul," Dena said.

Suddenly, time slowed.

I hoped Dena had been mistaken some how and Paul would walk into her office saying, "Hey, guys, you looking for me?"

"I don't know how he died." she said. "All I do know," she went on, "was that he was very happy at work these last couple of weeks. He was so proud about his weight loss, and he had just told me about you," said Dena.

I stopped listening to her. The world in front of my eyes seemed to whirl around, making me queasy. "I knew something was wrong. He didn't answer my calls."

"I'm so sorry," is all she could say.

I hung up the phone. I felt close to throwing up. I could taste bile in my mouth. I paced back and forth in my therapist's office.

I had felt especially pretty and happy when I had walked in there. I was eager to see Paul. I wore blue eyeshadow and mascara that made my eyes sparkle. Now, black and blue were running down my cheeks and onto my white blouse.

Michael looked on, disturbed and helpless. Nothing like this had ever happened in the thirty years he had counseled clients, he later told me. I was there to absolve my guilt, not to initiate grief counseling.

I lay on his couch sideways with my hands as pillows under my cheek: I was an inconsolable child. I fell to the floor in a tight ball, sobbing. Inhibitions were gone. Michael rubbed my back as I lay curled up on his Moroccan rug.

He watched with compassion as I transformed from a composed woman to a helpless baby, then to a tender child who had lost her father before she understood death, and finally to a distraught lover whose new life had come to a screeching halt. He held me for a moment before I screamed and beat my head on the floor crying "No!" I rocked myself back and forth. A guttural wail came from deep within me. I whimpered and buried my face in his shoulder.

Wisdom was useless. For me, at that moment, there was no fate, no karma, no religious conviction, and no useful clichés. There was just raw pain that spun my life sorrows back to front and center.

"Nooo! This didn't happen." I could only hold myself and rock, crying Paul's name. "He wouldn't do this. We didn't say goodbye."

He was going to save me, and now he's gone. That's what I thought as I walked out the door to face the rest of my life.

Two days later, Michael and I met again. He said that I was tougher than I realized. "That's what we have to be. That's what we are," he said. He was sure I would heal and cope. I wasn't so sure.

Into His Arms

AFTER LEAVING MICHAEL'S OFFICE, I DON'T REMEMBER driving home. I don't remember parking the car in the garage. When I came to awareness, I was at the back door, fumbling with the keys, at first using the wrong one to try to unlock the door.

Indi greeted me, jumping up to my knees. Her tale was wagging. She was happy to see me.

Aside from her, I felt like I was entering a house empty of love and filled with anger and disgust.

It was still daylight, but the house seemed dark. Joe was lying on the couch. He took a lot of naps these days. This was how he coped with stress.

I had rejected Joe; I'd told him he was no longer for me. He had started divorce proceedings. Even though I knew I didn't want to be with him, the word "divorce" made my stomach turn. No wonder Paul was avoiding telling his wife about us.

Now I needed Joe. I needed his touch and comfort. This was sick and wrong, but I had nowhere else to turn. He was the one who had known me forever. He was the one who lived with me, whether he liked me or not.

He asked me what was wrong, and all I could say was, "Paul is dead." He couldn't ignore me, walk away, and leave me with tears streaming down my face.

He stood up and reluctantly opened his arms, and I fell into them, sobbing. I don't know how long I cried but he didn't let go. I finally stopped, and my body was limp.

I was different at this moment. I was no longer Paul's woman, and I wasn't much of Joe's wife. But I needed relief from this emptiness, and Joe was my only answer.

Joe cried too—for the loss of us.

What do you do after your world comes crumbling down? Or at least the world you had imagined and hoped for. I didn't know about Joe's hopes and dreams anymore. All I knew was that I had lost the person who was giving me a second chance at happiness. I was convinced this imperfect love was perfect.

What would happen next? I wasn't sure. Maybe Joe and I would work something out, maybe not. All I knew was that I didn't want to be alone. But I didn't want to think about my marriage, only what I had just lost.

I wonder how Paul would have withstood this aching sadness if he were here and I wasn't. I wouldn't have wished this on him.

Sally Hutch … June

SALLY'S FACE WAS CARDINAL RED. AND AFTER I ASKED, "HOW are things?" I could see her chest flush under her deep-cut blouse. She had that Irish complexion that revealed her emotions. I really didn't need to ask.

Sally was Paul's friend, and the one who had found me through a series of email connections with mutual high school friends. I later found out Paul rewarded her successful sleuthing with tickets to see a rap artist of her son's choice.

The blood and heat left her hands almost while I held them to reassure her. Sally was in Denver to visit friends and seek consolation. I hated having to console her. I wanted the grief for myself. But Paul had been her friend, and theirs had been a long and loyal friendship since high school. And they had been roommates for a summer between college years.

I knew her sadness was serious. Her breathing seemed shallow; she barely exhaled. Her chest didn't rise. I didn't know how she was taking in oxygen. My own heart was thumping in the middle of my chest and echoing in my ears. My hands were cold, too. The blood had run to my brain. Do I hold her while she soaks the shoulder of my linen jacket?

I don't have time for this, I thought. Oh, no, no, no. There's got to be somewhere else I should be right now. She needed me to be right there. I picked up my teacup, and my hands started to shake. Too much caffeine these last couple of days. I licked my lips more than necessary. I felt a jolt of gratitude. She was in pain. And at that moment, I was numb.

I saw the perspiration dripping down her cheeks. Her pain had a sour smell. I wanted to go somewhere else. But she had a strong grip on my hand. It was my turn to help. She had spent so many hours on the phone saying anything and everything to help assuage my loss.

"What a bitch I am," I thought for just a moment and then banished my self-flagellation. What if I take her hand off my hand?

"To make life worse …" Sally said.

"How could life be worse?" I thought. "Hold that thought, Sally, I really need to excuse myself." I didn't need to use the facilities, but I needed to get away. I sat on the toilet and looked at the collection of mirrors on one wall and a glass bowl filled with floating gardenias. I wanted to stay there.

Sally brought us back to the counseling session. "Where are you, Jamie?" Sally's eyes squinted. "Your face is scrunched. You have a deep crease between your eyes. Are you all right?"

"No, no, I'm okay. I heard you. Now, what about life being worse?"

"Jamie, I think my son's drinking. He's only fifteen." Sally bit her lip until it almost bled. I had been biting my cuticles since Paul died. They were bleeding now. She added, "It's all horribly wrong. He thinks everything is fine because *everybody does it.*"

"*Everybody does it, Mom.* " I could hear my oldest boy's part persuasion, part reassurance explaining how he had been caught in the movie theater bathroom while he puked violently from binging alcohol. He shared a bottle of vodka in the park not far from his friend's house. The parents had thought the boys had gone to watch the movies.

"They do stuff, stuff we don't know about," I said. Sally's face flushed again. She swept her right hand as if she was going to behead me. Then she sat up straight. "I'm not you, Jamie. I go to all the soccer games. The kids come to our house to hang out, and I'm home all the time. I pay attention."

I retreated, a little. "No, we aren't the same. But we're terrified about our impulsive children and their well-kept secrets because so much of it is out of our control. We long for them to be nothing but safe, and we're grieving the loss of our friend. So maybe we are the same right now," I said to her with a bit of resignation in my voice.

"I'm so sorry for your pain, Sally." I propped my face with my right hand.

After some silence, Sally's demeanor changed, and she broke into a Cheshire cat smile. Sally recalled the time that Paul, her and Sally's friend Cee Cee pooled resources to live in a tiny house in Flagstaff, Arizona, for the summer. They were escaping the summer heat of Tucson.

"This probably isn't a good time to bring it up, but I have to confess that Paul was gross to live with. When I brought home dates, he was watching television in just his trunks. And he would cut out the underwear in his swimsuits so his 'preferentials' would be free."

"What's this 'preferentials'?"

"I don't know, I made it up or heard it somewhere, but you get the point, Jamie. He had no inhibitions. Maybe he just did that to be rebellious with his girl roommates. We wanted to look good and find rich boyfriends. Paul enjoyed sabotaging our dates. He was protective of us and made our lives hell."

Sally continued, "I tried to figure out why he was such a slob that summer. The pressure that his dad put on him to not finish school and come home weighed on him. Mr. Sutter feared that Paul was too serious about baseball, and that it would take him away from the family biz."

"Even more obnoxious, Paul never put down the toilet seat. Cee Cee, our more girly roommate and I would fall in the toilet almost every Friday night after an evening of getting shitfaced. Paul didn't date that summer. He made himself unappealing to the opposite sex, so he didn't have to spend money on them. He worked construction, played baseball and saved his money."

I'm not sure what Sally was trying to accomplish with her confession about Paul's college days, but it made me love him even more. Even though she was irked with me, I was glad for her visit and her candor.

Move On … June

"Move on," that's what Paul would say to me now. His wisdom and jokes remained in my memory like small gifts waiting to be unwrapped when I lay in bed.

"Move on." That was our advice to each other when we united in our courage to leave our spouses. We had had this discussion the day before he was to visit me.

"Move on." The back of my throat vibrated like a Hindu mantra when I said it. Moving on is a part of me now. Just a gentle reminder that life goes on, and I can go on with it. His last breath was a traumatic new beginning for me. I will move past the time when I could point to the part of my chest where the pain feels like either the end or a prod for the beginning. When my stomach was empty, and I didn't care.

I could move on. I could have fun. I could stop the shallow breathing where anxiety and less oxygen make my arms and legs itch. I can stand tall and be inspirational. I can remember why I am on this planet. "You have so much more to give," he said at a quiet tender moment.

I can see myself laughing and hugging and spurting out crude jokes. The more laughing, the clearer I see my life: my adventurous life, a loving life, my strong life. "Woman, why do you weep?" he could say now in his ethereal manner. He's right.

In a way, I loved him, so I could love me. It sounds good, and it's the only way to get over this empty, shithole sadness.

It's time to move on, Paul. I've had enough crying, laughing is the cure now. It's back to Girl's Night Out. They were the ones who were obliged to listen to my illicit tales. It's time to get loud, the wine spurring us on to more explicit conversations about men. The kind of stories that would make our spouses' proud peckers shrink.

I was lost in my thoughts when Sophie came through the back gate to have tea in my garden.

My garden was always a metaphor for living. The seeds I had planted in May would turn into sunflowers with giant yellow blossoms—bursts of sun in my backyard. They would peer over the neighbor's fence by the end of the summer. That would be me one day: tall, sunny, strong. I needed my happy life back. I wiped the dark, moist compost off my hands onto the breast pockets of my big white shirt and then onto the butt of my baggy jeans. I noticed my toe cuticles were filled with dirt.

"Levis last a long time. Youth doesn't," I thought.

"So, we've got to have fun," I said. "I've had these patched things with embroidered knee holes since the '70s. They've seen a lot," I said. "They look it, and you do too, little flower," said Joe. He popped out of nowhere. It was a stealthy entrance. These days, he was quiet coming and going: a more effective way to pick up intelligence.

"You can go now, honey," I sucked in air to catch anger before it let loose. Joe left, and I made sure I heard the back door close.

"I'm trying, Sophie, to be a loving wife. I'm trying to get along. I have to start over again. I'm thinking that if we are to survive this, we'll need a therapeutic tune-up, which he would hate. 'I don't analyze my feelings like you,' he's said to me."

"I don't get your marriage. Why do you guys hold on after so much hurt?"

"I'm not sure. But we aren't the movies. It takes a little longer to change behaviors and venues," I said. I keep thinking about our children and my employability. I grabbed a front hank of my hair to smell and comfort me as I sounded so contradictory and confused.

"You're going in the right direction, Jamie. I think you should try to work it out," said Sophie. It was a bit hard for Sophie to muster compassion for me these days, since she felt Joe, even with all his faults, was the victim in this situation.

I sucked the air in again. "I appreciate your opinion. I have a way to go to formulate mine," I said. "Check out these roses, Sophie.

I showed her my favorites. Every day, I smelled the roses in my garden. The fragrance erased the sadness for a little bit. I loved the pale pink ones with the fuchsia tips and yellow middles. They emitted a faint sweetness of cinnamon, so calming. My dog was very photogenic next to these. And they made an exquisite bouquet with the lavender.

"Are you going to work it out, Jamie?" asked Sophie, interrupting my garden digression.

"What were we talking about?" I asked, still distracted by the potential of my garden and the urgency of planting before June ends and the heat becomes hostile to new growth.

Clean Out the Cave ... July

MOVING ON WAS MAYBE EASIER IN THEORY THAN IN practice. I had made my declaration to stop crying and start laughing, but joy was not coming so easily. Time was not taking care of my pain as fast as I wanted it to. I was inpatient, but I didn't want to lose the memories.

And difficult questions kept going through my head. Was I there when he needed me? Should I have been more forceful about my concerns for his health? Did I love him as much as I could? What role did I play in his death?

Almost every day, there was a time when tears streamed down my face. I didn't talk about "loss" very often. Lidi taught me "No te enseñes tu ombligo." Don't show your belly button or your unbecoming emotions. And because of my illicit relationship with Paul, my mourning had to happen in private, mostly on drives in my minivan where I could freely express my emotions. The van was a good sounding board for grief. I could talk aloud to absent Paul until I was done.

Recently, I got a new phone, a smart one. I remembered I had saved a message from Paul. I wasn't ready to give up his voice. I found this on my cell phone:

Hey Ja ... Jamie, it's me. I just wanted to call and say hello... Happy Easter, tell you I love you. I'm on my way back from the

Gifted Guys now. And I'm going to stop at the pharmacy and get some razor blades and some stuff.

I'm going to go back and finish the laundry I did yesterday and I'm going to pack and I'm going to clean out my room. And that's my day.

Anyway, I just wanted to say hello. You know how it is, Jamie (laugh). Okay, I love you and I can't wait to see you. Hopefully on Tuesday. I love you. Say hi to Lidi. Love ya.

For a while I played that message, enjoying the everyday details mixed with love messages. Then I played it not so often until I finally deleted it by accident.

Did I really "know how it is?" I hope so. I relished the full declaration of "I love you" and the quickie comfort "love ya." All that love in one short voicemail.

Summer of Pink Impatiens … July

My tiny red stool was the perfect perch for contemplating my garden. I marveled how the impatiens had bloomed in profusion under the shade tree. The pale pink, pink and white striped, peach pink and barely whites were a solace to me.

"Time heals and that's about it. Just time and maybe accepting the sorrow that comes with loss," I said to girlfriends who would ask how I was doing. That's as far as I commented. Maybe that was even too much. It felt like no one wanted any more than that. Grieving was lonely but necessary to get on with life.

You must let it be. It's not fair to be hard on yourself. I realized that you're going to hurt, and you're not always going to be happy or even talk yourself into happy.

The flowers were dramatic this summer. There was more rain. The loss was getting easier to live with.

Sophie sipped her morning tea at the lime-green table in my backyard and watched me garden. This day we met early, because it was going to be over 90 degrees soon. The automatic sprinklers that drenched the thirsty garden before sunrise left drops of water on the flowers and their leaves. All were quenched, except maybe me. The sun was still closer to the horizon and bearable.

Growing new life gives a bit of hope with loss. I like to lie down in my garden and stare up and around. Sometimes Benny, the tortoise, ambles near my face. 'Why are you in my garden?' he asks. He eats a few dandelions then takes a nap in the sun.

I miss Paul. My body aches when I let myself think about him never coming back. I ruminate and fixate.

"I feel like a dog that regurgitates her food and then eats it again," I tell Sophie.

"That's sick, Jamie!"

I chuckled.

"I long to have my friend back, the whole of him. I'm grateful about the time we had. But sometimes I wish he had never called. I miss all the inflections of his voice: his stutter, the long pauses before a thoughtful answer, the 'God, I love you, Jamie' when I pushed too far."

"Jamie, I really hate to see you so sad," said Sophie.

"I know, it's sad being around sad people. Just let me throw up." Soon memories of Paul will fade. What will remain is a dream, an old email, and a buried phone message, not a gaping wound.

"Your eyes, Jamie, I know Paul wouldn't like to see those sad, puffy eyes."

"Don't worry. I'll get through it. Sometimes it makes sense to let the emotions take me where they may."

"I'm worried about you, Jamie."

"Don't be."

"Why not?"

"Because I'd rather you feel compassion from an emotional distance. Worrying about me and telling me so feels patronizing. Let me feel loss. When Paul knew me the first time around, I tried not to let myself feel or show much about losing my dad. But he knew something was up. I could have benefited from not waiting this long to accept my heartache. But I love Paul for being a part of this complexity of emotions.

Sophie sipped her lukewarm tea.

"There's one last thing, Sophie. I don't know how Paul died, but at least I know where he's buried. I'll figure it out sometime or decide it's irrelevant."

Sophie and I had ended the conversation. I noticed my hanging plants. They were on the verge of wilting with the slightest neglect. I pulled out the hose to give them a good drink. Why did I try to grow fuchsias here? They're exotic and fragile. They need just the right temperature, and Colorado doesn't have it. They're happy in California, not here.

Dirt ... August

"There is too much dirt in the vegetable garden," I said to Indigo. She led me as I wheelbarrowed the extra matter from the side yard to the alley, where my sign proclaimed, "Free Dirt!" The alley sifters will delight over the dry, cloddy dirt. The unleashed dogs and outdoor cats will shit all over it if it stays there too long.

Back and forth, back and forth, I pushed the wheelbarrow down the sidewalk on the side of my house. I hoped it wouldn't wake Joe from his afternoon nap as the rusted wheels squeaked by the back-screen door. Indigo continued to lead, even though she wasn't sure what direction I would take.

The sweat poured down the sides of my face. I licked the saltiness off my upper lip before sucking my water bottle almost to the bottom. The sweat dripped from my cleavage to my belly. I felt good and could swear that serotonin was making love to my brain.

I had a gardening uniform. I wore my hair in a sloppy bun. I didn't primp but felt my sexiest in my garden clothes. I loved the men's white button-down shirts, a black bikini top underneath and low-rider Levis inherited from my skinny sons. There is something sexy about gardening: feeling the heat of the sun, preparing a loamy soil to receive vegetable seedlings, and watching pollinators move their fairy dust from flower to flower.

To feel closest to the earth, I would imagine gardening naked. But gardening isn't an alone activity. There is only a chain-link fence between my house and the north neighbor.

I tried not to engage in conversation too often with neighbors, so I wouldn't divulge my secrets at a weak moment. It's optimum neighborly conduct.

I was careful with my back as I shoveled the dirt. I bent my knees as I lifted the weight of the composted soil. "How did we get so much dirt, Indigo?" I asked my dog.

"I don't know," Indigo replied in a "berf."

The garden time was when I retreated to creative thoughts and fantasies. Indi, being a loyal shepherd kind of dog, was willing to play along. Joe never would fantasize with me. "Oh, God!" He would say, exasperated, and he certainly didn't believe in God. It would agitate Joe. I mean, he would start to get those bug eyes. He couldn't relax into a semi-dream world of, say, an all-inclusive vacation to Mexico in the middle of February. That was a perfect winter fantasy to share while we lay on our worn leather couch cuddled with Indi.

"I don't want to talk about it," he would reply and then get up from anywhere he might be and go somewhere I wasn't. He called the fantasies "unfulfilled needs that he failed to provide for." I just thought it was fun. Maybe I should have told him the rest of my fantasy. If he would play along with my make-believe world, then I would play in his world of manly fantasies.

Indi's wagging tail told me she was receptive to my stories. "But it's good dirt, Indi. It has worms in it, and it's easy to dig, and it's dark brown. That's what keeps us coming back for more. It may be dirt, but it is good.

"Is that my marriage, Indi? I was thinking it was more like manure. But even cow shit is a good thing for a garden. Why am I thinking about my marriage? He doesn't think about it."

Indi looked at me and cocked her head to one side. She seemed to understand but didn't agree. She was loyal to Joe.

They took naps together on Saturdays. With her big brown eyes staring straight at mine, I could imagine what Indie was thinking. "Come on, Jamie, he's a good guy. He loves you, you know, and he's still here through all your big mess. He takes care of your computer and cleans the windows. He's a loving father. He can even dance when he loosens up. He pays the bills. He's an eager lover, if you would just let him pounce you."

"He gets his fair share of pouncing, Indi," I added. "Geez, Indigo, I didn't realize you noticed. Besides, we call that something different. And what do you know about being pounced, you're fixed," I couldn't help saying that to my dog, who just continued to stare at me.

Confusing Reality ... August

ONE EVENING I SAT IN MY VAN IN FRONT OF MY HOUSE. THE house felt bland, empty. I didn't want to go in there, at least until Joe was asleep

All I wanted was to have dreams about Paul. Night after night, I would ask for dreams about him: anything, good or scary. I ignored that my therapist said, "The people in your dreams are you." So, if I had a dream about him, it would actually be a message from my psyche.

In bed lately, I let my feet stick out of the sheets. That wasn't like me; I used to fear the boogie man grabbing my feet. But if he was the boogie man, then he could touch them.

Lately, I have been falling asleep fast, but I always think, "Please, no tripping over the log." I have those anxious dreams that startle me out of my sleep. I wanted them to be just about him.

Recently, I had two dreams, one after another." It's going to be all right," he said. The other was when we were young, and we were swimming in the ocean. The cold water woke me up and I had to go to the bathroom.

He could grab my hand when I turned out the light, I wouldn't be scared. He could grab me in the pitch-dark closet. I'd like to see his face floating through the glass shower door.

That won't scare me. This wasn't like me. But losing him had taken my mortal fears away, I was trying to find a place where his energy had settled, and I hoped it was close by.

A Letter to Paul … August

Dear Paul,

   I love you. When you died, I didn't stop loving you. You were all I could think about, except for having dinner ready before dark. For days, I sat in my garden talking to a Navajo bear fetish that reminded me of your protective spirit. I wanted you back just for one moment. I wanted to tell you I love you. I wanted reassurance.

   I tried to conjure dreams where you would talk to me. I had a feeling you would die because I cared too much. You nourished my soul, a soul that didn't recognize its own goodness any more. It was at this late point in my life that I blossomed.

   Can I do any of this myself? Being creative and being fearful are not optimal pairs. Thick skin works better. You had thick skin. You had to, with your business. Are you smiling because I'm trying? Maybe you're sad because I'm sad. I know you want me happy. Everyday I try to be happy. But I am angry. You fucking left me.
   Love,
   Jamie

Compelling Martha ... A Random Thought

REMEMBER MARTHA STEWART? FOR ALL HER FINANCIAL misbehaviors and gumption, I can't help but admire her. I want a Martha Stewart memory chip and a Martha Stewart app and her magazine. I just want a piece of her tenacity pie.

I want a piece of Martha to be implanted in my mind—the gutsy, never say never, damn with what they think. She is the Teflon queen—no crumbs stick to her. Martha is steadfast with her vision: one business after another, in and out of jail, her stock up or down. People's opinions don't stop her. She can whip up plenty of good from bad.

She's always right. To hell with everyone else.

But I will never be Martha. I cry too easily. Martha Stewart never cries, in public, at least. And I don't need to always be right.

After I wrote this, I pictured myself lighting up a cigarette from a pack of Camels, inhaling, but then coughing and putting it out.

Inclement Weather … August

IN AN INSTANT, THE NEIGHBORHOOD WAS LIT UP WITH A jagged bolt that seemed to electrocute the roof of the house across the street. We kids didn't blink. We wanted to see what happened next during this dramatic summer storm.

"Right in front of us!" We squealed.

Boom! It was louder than that giant drum in the symphony.

Currrack! As if the colossal shade tree was split in half. The frenzied pitter patter of heavy raindrops soaked the sidewalks. My older brother and I could see the steam rise from cool meeting hot. A breeze with the comforting smell of rain flowed through the screens into our room. The spectacle lasted way past our bedtimes. This was our favorite time of year.

My big brother explained electricity and the physics of sound. We shared this moment and a memory that seeped into our consciousness into our adulthood.

"Let's open up the blinds," I said to Joe," I want to see the storm. I want to smell the rain."

I was excited just like the old times with my older brother. To me, it was as if the turbulent weather was a four-star movie I was watching for free.

Weather wasn't the same for Joe. Where he came from, it was either icy or muggy.

"Let's watch the storm," I said. "We don't get many like

this." We put on our pajamas and lay in bed. When the lights were out, I opened the blinds and windows to get a front row seat for the light show. I sat up in bed.

He rolled over to go sleep. "Tomorrow comes too early to waste on a thunderstorm," he said.

I reached out to hold his hand. He tucked it under his stomach.

"He's tired and needs his sleep" I told the storm. I kissed him gently on the top of his head. Nature returned my affection with a boom and a bolt that lit up the clouds and the earth.

Abdul's Story ... September

JOE AND I WALKED IN THE PARK. IN THE LATE SUMMER, WE were trying to make a go of staying together. We had our reasons, even if they didn't make sense to our friends and family.

It had been three months since Paul's passing. Increasingly, we tried to enjoy each other's company. Somehow, at least not yet, we couldn't walk at the same pace. He walked fast, I liked to meander. Before long, we arrived at Station 5 on the fitness path.

"Let's try to do pull ups. If I could accomplish just one, I would feel strong," I said to Joe. Joe "humphed" and rolled his eyes as he swung his head left and right in a giant "No" expression. "Can't we just walk?"

"I want to try," I said. And I did, but my arms gave out before my chin reached the top.

A man came running up with a notebook in his hand. "Let me help you with your pull up. I can help you reach that tall bar," he said enthusiastically to Joe.

"No ... No thanks. That's all right," said Joe.

"I can get under your legs and push up and you will do it. Let's try it," said the guy. He had a Middle Eastern accent.

"No. I really don't want this." Joe glared at me. I smiled. "It was my wife who was trying."

The man gave up helping. He wasn't going to help a wife. So, he tried himself.

"I can't do this either," he said. My shoulder hurts. I think I injured it sleeping on the floor." He lay down his notebook. He told us he was writing a story about the suffering of his people.

"Where are your people? I asked.

"I am from Afghanistan."

"We need to go, Jamie. Now." Joe's voice was urgent.

"After he finishes his story. What's your name?" I asked.

"Abdul. I have been sleeping on the ground for one year to remind me of the pain of my people. That's how I hurt my shoulder."

I couldn't walk away with that intriguing information. Joe could.

"The only thing is my story needs to have comedy in it, so the people will read it. The readers need something funny. No one can bare all bad news. You must tincture it. You have to add a little of this and a little of that to make the right color."

Abdul told us his story of riding a friend's donkey in his small town in Afghanistan. "Donkeys are slow and stupid. They have no intuition, and they get scared by things underneath them. An ugly stray dog with matted fur and long brown teeth growled at the donkey.

This donkey kicked his hind legs and took off like a racehorse, jiggling me as it ran in potholes. I was no jockey, and there was nothing to hold onto but his coarse mane. My body shook, and my head flopped from side to side. Can you imagine that?"

Joe didn't laugh. I did, for the man's sake.

"I held on for my life. It could end soon. I heard my friends laughing and snorting, not caring that the donkey was running full speed straight for a bridge over a deep ravine. The bridge had no protection on the sides. The donkey was out of its mind with fear, ready to sacrifice himself and me to seek relief from the dog threatening to bite his heels. That was so funny and true. I think it will work in my story," said Abdul.

"Uh, huh. I'm ready to go, Jamie," said Joe. He glared at me. His eyes said, "You always get us in these situations, talking with wacked-out strangers."

"That was funny, Abdul. It sounds like a Borat movie," I said.

"What is Borat?"

"Oh, he's a funny character in a movie."

"Now!" demanded Joe.

"I am going to look him up," said Abdul.

"Oh, you'll like him."

As we walked away Joe said, "Why did you tell him that, Jamie? That Borat guy is crude."

"I couldn't help it. The donkey story reminded me of Borat. The guy said he needed something funny." I was trying to be spontaneous and fun-loving. Joe was still mad.

The Last Laugh ... September

MEANWHILE, WHO WOULD HAVE PREDICTED AN EARLY demise to a thriving business? Maybe Paul's wife, Joanne.

Paul's overextended belly was a harbinger for his wife and she had told him so much more than once. A short time after his death, Joanne made sure that all that was left of Paul's baby was a phone number with a recorded message leading nowhere and an empty school building with nails protruding on the walls where flashy show posters had once hung, reminders of Hollywood successes.

The kitschy 60s furniture in the reception area left smudges on the vinyl floors from being haphazardly dragged out the front door. Workers had placed the one-of- a- kind pieces next to a sign that said, *Free! Take This.* This would be like winning the lottery for low-rent apartment owners and other second-hand hounds.

Paul had turned an abandoned elementary school into housing for a successful entertainment business. He kept the school theme and decorated it with a sense of humor. The bathrooms were tiled and painted pink for the women, and the men's were all blue, even the sinks and toilets kept the gender color theme. The school cafeteria doubled as a lunchroom and editing room that provided 24-hour turn-around. Basketball nets hung at both ends to encourage decompression ball for the staff who pulled all-nighters.

The building, inside and out, was Paul's inspiration. It was his idea to use retro furnishings. This included a lime-green cocktail table decorated with fuchsia 60s flower power stickers. One could sit around the table on black imitation leather chairs.

There were *Rolling Stones* magazines with covers of Bruno Mars dancing and Pink suspended by ropes. Paul had spoken highly of these two performers calling Bruno "a nice guy" and Pink a "good person" who he really liked.

The walls were absent of brag photos of himself and famous people, not even one of his father. Paul was somehow humble in an industry that voraciously fed egos. "It was easy," Paul said. "It's about the music and nothing more: pop, rap, hip hop, jazz, Latin, reggae, rock, folk, punk, blue grass, soul and indie. It's about the latest."

Joanne wanted all that reminded her of his business, half hers too, to be gone. Her instructions were: "Sell the equipment. Trash the rest. Don't spare the sentimentality." Even the 11 by 14 photo hanging in Paul's office of their beaming family was tossed, hand-carved mesquite wood frame and all.

Her last reminder of his social habit, the antique wood armoire filled with unopened wine and vodka bottles, was put up for sale for one hundred dollars "as is" in the front yard of his school. Someone probably wondered, "What's the catch?" This was as good a find as a diamond ring in an old work boot at Goodwill.

Joanne was angry, "So furious that she couldn't see straight down the street," a mutual friend who was rescuing some of Paul's treasured tchotchkes told me. She wanted to stay mad, but she wanted relief. This wasn't the first time a person got retribution by throwing the absent offender's shit into the front yard. Maybe it was a little higher-end stuff and not appropriate for an impromptu yard sale in a business district. But as the "wronged wife," where she suffered the humiliation of being the last one to know, she was going to get the last laugh.

The Empress ... September

TODAY SOPHIE AND I WALKED TO THE PARK AT AN EFFICIENT clip. We shook our heads in tandem as we noticed new homes in our vintage neighborhood. The homes seemed out of character. Each block contained at least two houses where 1932 was scraped from history. In their place, huge homes erupted on tiny lots. Long-time neighbors lamented the loss of character in the neighborhood. "These monstrosities annoy me," I said to Sophie.

I could tell Sophie was itching to know what I was thinking these days. Our friendship had shifted. I had changed my thinking. I didn't need Sophie's opinion anymore. And I didn't need Joe's either. I wasn't a timid girl now. The woman who opened the front door of her house to greet Sophie was now a siren rising from the tumultuous sea. I had overcome.
Sophie didn't believe in anything but God. But she swears the devil had arrived on my portico last summer when Paul first emailed me.

Here I am now, holding the sword of a powerful empress in one hand and a rake in the other.

"Where am I?" Sophie asks.

"What do you mean, Soph?"

"I'm lost from the story. I'm not there anymore. You don't need me," she said as we walked.

"You helped me write this story, but I don't need you anymore. I don't need your questioning."

Sophie's eyes welled up.

"Was he everything for you, Jamie?"

"Then he was; he seemed to be. He was good for me. He was a moment in my life that made perfect sense, but was out of order, that made life urgent, that allowed me to be both nature girl and vanity glitz."

"It was a simple step, 'Come on Jamie, you'll have fun,' he would say. With no one pulling me back, I reached for his hand. He made me believe in happily ever after."

Gardening Garb ...
September, A Year Later

ONE YEAR PASSED. IT WAS A HOT DAY, MAKING EVENING A perfect time to clean up the garden. I put on my black bikini top with my cut-off jean shorts, my new "gardening garb." This year I was minus the white shirt and long pants. I whistled around the house getting ready for the job outside. I paused at the large mirror before exiting the front door. I turned my body and then twisted my head to check my butt. "Not bad," I said to myself.

"What do you think of my gardening outfit?" I asked Joe, not wanting his answer, since I had already formulated my own opinion. What the hell, I am who I am.

"Good. But you're not going to wear it outside, are you?" he said.

"That's what it's for, Joe."

"Please, Jamie. We have good relationships with our neighbors."

I look pretty good for a woman who's been through childbirth, a demanding profession, a few bouts of depression and children leaving the nest. Now I had everything going for me, except a six-pack. Still, it is a pretty mom tummy.

I blasted the stereo with Railroad Earth's *Bird in a House*. It was about a bird desperate to get out of a place where it didn't belong.

I started to trim all the baby aspens out of the flowerbeds. Then Joe appeared on the front porch. "What were you thinking?" he said in a stern voice. "Put your clothes on."

I learned to stop being insulted or hurt by him. I've learned how to get along and maybe take responsibility for my own feelings and needs. I felt more power that way.

"I'm at the beach, Joe. This is what I wear." "Besides, what's the difference with a bikini at the pool and one in the front yard on the hottest day of the year?" Joe turned around and closed the front door.

Paul would have laughed and taken a picture. I would have made him throw it away if I didn't like it, and he would have said, "No way. You're beautiful." I finally would agree. I'm older and more beautiful than I ever thought. "Thank you, my friend," I thought. Paul gave me the push I needed to change my attitude.

But I didn't want to antagonize Joe. I put my shirt on and turned down the blaring music. I didn't have to prove anything.

Paul and I learned something—both of us. Paul caught on quicker than I did: he before he died and I after. We couldn't help our mad love for each other. And then I knew I had to lose my whining ways if I was going to love myself and my life as much as we had loved each other for that short time. It's been a year that he's been gone. All the children are tucked in their college lives. For me, I'm not sure what comes next.

I dreamed I would have a glamorous life. And Paul would be healthy. I imagined a *Vanity Fair* article—a "Who's That Girl?" kind of thing. I would wear my one and only little black dress to that party, and we would be laughing with our glasses of wine, me in his arms. We would have the second chance. We would have joy. But he's gone, and I have a piece of him. The happy piece.

Reticulated Granite ... August

Over two years after Paul's passing ...

With a loud sigh, I took my first step and filled my lungs with the pine-flavored air. Out goes the bad air, in comes the good. Thunderheads were brewing, but the smell of rain excited my dulled senses.

I had walked twenty steps of my 40-mile trek in the Sierras where I planned to leave Paul's love trinkets for safe keeping. I didn't look back. Those bourgeois stresses of my urban life were gone. I breathed rhythmically. It made altitude gain so much easier. Songs danced in my head, and I sang so loud Mother Nature had to cover her ears. I stopped to marvel at a field of red Indian paintbrush. It was a good year for wildflowers.

Happiness was natural now: enough wallowing in hurt and boring my girlfriends with complaints. So quickly, I forgot what bothered me. Raindrops washed away the relevancy.

How could I explain that I never left Joe, and he never left me?

"I need time away to sort things out," I told him.

"That's original. What do you mean?" Joe asked.

"I'm going to a place that makes me feel good," I said.

"And just where would that be, happy hour at the bar down the street?"

"Good one, Joe." Sarcasm was going to be funny. I was mastering the art of quick comebacks—or at least non-reaction.

"You realize you're more considerate of the dog than you are of me?"

"I don't question the corgi's loyalty," he said, and after that Joe was silent. I was silent, too. I had no response.

A little time away would be good for both of us.

A solo backpacking trip in the California Sierra Nevada Mountains chilled and inspired me. "I'll work through the scary parts," I told my concerned friends. It had been years since I had hiked above timberline. But I remembered how to light a stove without burning my hands and how to sort out the strings on my REI tent. I relished the sight of high-flying eagles, turquoise skies, and naked dips in snow-fed lakes.

"But what about black bears that love toothpaste, and what about dark nights with no moon? What about creepy mountain guys with long scraggly beards?" I admitted those fears.

After my first day of hiking, I set up camp at 10,000 feet, at the edge where pine trees stop growing. I filtered my drinking water from an icy stream. I cooked a gourmet meal of freeze-dried beef with noodles. I gazed at a granite peak that turned pink as the sun set over the opposite mountain. I put on my long underwear and stocking cap and settled in for a long, chilly night.

Unfamiliar sounds woke me up twice. The wind was blowing hard that night. Both times, I squeezed my face against the thin screen of the tent to look around, then retreated inside my warm sleeping bag, waiting for morning light to venture out.

In the morning, I unzipped my tent and stuck my messy head out to view the world. Putting my palm to my face, I discovered my breath smelled like horse shit. I pinched my nose and shook my head. A person couldn't have such bad breath.

I climbed out of the tent, slipped on my sandals, and ran to the protection of the nearest tree to relieve myself.

Then I wrapped my arms around my waist and stood looking in the direction of a steep wall of granite carved by a glacier millions of years ago. Grateful for this magnificent view, I stretched my arms up as high as they would go, then to my sides and almost down to the ground. Finches cheered me on, a pika squeaked, and a hummingbird zoomed by. A mosquito tried to end the moment by zeroing in on my forehead. I slapped my forehead too hard.

On my fifth day of hiking, I met a man—of medium height with longish brown hair. His approach had awakened me from my nap on a warm granite boulder. His caramel-brown eyes were expressive and, for some reason, lessened my hesitance about talking to a stranger. I was ready to chat, having kept mostly to myself for many miles. The man and I sat on the giant rock under the shade of an evergreen.

"How long have you been hiking?" he said.

"Five days and about 35 miles," I said.

"That's a rigorous schedule for a lone hiker."

"Everyday gets easier and more fun."

"What's your name?" he asked.

"Jamie." I put out my hand to shake his. "And yours?"

"Henry." He shook mine, careful not to squeeze a woman's hand too hard.

"Nice to meet you, Henry. You're the first person I've said more than 'Hello,' to in five days."

"Wow. You must be lonely."

"At first, but I've gotten to like my company. But I'm ready to have a conversation with a real person."

I watched Henry dust himself off. He had long fingers and curious scars on his hands and feet. He was wearing those hiking sandals. He had an accepting smile. We continued to talk, appreciating our surroundings. Each of us waited with long pauses, contemplating what the other had just said.

"You're a good listener. My husband says he hears everything. But it doesn't matter. He doesn't reply. He walks away in silence and retreats to his garage where there are no demands, where he can build something and numb his brain. Sometimes he stays in there overnight, sleeping on a fold-up lounge chair and watching his tiny garage television. Damn! There I go again!"

"Do you want my opinion?" Henry said hesitantly.

"No, no, I don't mean to complain, especially on such a beautiful day."

Something about this man's sincerity made me want to delve deeper into his thinking. "What draws you to the mountains on a solo trip?" His eyes seemed to search for a thoughtful answer.

"Oh, I don't know … hiking by myself reminds me not to cling to worldly things like people, possessions, and my routines. I love my patients, but I need breaks. I need to remember to be thankful, especially for the small stuff that you can overlook when you're busy." He scratched his head, and then rubbed the palms of his hands as if he would find the right words that way. "Hiking through the beauty and the challenges of nature reminds me how precious life is. When I'm out here, the mundane world shrinks away."

I nodded in agreement, "Yes! So true. I don't often meet someone who thinks like I do," I said. My body tingled in the presence of someone who felt so familiar and to whom I could instantly relate. "My husband hates when I get too deep. 'No more bullshit. Please!' he begs."

"I haven't heard any of that from you," said Henry. "But I drive my wife nuts, too. She thinks my curiosity and storytelling are over the top."

I saw goose bumps work their way down my legs. Have I met this person before? Maybe we went to the same high school. "Few people are willing to bypass mindless chatter," I said. "I can only partake in so much small talk."

Henry nodded in agreement.

He took out his crackers and canned sardines. "Take this, it'll nourish you," he said. He put the snack in the palm of my hand and briefly held his hands over mine. I stuffed the treat into my mouth. I chewed twice and swallowed. My manners were compromised after being alone so long.

Even without the food, I felt nourished by the direction of the conversation. I would've eaten canned anything to keep Henry in my company.

"Yes, thank you. That was great," I said. "And I've some powdered lemonade and some salami."

"A little meat, fat and sugar, some of my favorite mountain treats," he said as he reached for a piece of salami. "Isn't that cracker awesome? It's unleavened bread. It's kind of like a cracker, but without the salt. Do you want more?" he said.

"Yes, would you break a piece off for me?"

For a few moments, we ate the simple meal in silence, not worrying about dropping crumbs or cleaning up wrappers.

"I hope this isn't too personal, but it's been on my mind for the last five days." I waited for his reaction with my eyes looking down. I felt shy about going deep, but still very safe in this man's company. Something seemed otherworldly-wise about him.

"Go on." Henry's face lit up with a big toothy smile, and his soulful brown eyes seemed to twinkle. I teared up, but he didn't notice or didn't acknowledge the tears.

"Okay …"

"I'm listening," said Henry.

"When you allow yourself to be loved deeply, it gives you strength."

"Oh, yes."

"Your inhibitions are set free when you love with all your heart. But when the person you love ceases to be, love doesn't stop. Somehow that deep love, and its loss, can make you more compassionate toward others and more accepting of one's self. Do you think that's true?

"Yes, I would bet my life's work on it." Henry said.

"And what's your work?"

"I heal the broken-hearted. I'm a cardiac surgeon," He looked left and crinkled his forehead up as if hoping that his bad pun would not change the tone of the conversation.

"No shit!" I boomed. I pushed him on the shoulder. "I had sized you up for a furniture maker or creating something with wood. I figured you had a mishap with nails. I pointed to his hands and feet."

He didn't comment, but I knew he heard me. He changed the subject. "It's funny, I'm usually the curious one, but you're asking all the questions," Henry said.

"Probably cause my need to know is greater than yours."

"Yes, maybe this chance meeting is about you," Henry said.

"You don't curse, do you?" I said to Henry.

"No."

"It's a habit for me."

"I forgive you," he said with a mischievous smile.

"You wouldn't if you knew my whole story."

"Yes, I would, I'm just that way," Henry said.

"That's a good way." I could have spent the whole day with this guy. "Would you like to hike with me a mile or two?" I boldly asked.

"Oh, I would, but I need to return to my flock. He looked up and slightly grimaced knowing the metaphor was kind of sappy.

"That's cute. You mean your patients?"

"I've so much invested in their lives that I feel like they're my flock to treat with loving care."

Henry and I gave each other a vigorous handshake, he with two strong yet gentle hands. Then we parted. "I'll be with you in spirit," he said, waving in a silly way, as though he was my best friend who I wouldn't see for a long while.

I smiled and laughed. I put my hair behind my left ear.

Henry turned right to the well-worn trail where he said he hoped to meet wandering hikers to help them find their way. "What a decent person," I thought. I hoped we'd meet again.

I decided to take a nap on the boulder before I set off for the rest of my hike.

Soon, the heat of the noontime sun woke me. I stretched out my arms and legs and yawned, feeling the warmth of the smooth rock. I listened for people. There were only the sounds of birds chirping and mosquitoes buzzing.

I sat up and realized I was hungry; I hadn't eaten anything since breakfast. There were no crumbs or wrappers, no sign that I had enjoyed lunch with a fellow hiker.

It had seemed so real …

It's what I needed.

I yawned again and noticed that across from the boulder was a patch of wild pink primrose so showy, yet so delicate. I smiled and thought of Paul Primrose Sutter, showy, delicate, funny, and kind. Thoughts of Paul came and went like clouds in the sky. I thought of my daddy too. He did the best he could and maybe Joe did too.

I remembered my brother told me that the rock I was sitting on was reticulated granite, a kind that appears strong but can crumble easily. I had had my moments, but now that was not me. I left a music box that Paul gave me which played *You Are the Sunshine of My Life*. Now, I was ready for the rest of the hike.

Hope

THE MOMENTS BETWEEN THE END OF DAYLIGHT SAVINGS time around November 1 and the winter solstice on December 21 are dark. Even though it's the beginning of winter, the day after deserves more celebration. It's when days start to grow longer.

In the winter, my garden is still. It looks brown and lifeless, even hopeless, as though nothing will ever grow again. But right around the end of February and my birthday, I can walk out the door and there, under a crisp brown leaf, is a tiny yellow crocus trying to reach the sun. Soon the purple Grecian windflowers sprout under the dead aspen leaves.

The flowers live even if nature dumps a giant mound of snow on them. And they come back year after year. Each season is a present from nature. The end can also be the beginning. It must be. You have to have hope. Hope that the pain will be less and then almost nothing over time. Hope that you will laugh more than you cry. Hope that the present will be as good as the past.

Acknowledgments

My appreciation to my husband, Wayne. You were my male muse. You helped create my "naked room" where I could be vulnerable and express myself. I am grateful to Gigi, my mom, my biggest fan. Thank you for the pushes and shoves. To my sons, Max and Sam, and daughter-in-law Emily, your hard work and passion for life motivate me. So do the spirited lives of Eszter and Taylor.

To Evon Michelle Davis, my teacher, you helped me free my wild subconscious from its cage and to Meagan, for your gentle critique at the beginning. To Katie Paganucci and Randee Stapp, you inspire me.

To Stephen K, your book gave me the courage to let loose—very satisfying. To Anne L, your book validated my writer anxieties and encouraged me to keep going. To Suezy K, you were right. To the wasps, you distracted me. To Peg, "Just write, b-tch!" always felt encouraging. To JW—you reminded me "Being creative is fun."

Thanks to my Girl's Night gals: Barb, Cindy, Deb, Donna, Jean, Kathy, Pam P., Pam G. for not wondering aloud too often about when I was going to finish this book.

Special thanks to Dianne Moore Bret Harte, Pam Guiry, Julie Yuvienco, Doug Farquhar, and Nat Fraser who reviewed early drafts. Also thanks to Claudia Avitabile, Susan Kolodin and Donna Senn for their first impressions.

I am grateful to Barbara Yondorf, Katharine Rasé and Beverly Armstrong for their critique, encouragement and listening. Thanks to Marcelle for her medical knowledge. Thank you to Nicole Duggan for her thoughtful review and to Leann Stelzer for her expert designing, editing, formatting and coaching.

This is a work of my inspired imagination.

Made in the USA
Monee, IL
02 February 2023

26960945R00166